# My Heart Belongs in the Blue Ridge

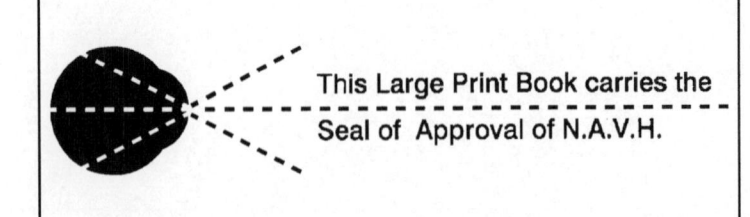

This Large Print Book carries the Seal of Approval of N.A.V.H.

# My Heart Belongs in the Blue Ridge

## LAUREL'S DREAM

## Pepper Basham

**THORNDIKE PRESS**
A part of Gale, a Cengage Company

GALE
A Cengage Company

Farmington Hills, Mich • San Francisco • New York • Waterville, Maine
Meriden, Conn • Mason, Ohio • Chicago

**GALE**
A Cengage Company

Copyright © 2019 by Pepper Basham.
Scripture quotations are from the King James Version of the Bible
Thorndike Press, a part of Gale, a Cengage Company.

**ALL RIGHTS RESERVED**
This book is a work of fiction. Names, characters, places, and incidents are either products of the author's imagination or are used fictitiously. Any similarity to actual people, organizations, and/or events is purely coincidental.
Thorndike Press® Large Print Christian Romance.
The text of this Large Print edition is unabridged.
Other aspects of the book may vary from the original edition.
Set in 16 pt. Plantin.

---

**LIBRARY OF CONGRESS CIP DATA ON FILE.**
**CATALOGUING IN PUBLICATION FOR THIS BOOK**
**IS AVAILABLE FROM THE LIBRARY OF CONGRESS**

---

ISBN-13: 978-1-4328-7063-8 (hardcover alk. paper)

Published in 2019 by arrangement with Barbour Publishing, Inc.

Printed in Mexico
1 2 3 4 5 6 7 23 22 21 20 19

To my real-life family of storytellers who have all inspired my writing in one way or another.

# ACKNOWLEDGMENTS

This story is close to my heart because so many of the stories, people, and descriptions were inspired by tales my Granny Spencer told me of our ancestry in the Blue Ridge Mountains. Though my Granny Spencer isn't on earth with me anymore, her spirit still lives on through these stories and through the faith she showed to her children, grandchildren, and great grandchildren . . . and to everyone who knew her. I couldn't have written this novel without her inspiration, and someday, I'll tell you the rest of the story — Sam McAdams story and Kizzie's story. They need to be told, because, not only are they unbelievably true, but also because they point to an unbelievably amazing Savior.

Most stories involve people on a journey, and the creation of this novel also includes many wonderful people who've helped bring this story to life.

Thank you, Katie Donovan, for using your excellent reading eyes to be an early reader for this story! You made it better!

Carrie, Rachel, Beth — I am daily humbled and grateful to have you as part of my life and writing journey. Your encouragement and faith in me bring such joy to my life. I can't tell you how much your love means to me. And Rachel, THANK YOU for loving boxes much more than I do.

Author extraordinaire, Heather Gilbert, thank you for letting me pick your brain about our heritage to make sure I "do our culture proud."

Thank you so much to Becky Germany and the Barbour team for seeing the potential in this story.

To my Alleycats, who pray for and encourage me, my writing, and even my imaginary friends. Thank you!

I was blessed to grow up surrounded by a loud and wonderful Appalachian family, who tried to keep me straight, show me Jesus, and just love me big! To my amazing Spencer family, where so much of the culture in this book and love of family originated — thank you!

To my crazy crew of hubs and kids. You all make my life beautiful and daily inspire me with stories. God couldn't have blessed me with anything, apart from salvation, as amazing as YOU!

And to the redeeming Savior, who can turn the darkest moments to dawn, thank You for the opportunity to show Your bigger story through the fingerprints You place on the lives of Your kids — even the fictional ones. Thank You that Your dreams for Your children are always bigger and more beautiful than we can ever plan. I'm so thankful You called me to be a storyteller.

# Chapter One

*September 1918*

"He's bringing nothin' but trouble, Caroline McAdams. Make no bones about it."

Imogene Carter's voice clapped like thunder into Laurel's solitude and sent her scuttling deeper into the recesses of the barn's loft. She tucked her precious novel within the folds of her skirt and peered around the mound of straw blocking her from the unwelcome visitors below. Her deep sigh fanned the loose straw nearby.

All Laurel wanted was a few minutes of peace and quiet from a day full of chores to disappear into the pages of a good book. What was the use of being a grown woman if she couldn't even hide long enough to read one chapter?

She held her breath. Maybe the women would go away and kindly leave her be.

No such luck.

The barn door groaned with their entrance, almost as though it hated hearing Imogene's complaints as much as Laurel and half of the mountain did. One quick peek around the straw mound showed three heads: long-and-lean Imogene, round-and-rosy Pearl Jacobs, and Mama, sweet as honeysuckle and strong as pine.

"You know I don't want to gossip 'bout nobody, Caroline."

Laurel rolled her eyes to the ceiling and prayed God wouldn't strike Imogene down on the spot. That woman could stretch the truth from here to the horizon and back again. Laurel gave up hope for peace and quiet.

"I gotta bad feeling about this missionary teacher." Imogene's voice bounced off the rafters. "Something's wrong with him. He's come all the way across the ocean, London or some city like that, and you know what kind of folks comes from them places? Rascals, Caroline. Rotten to the core."

Him? The new teacher was a *him*? Laurel scooted closer to the edge of the loft. Why on earth was a foreign teacher coming to Maple Springs? And a man besides? Sure 'nough they'd gotten used to the ways of Reverend Anderson from England, but it had taken two years at least, and he was doing heaven's work, so he was supposed to stretch God's net to the ends of the earth.

And for an Englishman, Maple Springs probably looked a whole lot like it teetered on the very edge.

"Now, Gene, we can't go jumpin' to conclusions about Mr. Taylor." Mama responded with her usual calm. Laurel couldn't help but smile. "I heard tell he has connections with Reverend Anderson, and you know what good work he's done for folks in these parts. Besides, it don't make sense, a young man comin' all the way here just to lead our young'uns astray."

"Ain't that the truth, Caroline." Imogene's voice edged a pitch higher, like an off note on the fiddle. "Why would such a man spend his idle time in Maple Springs instead of fightin' the war like every other man within fightin' age? No siree, I got a bad feelin' about this, and make no mistake. Wouldn't be surprised none if he was runnin' from the law."

Laurel shook her head at the notion, but Imogene's mention of the war shot a chill over Laurel's skin. Jeb was over there. Somewhere. She'd heard horrible accounts from her great-granddaddy about the war betwixt the states, but what did war look like in a whole different country? Worse, she'd wager.

"Let's not go makin' our minds up about the boy before we even lay eyes on him. I reckon he's gonna get a shock movin' from a city nohow, so we ought to try and make things easy on him." Mama's reasonable request smoothed like sugar in butter.

"There ain't nothin' *good* come from the city. Nothin'." Imogene bellowed on, her voice as harsh as Mama's was easygoing. "He even looks like trouble. Pearl saw him last evenin', didn't ya, Pearl? Comin' up the stretch from the train depot."

"Came right down into Mrs. Cappy's store," Pearl replied. "Fanciest getup I ever did see, and a face as smooth as his voice." She sniffed. "Smelled like the city."

"You mean he smelled like sin." Imogene preached louder, causing the cow to scuttle. "Drawing you in and sickening your soul. That's what he's gonna do, Caroline. You just wait and see. What we need is to —"

"Thank God for answered prayer?" Mama's words stopped the conversation dead. "I couldn't agree more, Gene. We've been prayin' for a new schoolteacher all summer long. School's already starting two weeks late for lack of one."

At least one woman in that gaggle talked sense.

"And I reckon being from the city he's

gonna dress different than the likes of us. We need to learn 'bout the world outside of here. How many of our boys right now are plumb across the ocean fightin' in this war and —"

"Anything we can't get or make back on our mountain, the good Lord ain't meant for us to have."

Laurel balled up a fistful of skirt and almost threw her book from the loft, just to see if it would knock a clear thought into Imogene's mule-head. But there was no use in wasting a good throw, or a good book. Of all the narrow-minded things to conjure up! Imogene Carter ruled the mountain, and if somebody didn't take a mind to help that new teacher, Imogene would have the whole hill and hollow convinced he was a no-account peddler of sin.

"Gene, Pearl, I heard my rooster crowing last night, and would you just look at that sky." Her mama tsked. "Sure enough. That old rooster musta been right. Looks like rain."

Laurel glanced through the loft window at the afternoon sky. A few clouds passed over the sun, but nothing serious. Sure as shootin' her mama had a plan. Honey-coated clever.

"Y'all might want to get on home afore

the rain starts. Ain't you wearing your new store-bought sweater, Gene?"

Laurel caught her snicker in her palm. Someday, she'd like to be as genius as her mama.

"Well now. If that rooster of yourn crowed, no need to chance it." Imogene hesitated, and Laurel could almost see the woman tugging at the ends of her sweater. Sounds of shuffling feet moved toward the barn door. "We'll see ya at church then?"

"If Sam don't have other plans for me, I'll be there."

"That husband of yourn needs to git into church, Caroline. Him and his work ain't gonna save his soul."

Laurel nearly stood to her mama's defense. As if the whole house hadn't been praying for her daddy for years, Mama the fiercest of them all!

"But I reckon that's a talk for another day," Imogene's voice conceded, and Laurel relaxed back into the straw. "Have a good night, ya hear?"

The women's muffled goodbyes disappeared behind the closed barn door, and welcome silence returned. Laurel sighed and opened the novel, searching for her spot in *Little Women*. Jo had just met Laurie. No doubt romance would follow betwixt the two of them, and then . . . well, most likely, Jo would change.

Dreams would change.

She grimaced down at the page, her thoughts flitting to her sister Kizzie and a whole host of other girls she'd once known. Romance sure had a way of messing up dreams.

Laurel's attention darted to the far corner of the barn where her precious stash of savings hid at the base of the post. Six more months working for Mrs. Cappy was all it would take for Laurel to have enough room and board cash for college — a dream she'd never considered before her teacher last year planted the seed. Miss Brayton talked of possibilities. Of sending out mountain folks to bring learning back to the hollows, and there wasn't no romance on the planet gonna stop her. She'd turned down two marriage proposals in the last year to hang on to this new dream — a hope swelling bigger in her chest than the whole eastern side of her mountain.

Her attention flipped back to the closed barn door. *Wonder what the city teacher knew about college. Maybe he even got a two-year degree.* She hugged her book and fell back into the scratchy straw, eyes closing to daydream. A two-year degree in a real college. *Imagine the books!*

"Come on down, girl."

Laurel shot up to a sitting position and snapped her book closed.

She stifled a groan, scooted to the edge of the loft, and peered over. "How'd you know I was up here?"

"I'm your mama. I've known you better than anybody else for nineteen years now." Mama placed her hands on her hips, but the hint of a smile played on her pressed lips. "I gotta job for you to do."

Laurel tucked her book beneath her arm and shimmied down the loft ladder. What other job could Mama possibly have for her? She'd finished all her morning chores well before breakfast and helped clean up after lunch hours ago.

"You need to get down to the mission house and invite the new teacher for supper."

Laurel almost missed the last ladder rung, she turned so fast. "What?"

Mama clicked her tongue. "Ain't no tellin' what welcome he'll get with ladies like them on the lookout. Besides, if we show a little kindness from the start, other folks'll follow."

Laurel didn't argue but cast another look up the ladder and then back at her book.

Mama's hand warmed her shoulder. "I know you work real hard, and if Jeb was here, I'd send him."

At the thought of her brother fighting in some faraway place with machine guns and cannons and heaven knew what else, Laurel pushed her disappointment away. "I don't mind none, Mama."

"Preacher Anderson's plumb over the mountain in Yella Hill on a call, so I reckon he missed pickin' up the teacher at the train depot."

"You mean the new teacher walked from the station to Maple Springs on his own? That's five miles, if it's one."

"Which says a lot about his strength of character. Determined."

Or crazy. But city folk were a sight bit different than country folk.

"And I reckon he slept in the mission house last night."

Laurel's mouth slipped open. "Surely not, Mama. It ain't fit for a family of coons."

"Which is why you're gonna invite him to stay here while the menfolk make the mission house fit for a schoolteacher."

Laurel stopped dusting straw off her skirt and stared at her mama. "Stay here?" Heat drained from her face and left a trail of cold down her neck. The back room of the barn had been home to many a stranger, but not this late in the year. "It's been 'bout six months, Mama. High time for Daddy to —"

"Your daddy's fine for a while yet. It's the dark days that cause his dark mood." Her mama looked out the barn window, a sliver of sunlight haloing her sky-blue eyes. "We'll see the signs beforehand." She turned back to Laurel and shooed her toward the door. "Go on now, it's gonna be evenin' afore long."

Laurel hesitated only a second longer before she headed out the door and down the steep mountain path toward the church schoolhouse. The trees were only beginning to shift into autumn colors, with hickory and beech displaying their golden glints first. She breathed in the earth's fragrance, still fresh from morning rain. The scent mingled with the faintest hint of wild rose and moss, faithful companions through the dense woods. Sunlight created a patchwork against the leafy trail as it slit through the mature forest and led the way down the mountain. Small glimpses of horizon showed between the trees and offered an endless view to uncharted lands of colleges and city streets and millions of other things she'd only seen through the pages of books.

What had Mama called the new schoolteacher? Mr. Taylor? Well, if he was anything like Mr. Brickner from five years ago, bald with a voice as perpetually vacant as his expression, Laurel might have to pinch herself during supper to keep awake. Besides, with eight different teachers in as many years, only two stood out from among the others — two who didn't enter Maple Springs on a rescue mission to save the backwoods heathen mountaineers from their ungodly and sinful ways.

They came to truly teach . . . and learn.

Miss Skoondyke from three years ago stirred the spark of Laurel's curiosity about college with her personal stories of massive libraries and engaging lectures, but Miss Brayton, two years later, fanned the flicker to flame. The young, raven-headed woman saw potential in all her students but recognized Maple Spring's need for a consistent teacher, particularly a native with the courage to get a college degree and bring learning back to her people.

And Laurel planned on becoming that teacher.

# Chapter Two

Perhaps Jonathan Taylor had made a terrible mistake leaving England for a chance at redemption.

He attempted to shove the dying flames back to life in the hearth of the dilapidated mission house, but the last firewood he'd scrounged up before nightfall barely smoldered at dawn. He reached for the accoutrements the local store owner, Mrs. Caparila — or Mrs. Cappy, as the locals called her — had given him the evening before . . . after she'd greeted him with the end of a shotgun. Jonathan's skin chilled at the tangible memory.

He'd take better care to arrive before dusk to keep from having his life flash before his eyes at the vision of a double barrel. Thankfully, once he'd identified himself as the new schoolteacher and not some thief who'd been stealing from Mrs. Cappy's store, she greeted him with a reluctant acceptance, gave him bread and supplies for breakfast, and ushered him toward his new home.

The mission house.

Part of his uncle's mission, when he came to Maple Springs, was to first build a church then a school — and then the mission house, a structure for the resident schoolteacher. Jonathan looked about the stone cottage in the faint light of morning, weariness seeping to his core, especially in his weak leg. A single room made up the sitting room and bedroom, from what he could tell. A small kitchen attached to the back, with the roof partially collapsed, and a broken ladder led to what he assumed was a loft area. If he hadn't been so cold, he'd have chosen to explore the possibility of sleeping on the broken floor, what with unknown amounts of things creeping from the holes in the split wood. As it was, he'd placed his cot by the fire, grateful for the three months of soldiers' training he experienced before they'd rejected him as unfit for combat.

Dismissed as too broken to even defend his country.

Jonathan shook off the melancholy and made quick use of the hot ashes to scramble an egg, drawing his wool blanket around his shoulders as he cooked. His uncle had written to him that the house hadn't been occupied for a few years, since the female teachers usually boarded at Mrs. Cappy's. The memory of Jonathan's four-poster bed in his family's electric-heated London town house taunted every aching bone in his body.

Perchance he'd gone to exaggerated lengths for an opportunity to prove he wasn't the useless invalid his father thought, but his uncle's faith in him to teach in the rural Blue Ridge Mountains had dangled hope.

Hope that Jonathan could offer service in a world where "whole" men proved themselves in battle and broken men carved their purpose by other means — even those that pitched them into a foreign world, in the middle of the wilderness, with an absentee uncle.

His younger brother had called him mad when Jonathan shared his plans.

His mother had wept for him as if his death was imminent, before accepting her son's fate.

He could imagine his elder brother's skeptic reaction all the way from the front lines of war-torn Europe.

His sister, in all her youthfulness, had laughed and asked him to write letters of his many adventures.

But his father, stoic and distant as always, bore a silent verdict Jonathan felt to his core. Failure.

Despite the optimism lacing his uncle's letters, Jonathan felt another failure creep over his skin like the chill in the air. He didn't belong here, did he?

With stiff movements, he retrieved his bags and stepped onto the front porch of the house, breathing in the pine-laced air. Birdsong brightened his mood and drew him further onto the porch, without much shift in the temperature.

He cast a look down the hill. Through a light veil of trees, Mrs. Cappy's two-story white clapboard store stood, an odd structure in the middle of these woods. Another cabin or two scattered along the road in what appeared to be a random toss of wood or stone, making up the town center, if such a place could even be referred to as a town. Was one of those homes his uncle's? Where was his uncle?

His gaze traveled back to Mrs. Cappy's store, settling on the second floor where the boarders stayed . . . one of them Miss Danette Simms.

Within two minutes of their meeting last evening, with Jonathan at gunpoint, he understood two terrifying things about the buxom brunette. One, she was in search of romance, and two, she'd chosen Jonathan as her prey. Thankfully, this younger-grades teacher hinted at her whereabouts by the strong scent of her lilac perfume and the unnerving high pitch of her laughter.

A steeple rose up the hillside away from the store, drawing him toward the place of his new occupation.

The whitewashed schoolhouse stood on a small grassy knoll, and as Jonathan crested the hill, morning dew misting his face, the forest fell away to reveal an endless horizon.

Stretching as far as the eye could see, layer upon layer of misty blue mountains extended into a golden splash of orange-hued sunrise. He pressed his palm to a nearby oak, the magnificence of the scene grasping at his breath. After a night of staring in the darkness at a broken ceiling and cracked floor, this view upended his perspective . . . or perhaps set it straight. God was here too. In the sunrise, the morning mist, even the mission house.

And God had brought Jonathan to this very place.

He stood a few moments, bathing in the revelation with some internal thanksgiving, and reminding himself that God knew what

He was doing, despite Jonathan's current misgivings. With purpose in his stride, he finished his walk to the schoolhouse, taking in the subtle changes of the waxing sunrise as the orange swelled and spilled over the horizon like molten gold. Warmth covered his chilled skin with a fresh wave of energy and he took the school steps two at a time, breathing in the scent of fresh pine and woodfire.

A simple entry greeted him with a whitewashed wall and two doors. The room to the right carried the faint hint of gardenias and featured a large chalkboard with the alphabet on display at the front of the room. Miss Simms's room.

He reflexively shuddered and turned to the room on the left. Small, but clean. The pine floors led up to a large wooden desk with a chalkboard taking up space on the wall behind it. Desks stood on either side of the aisle, and three large windows covered the left wall, revealing more of the breathtaking mountain range.

His shoes clipped against the floor as sunrays beamed through the windows lighting his way to the front of the room. Jonathan placed his bag on the desk, claiming his position among the stack of red primers, and uncertain wilderness.

Were those the only tools he had? A set of primers and a chalkboard?

He studied the barren-walled room, his attention settling on an alcove in the back wall where three tall bookshelves waited, filled to almost overflowing. Books! He approached the shelves, his grin peaking as if someone had thrown him a lifeline. This small mountain school had an impressive collection of classics as well as fiction published as recently as 1915. He uncovered a few encyclopedias and geography books, two texts on vegetation of the United States, and even one flower book with color pictures. He pored over the choices, his thoughts rushing into how to use these small treasures in his lessons. Some teacher before him had left a precious gift for these people. Did they realize the cost? The wealth of information behind each page? Did they even read?

Jonathan set to work, making two lists — one of his current supplies and another of items he needed. Later in the morning, when his three large trunks arrived from the depot, much to the complaints of Mr. Mundy, a man he'd hired for the job, Jonathan began adding some color to the barren walls and shelves of the schoolhouse. A globe. A framed bug collection. A massive map of North Carolina that he'd purchased when he'd passed through the last town. He placed a few of his personal favorite books on a shelf near his desk and finished his unpacking with a blown-glass apple paperweight his mother had bought for him as a going-away gift.

With each hand-chosen addition to the room, Jonathan accepted his new position, pushing the doubts away. He worked the entire day, ignoring the occasional pangs in his weak leg incited by the long walk from the day before and his refusal to sit down for very long. He couldn't allow his weaknesses to impact this opportunity.

But it was no use. The weariness from his long travel and lack of sleep finally weakened him to his desk and he collapsed, pressing his face into his hands with a groan. *Dear Lord, please give me strength to help make a difference.*

A resounding thud from across the room woke him from an unexpected but much-needed rest. A girl, probably no more than fifteen, stood in the doorway, afternoon sunlight framing her silhouette. Jonathan blinked his bleary eyes. Had God answered his unvoiced prayer for help with an angel straight from heaven?

She stepped forward, closer. No, her

simple green dress and freckled face suggested an earthlier abode than the twinkle in her eyes attempted to contradict. An angel? Ridiculous.

The stranger's expression held none of the suspicion he'd experienced yesterday from the women in Mrs. Cappy's store. She approached, confidence in each step and a welcome smile drawing him in, as if they'd already been acquainted and she stopped in for a friendly visit.

*How unusual.*

He stood so abruptly his chair tipped backward and slammed against the floor, sending a slight cloud of dust dancing into the sunbeams between them.

"You're a might bit skittish, ain'tcha?"

"Excuse me." He turned to set the chair upright, making a fumbling mess of it. "May I help you?"

Her gaze roamed before she whistled low. "Mmhmm, somebody's been sprucin' up this place for sure." She stepped to the side and glided an appreciative hand over the globe. "What a wonder!"

"The world is a fascinating place."

Her gaze flipped to his, direct, almost unnervingly so, and then looked back at the globe. "Well, I ain't seen a whole lot of it, but I sure like visiting through books."

"One of the best ways to travel."

She looked back up at him, her face lighting with another smile that nearly unfurled his own.

"Sure is." She studied him in silence, fidgeting with the end of her golden braid. "Would you happen to know where I can find the new schoolteacher?"

He took a step forward, keeping his gait as steady as possible. Her attention flitted to his uneven step and then back to his face. He hated the recognition of his weakness.

"I'm the new teacher." He closed the gap between them and held out his hand, drawing her focus away from his leg. "Jonathan Taylor."

She tilted her head ever so slightly, golden brow angled high and pale blue eyes reexamining him from shoe to head. Maybe she wasn't as young as he'd thought. Those eyes held more years than her face.

"You're the new teacher?" She peeked around his shoulder and scanned the room, then turned her gaze back to him with a crooked grin attached. "Are you joshin' me?"

"I assure you, miss, I'm the new upper-grades schoolteacher."

She took his hand and shook it with the firmness of a man. "Ain't you a bit young for a city schoolteacher?"

His brows rose as he stepped back, her directness throwing him off his guard once again. Did all the mountain folks speak with such candor? "I'm old enough to have a degree in education as well as having completed some training in medicine." And medic training until they dismissed him when they uncovered the limitations in his mobility.

"A degree?" Those pale eyes sparkled afresh. "How many years is that in school?"

"I completed mine in four years, and am well qualified despite my age to teach chil—"

"Four years?" she murmured to herself. "Ain't too long, is it?" She glanced back up at him and shook her head as if to console him. "Now Mr. Taylor, don't get your back up. Round here our teacher history has been a mix of young women and *old* men. That's all." Her crooked grin resurrected, along with another appraisal of his person. "I reckon you'll cause a stir for sure with your good looks and all." She didn't give him a chance to respond to her comment, even if he'd wanted to. Her smile faded and concern creased her brow. "Did you sleep in that ol' mission house last night?"

He was still trying to come up with a

rebuttal to her "good looks" comment and only managed a nod.

"Shucks, it's a good thing the coons didn't join you for the night. From the size of them holes in the walls, they could've crawled right in your bed."

Jonathan's stomach dropped. Perfect. Her comment assured him of another sleepless night. "What grade are you in, Miss . . . ?"

"Laurel McAdams, and no sir, I ain't . . . pardon me, I'm *not* one of your students. I graduated last spring, but I've offered to help Miss Simms with tutorin' some of the young'uns when I have a chance. She pays a nickel a week."

"You've graduated?"

"We're quite a pair, aren't we? I'm thinkin' you're older and you thinkin' I'm younger. You can't blame me, though. The last male teacher who came from the big city wasn't near as green as you." She leaned forward, adding a whisper to the conspiratorial glint in her eyes. "In fact, some of us thought he came over on the Mayflower."

He couldn't hide his grin this time, and a feeling as warm as the sunlight through the windows pressed against his chest. He hadn't expected the mountain people to be charming. Rude, ignorant, filthy, poor, maybe even dangerous, but charming? She stared up at him, offering raw friendliness.

*"Kindness is always a right choice."* His mother's phrase peeled through his fuzzy thoughts and attached to Laurel McAdams like a missing puzzle piece.

"Do you have plans beyond graduation, Miss McAdams?"

"Laurel." She corrected and then looked out the window with a shrug. "My plans right now are to invite you up to my home for supper and a better place to sleep. Mama sent me straightaway. She said your uncle's gone over the mountain to hold service for a dear saint who died in the night, and Mama figured you could do with a hot meal too."

"That's very kind of your mother." He paused to consider what supper might consist of at her home, or what sort of environment awaited him, but then the unnatural trill of high-pitched laughter drifted from outside.

"Yoo-hoo! Mr. Taylor. Are you in that schoolhouse all alone?"

Jonathan met Laurel's wide-eyed expression with one of his own and quickly snatched up his jacket from the desk chair. "I'd be happy to come."

"Mr. Taylor?" Danette Simms's voice called from the other side of the school.

He lifted his hat from the rack by the back door and gestured toward the exit. "Let's hurry, shall we? I'd hate to keep your mother waiting."

Laurel's periwinkle gaze filled with mischief enough to sparkle. "How 'bout we take the back way up the mountain to avoid any . . . um . . . unwanted company?"

He almost ran to keep up with her pace, his leg hitching his steps. "Brilliant notion. Lead the way."

"She get her hooks in you already?"

Jonathan pushed a hand through his hair before smashing his hat down on top of his head. "It's safe to say I've been sufficiently introduced to Miss Danette Simms."

"I don't blame you for bein' scared of her. She's a whole lot worse than a hungry bear in March. I ain't never seen a woman hankerin' for a husband so bad." She shook her head and chuckled, a sound as at home along the path as the cool breeze.

He liked the sound. Gentle. Genuine. It inspired some sort of peaceful response in his chest. Somehow having an ally in this desolate place didn't make it seem quite as lonely, especially with his uncle's absence. Laurel McAdams was certainly an unexpected ally, though. Her shock of golden waves danced in the breeze like the leaves across the autumn ground, and though her grammar was questionable at best, she held herself with more kind confidence — a natural assurance — than most women he'd met in his parents' social circles.

They walked in silence for a while, birdsong and rustling leaves their only companions. The path took a narrow and steep twist up the mountainside. His leg gave its gentle protests as the trail became more rigorous, but he pushed forward, refusing to comply to its complaints.

Afternoon glow faded by slow degrees, lengthening the trees' shadows across their way and causing the forest to close in around him. Laurel didn't seem to notice.

What did people do this far from the world? The silence itched at his comfort. "What does your father do?"

Laurel kept her eyes forward. "He works at a furniture shop in town."

"Town?"

"Yeah, I reckon you're wonderin' where a town might be. Ain't nothin' but trees and sky around here, is there?" She grinned. "Wilkesboro is 'bout an hour east of here. He works there."

"He travels there every day?"

Laurel's brow furrowed in confusion and she came to a stop in the path, head tilted.

"He goes where the work is. Can't be too picky when there are mouths to feed."

Jonathan surveyed the winding trail as it disappeared farther up into the mountain forest. "And how many mouths?"

"I got you scared now, don't I?" She smiled and resumed her walk. "Well, I ain't sayin' you shouldn't be a little scared. We got a whole passel of crazy young'uns in my house, the twins bein' the biggest handful, but they ain't got all their teeth yet, so I reckon you're safe."

His laugh burst out before he could catch it. "That's a relief. I'd wondered how to manage the natives but had no idea they'd come with teeth bared."

It was her turn to laugh, a light, airy introduction into the fading light. "Well, there's some who might, and that's the truth. Our family's a bit different than other folks in the mountains on account of Mama's daddy running the campground for folks traveling through from Wilkesboro over the mountain. Strangers would stop in and sit a spell to tell their stories, so she grew accustomed to welcomin' folks with curiosity. That ain't . . . isn't true for some round here."

Her admission matched his uncle's letters, which was probably the reason Laurel's ready friendliness surprised him so much. When his uncle had arrived in the Blue Ridge years ago, it had taken him months to even make it into someone's home, let alone earn their trust.

"And as far as mouths to feed, let me see . . ." Laurel tilted her head to the side in thought. "There's Daddy and Mama of course, and then nine." She hesitated, smile fading for a second. "I mean the eight of us young'uns, but two don't live at home no more. My older sister's married and expectin' her first baby come December. And my brother's off fightin' in the war, so there's really only six young'uns at home."

*Only six?* He watched her profile as they walked. "My brothers are fighting in the war too."

Understanding lit her eyes. A comradery. "France is a long way off, but so is England."

A question slid in between her words.

"No place is too far to bring the gift of education."

She took his answer with a nod. "And there's all types of education, ain't . . . isn't there?"

He turned to reply, but the view up ahead stilled his movements. Sunrise had been beautiful, but the benediction of the day, purplish-blue hues spliced with fading amber, stole his breath. A sea of mountains reached to touch the tawny sky, the peaks veiled in intermittent clouds in an unearthly and mesmerizing beauty.

"It's pretty, ai . . . isn't it?"

Laurel's attempts to correct her speech somehow made her more endearing, and in this quietness, cloaked in sunset, Jonathan felt more comfortable in a woman's presence than he ever had. Perhaps it was her easy friendliness or her simple charm, but as he stared over at her, her skin alight with the golden hues from the horizon, a curious sensation tightened his chest.

He turned his attention back to the view, heat crawling up his neck. "Yes."

"This is my favorite spot in the whole world. Ain't nothing better than watching a sunset grow quiet over those mountains, except maybe viewing a comin' storm or snowfall. Makes a body feel closer to the Almighty. Like you're seein' Him paint a picture right before your eyes."

He was the teacher, and yet she found words to express something he'd been trying to voice since sunrise.

A sudden wail broke through the serenity, echoing from the darkness of the forest like a fabled banshee. Chills fingered up his neck. His gaze locked with Laurel's. She'd heard it too.

The cry came again, adding an eeriness to the dense and dusk-lit forest. Jonathan's pulse stumbled into a faster pace. "What . . . what is that? A child? Did you —"

She raised her hand to stop his words, her head lowered, listening. The cry came again, nearer and a bit deeper, more like a woman's call, haunting. Hairs rose on his arms.

"That ain't no young'un." Laurel's harsh whisper bit into silence. She bent to the ground and began to unlace her boot. "Mr. Taylor, you see that trail up behind you?"

"Why are you taking off your boot?"

"Do you see that trail, yonder?" She nodded behind him, her voice strained.

It took a moment for her words to sink in. "The trail?" He turned and noticed a faint path cut between the trees up the mountainside, stretching away from their current position. "Yes, I see it."

She took a quick look at his weak leg and pursed her lips together, pulling one boot off and moving to unlace the other. "Run as fast as you can up that trail. My house is at the top of the ridge. Get my daddy. Tell him to bring his gun."

"I'm not leaving you here alone." Though Jonathan had no experience fighting spirits, or whatever haunted these mountains, he certainly wouldn't leave some young woman to do battle alone.

The wail echoed closer, farther down the mountain toward them. Laurel glanced in the direction of the sound and then stood, grabbing his arm. "We ain't got time to argue. I *know* what it is." She looked back down at his leg. "Run, and don't look back. No matter what you hear." She pushed him toward the trail and then started pulling at her stockings, wild eyes still fixed on his. "Teacher, I said *go.*"

Her urgent command propelled him into motion. He didn't know why he was running, or from what, whether a vengeful spirit or one of Doyle's Baskerville hounds, but he ran as if his very life depended on it. From the look in Laurel McAdams's eyes, it did.

# Chapter Three

The cry came again. Closer.

Jonathan ran up the hill, his lungs ready to burst and his body screaming for relief. Dusk crowded his vision, overshadowing the trail as he stumbled for the tenth time. Bushes snatched at his clothes like hundreds of angry claws to slow him down, but he couldn't stop. He had to get help for Laurel. He mounted the hill and chanced a look back the way he'd come. Whatever hunted in the forest had probably reached the spot where he'd left Laurel. Pain knifed through his chest — whether from exhaustion, fear, or the fact he was a complete and utter coward, he wasn't sure.

What sort of gentleman was he? He turned back toward the trail and almost retraced his steps to rescue her and regain his honor, but the urgency in her voice and expression halted his return. Classes on the Pythagorean theorem and early eastern civilizations hadn't prepared him for this. Medical courses? Doubtful. Dickens's novels? Maybe.

He stumbled against a rock and slammed his knees into the ground. The cry echoed toward him again, deeper and with a growl in it. Pinpricks tingled up his neck to his scalp and ushered a shiver through his body. *Dear God, what is it?* The trail was silent except for the eerie rustle of dry leaves — and no sign of Laurel.

He had to get help.

He pushed himself off the ground and ran forward. . . .

Directly into the barrel of a shotgun.

The second time in as many days.

"Mighty late in the evenin' to be sneaking 'bout the woods, boy." A sturdy man, medium height, emerged from the thicket like a shadow, his gun trained on Jonathan's chest.

Jonathan's knees, already weak from his flight, almost gave way altogether. Maybe he *was* in a Dickens novel. Or worse. Edgar Allan Poe.

He instinctively raised his arms and stepped back.

The man moved slowly, his leathery hand pinched near the trigger. Eyes narrowed just behind the sight of the gun, he tilted his head to the left and spit into the forest. "What's yer business?"

Jonathan swallowed to wet his dry throat. "I need to find Mr. . . ." His mind went blank. What was Laurel's last name?

The cry split into the silence of their conversation and shocked Jonathan out of his inertia.

"McAdams. Mr. McAdams. I'm the new schoolteacher, and his daughter Laurel is down . . ." Jonathan looked back down the trail. "Down the . . . the path."

The man measured Jonathan with a long stare, then without so much as a glance back, he marched down the trail at a rapid pace until he disappeared into a coat of dusk and forest. Jonathan's legs gave way. He collapsed to the ground and released a long breath. Ghosts? Men lurking in the shadows with guns, ready to kill?

Oh yes, this was much more reminiscent of Poe. Jonathan preferred lighter, less life-threatening reads.

Darkness crowded the last remnants of sunset back into the pitch black of the forest, and the sounds around him grew increasingly less familiar. The eerie call of an owl, he knew, and . . . something akin to a cricket noise? Perhaps even a frog. An explosion of gunfire shook him to a stand, and he turned to stare in the direction of the sound. With the events of this evening, he may never sleep through the night again.

As if to confirm his conclusions, a movement down the path caught his attention . . . and turned his blood cold. Approaching, cast half in moonlight and half in shadow, came an apparition in white. A gown fluttered around it as the specter closed in on him like a vampire. If Jonathan could have felt his legs, he would have moved, but numbness stole through him, paralyzing him in place.

"Teacher?"

Jonathan blinked. Was it Laurel's ghost? Come to exact revenge upon his cowardice?

"Teacher?" Her pale face came into view, concern crinkling her brow. "Are you hurt?"

Well, he doubted a banshee or vampire would ask about his welfare before killing him. Laurel drifted forward, barefoot and in nothing but her under dress. The thin white material did little to hide the curves of womanhood he'd failed to notice upon their first acquaintance. No, she most certainly was not a little girl. A surge of heat warmed him from his toes to his forehead.

"Wha . . . what happened?"

She crossed her arms in front of her and rubbed her hands against her skin as if to keep warm. "Daddy's been trying to get that nasty lion for ages. I hope he won a good shot."

"Lion?" Jonathan loosened his collar from its choke hold on his throat and stepped forward, slowly unbuttoning his shirt. "There are lions in the Blue Ridge Mountains?"

Laurel's attention went to his open shirt and then shifted back to his face, confused. "Mountain lions. You ain't heard of them? Cougars?"

"Cougars?" He slid his arms from his shirt and draped the material over Laurel's shoulders, pulling it tight around her. "You have cougars in the Blue Ridge Mountains?"

She studied him, then looked down at the shirt, before returning her attention to him. "What in the name of Sugar Loaf are you doing givin' me your shirt?"

"I . . . I thought you may be cold, and this was the very least I could do."

Laurel's gaze searched his, the confusion dissipating into understanding. Streams of moonlight sliced through the trees and haloed her wild golden curls. The faintest hint of a smile touched her lips, and she tilted her head ever so slightly to the right, a sweet look of trust on her face. It was one of the most beautiful sights he'd ever seen.

"Thank you, Mr. Taylor," she whispered and pulled the shirt more closely around her shoulders. "That's awful nice."

She didn't move closer, but she didn't step away either. They both stood, suspended in the moment — both holding on to the front of Jonathan's shirt, fingers inches from touching. Something powerful and pleasant swelled up through his chest. Perhaps it was mere gratitude at her being flesh and blood, and alive. Whatever the feeling, the shock of it pushed him back a step and broke the moonlit spell.

"I should have stayed behind to protect you. I'm sorry."

One of Laurel's hands flew to her hips while the other pinched his shirt in place. "You're talking crazy now. You did the right thing." She pointed her finger and grinned. "You listened to me. Shows you're smart."

He couldn't help but return her smile, his pulse slowing back to a normal rate. "After tonight, Miss . . . Laurel, I'll heed any advice you give me."

"Is that so?" She gestured with a nod up to the right. "Then let's get out of the dark and move on inside so the whole family can lay eyes on you."

Jonathan hesitated, a little mesmerized by the innocence and beauty of this foreign creature before him. She'd risked her life for him, unwaveringly so.

Laurel stopped in her turn and studied him. "You've had a humdinger of a day, ain'tcha?"

"Quite." An understatement of the decade. He drew in an unsteady breath and pushed a palm through his hair, his gaze traveling back down her body as she moved ahead of him on the path. "Might . . . might I ask what happened to your clothes?"

Laurel shrugged, face forward. "It's one of the first things you learn when you know a cougar's got you in his scent. You try to slow him down."

"By removing your clothes?"

Her grin hitched up on one side again, her humor marker. "Well, I'd rather learn another way, ain't no mistake, but it's all I got right now. If the cougar has to stop and sniff each piece of clothing, then it will —"

"Slow him down." Jonathan felt his own smile bloom. "That's brilliant."

"Book learnin' ain't the only kind of smarts you need, is it, Teacher?" Her brow lifted to match her smile. "Come on. My house is at the top of the ridge."

"What about your father?"

She sent a look back down the path and sighed. "I almost feel sorry for that cougar."

Jonathan shook his head, still trying to convince himself that he was awake . . . and alive. His sister would take the entire account of his day as if pure fiction in his next letter. In truth, if he hadn't lived it, he'd probably not believe it either.

A shadowy structure rose before them, hugging the mountainside with various rooflines jutting into the night. The sight of smoke and flickering light through a window promised heat against the evening chill in the air, Jonathan hoped.

"You got 'im?" a young voice called through the shadows. The silhouette of a child shuffled across what appeared to be a front porch.

"All in one piece too," Laurel called back, then shot a grin over her shoulder and tapped the shirt she still had draped around her shoulders. "Well, mostly."

His lips relaxed into another smile, effortlessly. Her easy comradery and humor provided a buffer against the residual shock of the past hour. His sister would find Laurel McAdams fascinating.

He followed Laurel up steep stairs onto a porch and toward a dimly lit entry.

"We thought that lion done got you and Teacher," the young voice said from ahead of them, stopping in the doorway to reveal a sunny-headed youth. "I was lookin' forward to eatin' your portions for supper."

Laurel tousled the boy's thick head of curls and pushed him through the door. "We got fried chicken and taters. You really think some mountain lion's gonna stop me from those vittles?"

Even in the pale light of the moon, Jonathan could see the simplicity and aged wear of the log house. Eight people, or more, in this home? His uncle's letters had detailed the economic differences of the Appalachias, but seeing the truth in flesh, wood, and stone made a humbling difference. No, he knew nothing about this world. The scene continued his mental comparison to some fictional world in Dickens, unreal. Yet, a warm swell of laughter tumbled from the front door — a type of laughter he rarely heard in the grand halls of his family's town house. Heartfelt.

The lantern lit their way into a large front room, alight with a fire's glow from a massive stone fireplace. The air tinted with the thick scent of something frying. Jonathan's stomach answered the call.

Log walls framed the room patched with bits of . . . newspaper. Newspaper? As wallpaper? Two beds stood at each corner, and a wooden rocker along with a few ladder-backs surrounded the fireplace. Did everyone sleep in this one room? Surely not.

A doorway opened into another room, where he caught sight of a long table surrounded by chairs. At one side of the fireplace, a narrow staircase disappeared out of sight.

"This here rascal is Isom Tarleton McAdams." Laurel's words brought his attention back to the lad at her side. "He's in Miss Simms's class right now, but if there's ever any help you need navigatin' these mountains, he's the best."

The tow-headed boy stood a little taller, a similar spray of freckles dusting his nose like his older sister's. "Know every cave and holler from here to Yella Hill." Then his eyes grew wide. "What in blazes happened to yer shirt, Teacher?"

Laurel laughed. "He was bein' all gentlemanly when I had to skin down to outwit the mountain lion." She shrugged out of Jonathan's shirt and passed it to him.

Isom's nose crinkled. "I don't think I wanna be no gentleman, if 'n it means you have to give your clothes away. I'd have to wear my Sunday shirt ever day."

Jonathan's mouth slacked. Did the boy only have two shirts? More information from his uncle's letters surged to the forefront of his mind. Large families. Hardworking. Poor.

Jonathan removed his hat and took inventory of the room again, following Laurel over the threshold into a brighter space, alight with lanterns.

"You look plumb dumbstruck, Teacher," Laurel whispered.

"I just can't imagine how all of you can sleep in one room."

"Gracious sakes, we don't all sleep in there. That'd be a crowd, wouldn't it?" Laurel gestured toward the larger bed to the right. "Mama and Daddy sleep there, with Suzie. The twins are in the other bed. Isom shares the lean-to with my brother Jeb usually, but tonight I reckon he's gonna be sharin' it with you." She nodded to the stairway. "Me and Maggie take the loft. Don't you share with your brothers?"

He didn't meet her gaze, the image of his immaculate space almost shameful in the sight of the surroundings. "We have our own rooms."

Laurel's chuckle brought his gaze back to hers. "Shucks, Teacher, I ain't never had my own bed, let alone my own room, 'cept when I stay at Mrs. Cappy's, and then I'm living high." She dropped her voice again. "I ought to warn you. Isom is as rowdy at sleep as he is in wakin' hours, so I'd scooch to the far side of the bed if I was you to keep from gettin' bruised."

After last night on a cot on the floor of the derelict mission house, sleeping in an actual bed, with or without a rowdy bedfellow, sounded like an improvement.

She led him through the doorway into what appeared to be the kitchen. A woman stood by the stove, cutting up some golden breadlike food. A girl, not much younger than Laurel, waited near the table, plates in hand. A small girl with braids the same gold as Laurel's stood beside her, and two boys sat at her feet playing with spoons. Their matching mass of red curls and dark eyes marked them as "the twins."

"Look who I found."

All eyes turned to the doorway.

"Well now." The woman at the stove smiled, hair a little darker than Laurel's and pinned back in a tight bun. She stepped forward, wiping her hand on her apron before presenting it to Jonathan, her blue eyes blooming with the same welcome as Laurel's. "Pleased to meet ya, Mr. Taylor. Welcome to Maple Springs."

Poor Teacher looked paler than a ghost. No doubt he was still addled by the incident with the mountain lion and who knows what other shocks since arriving at Maple Springs. She'd read a host of books, and none of them came close to describing her world.

Laurel studied him from across the table as she placed the bowl of mashed potatoes in the center. He sat talking to Mama, his manners as kind as anything she'd ever seen, and even with his pale complexion, he wore handsome like a prince . . . or at least how she imagined a prince must have worn handsome. Refined. Clean. Smelled like spring.

What on earth was he doing in Maple Springs? His welcome had been a hard one. She worried the collar of her dress, having run upstairs to get respectable. Would he return to England as soon as daylight touched the trees? She frowned at the thought. The last thing they needed was another quitter.

Half the young'uns in the lower school couldn't even read letters, and most of the upper-school students kept their heads full of courting, proof they'd been without a teacher for much too long to remember how to dream bigger than the next day. Since Miss Brackston left in early April to get married to her Asheville sweetheart, Miss

Simms had about lost her head trying to teach all the grades. She sure could scream better than any mountain lion.

"Maggie here" — Mama placed her palm on Maggie's shoulder — "she'll be in your class."

Maggie barely lifted her eyes to the teacher, in her usual shy way. "Good evenin'."

"I look forward to getting to know you better, Maggie."

Maggie's face turned plumb crimson.

"And this is Suzie." Mama touched the head of the youngest girl in the McAdams family. With her regular cheerfulness, the golden-haired cherub sent Mr. Taylor her widest grin, double dimples and three front teeth missing.

"You tawk real purty."

Mr. Taylor's smile spread wide and he knelt to meet Suzie at her level. There was something sweet about a man down on his knees with a young'un. Laurel hadn't seen a whole host of gentlemen. Most of the menfolk in these parts couldn't afford to be gentle, except Mr. Ward with his wife and daughters. Heaven and all its angels, that man could melt away a storm when he smiled at his family.

Laurel hadn't reckoned there were too

many men like Mr. Ward in the world, but Mr. Taylor might be one of the few. Jeb had said a gentleman was a weak man. Laurel's gaze shot to Jonathan's leg. Was he? When he'd had his shirt off, he'd looked about as stout as her brother.

"Well, I like the way you talk too," Mr. Taylor said, his soft voice dripping over the words.

Maggie looked at Laurel, her eyes wide as saucers, most likely envisioning a little bit of a fairy tale.

"You done met Isom," Mama continued. "But these two on the floor here are James and John."

Mr. Taylor's smile spread into a chuckle as one of the boys threw a spoon at him. "Sons of thunder?"

Mama nodded. "And maybe a hurricane or two."

Laurel walked over to the shelf and took another plate to add to the table. "Mama's people are from the English way, ain . . . aren't they, Mama?"

Jonathan slipped his soft brown gaze from Laurel back to Mama. "Your people?"

"My granny. She come over with her daddy from Derbyshire, but he died real soon after gettin' here. Her mama remarried rather quick to a mountain man, 'cause he'd help provide for the young'uns. Settled in Maple Springs and that's where we been ever since." She nodded toward her special cabinet. The one with the curved glass and the wood carvings. "That's from my granny and so is the tea set inside."

"Mrs. Cappy even special ordered some English tea one time for Mama's birthday as a thank-ya for sending me and Maggie down to stay with her." Laurel sighed at the memory. "It was the best thing I've had to drink in my whole life. Do you remember the sugar cubes, Maggie?"

Maggie almost smiled.

"Mmmhmm, sweet and creamy." Laurel closed her eyes for a minute to savor the recollection.

"It's nice to know you have one good thought about England, Miss McAdams."

Laurel's eyes flew wide. "Well, now I have another." She gestured toward him with the plate before setting it on the table. " 'Cause I just know you're gonna work wonders with our school."

Mr. Taylor stood slowly, clearly uncomfortable but determined not to show it. "I certainly hope you're right." His gaze flipped to Mama. "Because I want to be of service."

A loud commotion came from the front

room. Butter, their greyhound, entered first and went directly to Teacher, sniffing for trouble. Daddy marched in behind, a bundle of cloth in one hand, his gun in the other, and a thundercloud on his brow. He tossed the cloths to Laurel. "I wisht I was as smart as that dad-blamed cat."

He released another growl, set his gun against the wall, and then turned to offer Teacher his hand. "Sam McAdams." Her daddy stood about as tall as Teacher but was an extra few inches thick in about every direction. "I bet you never hunted a mountain lion before, have ya, boy?"

Teacher took Daddy's hand without flinching. "No sir, but after tonight, I'm keen to learn."

Her daddy stared at Teacher for a good five seconds and then burst out with the loudest ruckus of a laugh one ever did hear. He smacked Mr. Taylor on the back and nodded. "I reckon you are." He gestured toward the table. "Come on. Let's eat before all this hard work gets cold."

Two hours later, as Laurel lay in her bed, she stared out the tiny window toward the barn. The light in the lean-to had gone out half an hour ago. Perhaps Teacher would get some sleep since Mama made Isom sleep with the twins. She snickered. Well, she knew a nine-year-old who'd wake up bruised in the mornin'.

And even though Mr. Taylor nearly fell asleep in the rickety old rocking chair as they'd played music after supper, she could tell he'd liked listenin'. He'd smiled several times at the words to the songs.

He wasn't afraid to ask questions either. Unlike Mr. Davis, the teacher from five years ago who talked more than he listened, Mr. Taylor seemed to thirst for information about the mountain people and their ways. And Daddy loved giving it.

"He does talk purty," Maggie's voice whispered into the cool air of their room. "And he smells good too."

Laurel rolled her eyes but couldn't deny it. When he'd wrapped his shirt around her shoulders, he'd left the scent of sweet leather behind, made her want to hold on to his shirt a little longer.

"Kizzie would have been undone at the sight of him," Maggie whispered, shifting to snuggle against Laurel's warmth.

Laurel pinched the quilt close to her chest against the ache that always accompanied the thoughts of her sister. "Well, he's definitely a sight prettier than most fellas she ogled over." Oh Kizzie. She'd love a handsome face and sweet talker. She wouldn't have heard one word Mr. Taylor taught in school for pining away after him.

"You reckon he'll stay?"

Laurel drew in a long, quiet breath, weighing her reply. As kind and interested as Mr. Taylor seemed, he wasn't fit for these mountains, but voicing the thought wouldn't help anybody, especially her sister who desperately wanted to learn more about science and nature. She had a curiosity about it all and a unique gift for drawing what she saw. "If Daddy and that mountain lion didn't scare him off, I think we got a good chance to keep him awhile."

Silence whispered with the wind over the wooden rafters.

"Do you think she's alive?"

Laurel pressed her eyes closed, forcing the burn away. "I hope so."

"Me too."

More silence as Maggie pushed closer into Laurel's back for warmth. "Do you think Daddy will ever let us talk about her again?"

Laurel hesitated. Down deep, their daddy was a good man, but the betrayal of family was the worst kind with certain expectations she knew her daddy wouldn't shake. Laurel squeezed the quilt around her body like a hug, adding a prayer to her thoughts. "Maybe so, Maggie. Maybe one day."

# Chapter Four

The faint gray of predawn brought Jonathan's sleeping quarters into a hazy view. He rolled over on his side and reached for the pocket watch he'd left on the crate used as a bedside table. Shadows of night still obscured the sight of his watch's face, but he'd guess from his short acquaintance to North Carolina that it was before six. He lay back and reached his arms up by his head, his palms pressing into the wall above his bed and his feet nearly touching the room at the other end. The lean-to was about as long as it was wide, but with stone walls and a tiny potbelly stove, the room remained comfortable all night.

Despite his exhaustion, he'd stared into the darkness, wide-awake, long into the night. He'd stepped into a world like none he'd ever known. Yes, there were terrifying chasms of differences and some daunting challenges to meet, but something about a family gathered round a table for a meal, children and parents, offering their meager options, fueled his determination.

He'd come for a purpose.

He looked up at the wooden ceiling, his smile stretching wide at the memory of the McAdams family gathered around the fireplace, singing together. All ages joined in, as Mr. McAdams played the banjo, Laurel the violin, which she kept referring to as a fiddle, and Isom the spoons. The spoons? But the boy had played them with confidence and rhythm.

Then there were the songs. Some deserved a good dance, and others? Others swelled in almost mournful tones, calling to a deep place in his soul. They recounted tragic tales or fathomless longings or sweet romances or tender requests to the Almighty, and the way the family's voices ebbed and flowed in tight harmony moved him.

He closed his eyes, ushering a prayer. *Equip me for Your service in heart and spirit.*

The high timbre of young voices drifted through the door of the lean-to. Jonathan pushed to a stand and peered out the small window above his bed, squinting to see in the morning dimness. Lantern light glowed from one of the small side windows of the house, its true image beginning to dawn with the faint hint of morning. The log cabin appeared much smaller on the outside than it had felt from within. Metal sheets made up the steeply slanted roof, and a back part of the house looked as if it had been added on at a different time due to the unpaired look of wood and roof pitch.

Two silhouettes, one tall and the other small, walked through the forest away from the house, a hound with them. What was its name? Something odd. Butter.

Last night, when asked why they had named the dog Butter, Laurel answered that their father always named an animal after whatever he traded for it, unless he used "cash money" to buy it. Throughout the remainder of the evening, Jonathan had also met a cat named Molasses and a shepherd named Boots.

He squinted into the growing light to identify the pair of silhouettes. Laurel and Isom? Laurel had a rifle resting easily on her shoulder. His grin resurfaced. More fodder to add to his letters to his sister, Cora. He could imagine her reaction — pale gray eyes wide just before she burst into laughter. An ache squeezed his breath, and he turned away from the window, quickly dressing into his warmest clothes.

The morning air smelled of woodstove

and pine. Jonathan pulled his jacket close around his neck and took off in the direction he'd seen Laurel walk. What would the two do so early in the morning? He glanced back at the house and barn. The chicken coop stood near the barn, so they weren't collecting eggs. And since they were going in the opposite direction of the barn, they weren't taking care of the cow or horse.

Glints of dawn twinkled into existence and shoved the gray of predawn away. The trees and tall grass around him sparkled with a glossy coat of dew. Over a hill and down the other side, Jonathan caught sight of the pair kneeling, Laurel's blond head bent over something with Isom at her side.

His footfall against the leaves must have alerted them to his presence. Butter darted toward him in a run. Laurel shot to her feet and spun around, rifle gripped to her side. Thankfully, she caught sight of him before she raised the gun. He wasn't certain if he could manage gunpoint greetings for a third time.

"Heaven sakes, Teacher, you ought to make more noise if you're gonna follow folks around in the woods." Laurel released a long breath and shook her head, her expression serious though her tone sounded light.

"Forgive me. I didn't mean to startle you."

Her shoulders relaxed with a sigh. "I reckon I got my back up after we had a meeting with that mountain lion last night." Her grin flickered alive, a common fixture for her. "Mama thought you might lay in a bit this mornin', but I see you're up with the sun. Daddy would say that shows good character."

Jonathan took the compliment with a taller stance. "There's much to be done. If your father is going to gather other men to mend the mission house, I want to be available to help. No use dillydallying about."

She gave him a measured look and then nodded as if he'd passed some unspoken test. "Daddy was sayin' they're gonna make repairs out of fieldstone taken from the old Carson place. It won't make the house no bigger, but you'll keep warm and dry this winter. Stone holds heat real well."

"I like the sound of warm and dry."

Her smile bloomed again, settling over him with a sweet calm. "And I'm sure you'll miss the coon holes."

Her quick wit set him at ease. "I feel certain I can live without them quite happily."

She chuckled, a sound that somehow brought an added glow with it.

"Quit ya jawin' and let's git these rabbits fit for Daddy afore he comes lookin' for us." Isom looked up, face pinched in frustration as he wrestled something from a strange-looking little box into a cloth bag.

High-pitched peeps came from the bag as Laurel reached to take the undulating sack from her brother.

"What are you doing?"

"We're checking our gums," Isom answered and took off walking in the opposite direction, as if Jonathan understood the routine like a native. "We gotta get 'em done afore Daddy leaves."

"Gums?"

He ran to catch up with Laurel, who'd moved on to follow her brother over the next hill.

"Rabbit gums. Daddy takes rabbits to either Mrs. Cappy's store or into town to sell. Seems that they're a delicacy for rich city folks."

Jonathan looked around the forest, the air cool and shaded with early dawn. "You do this every morning?"

"Most mornin's. It's good money."

The majority of people in his social world weren't even awake at this time of day, let alone in the forest catching rabbits.

They slowed near another "gum," its

design a simple wooden rectangle with a notch on one end. Kneeling low, Isom carefully raised the door of the trap, but even before the door opened completely, Butter sent off a series of rapid-fire barks.

"What in the —"

"Run!" Isom yelled, interrupting Laurel's exclamation, and scooted from the box at a fast back crawl. "Polecat! Run, afore it's too late!"

"No, Butter —" Laurel's words cut off as a hiss sounded from the box.

Almost in synchrony, Butter yelped and shot back. Isom turned his face toward the ground, continuing to army crawl a retreat, and Laurel whipped around and snatched Jonathan's hand, tugging him into a run.

What was happening? A polecat? How many types of cats did these Appalachian people have?

As the thought solidified, the most detestable, pungent aroma clouded every space around them, turning Jonathan's stomach with its potency.

Laurel brought her apron around her nose, so Jonathan took the hint by pulling his jacket up to try and block the scent. As he glanced over his shoulder, the most unusual furry black-and-white creature emerged from the rabbit gum, like no cat he'd ever seen. Furry, black tail flagged high, it continued its misty assault even though both Butter and Isom were clearly out of range.

"Oh, he's real mad." Laurel increased her pace, bringing Jonathan along with her.

Yes, they needed to outrun the horrendous odor.

But no matter how far away they ran from the scene, even all the way back to the barn, the scent followed them, growing in intensity when Butter or Isom neared. Laurel slowed and looked behind her, pressing her palm into her stomach and bending over as if she might become sick. He understood. The smell continued to unsettle him too.

But then she looked up and started . . . laughing, and the very sound somehow took the sting, though not the stench, out of the situation. It was one of the sweetest sounds — a gift into this wild, impoverished place, and he welcomed it with a sense of wonder.

She had so little compared to him and yet, somehow, he wondered if she didn't possess something more intangible and precious than he'd ever known.

It was like all of creation was dead set at scaring off the new teacher from Maple Springs before he even taught one lesson.

The soft-spoken man didn't seem to be a troublemaker, but in the past day since Laurel had known him, they'd run from Miss Simms's pursuit, a hungry mountain lion, and now the spray of a scared skunk?

She looked over at him as they created distance from the ol' polecat. He kept looking over his shoulder, caramel-colored eyes wide, as if another cougar stalked their trail. Poor man. They may have outsmarted the mountain lion, but there was no way they'd outrun what that polecat left behind.

Laurel slowed her pace with Jonathan coming to a stop by her side. He leaned over, hands on his knees, and finally glanced at her. "I . . . I . . . have never seen a cat like *that*."

The stench was overwhelming, and Laurel really shouldn't laugh, but the man was about as prepared for Maple Springs as she was for a visit to King George. It was either cry out of sheer pity for poor Jonathan Taylor or laugh at the ridiculousness.

She preferred laughing.

The man looked at her as if she'd lost every bit of sense she had, and he might be right, but the absurdity of the past two days didn't make a lick of sense . . . and only a crazy man would stay for more.

"I reckon you'd better git on back to

England before something worse happens to you, Teacher, 'cause the whole forest has come out in protest, it seems." She coughed through another breath of putrid air, attempting to quiet her chuckle.

His brows shot high, and then he seemed to catch on to her humor, because his grin spread like sunshine. "I do feel rather important to garner such special attention."

Her laugh shook through her again. Well, that sense of humor would sure come in handy from the looks of things. "And I hope you're mighty stubborn too, 'cause we're in need of a good teacher."

His smile softened, his gaze fastened on hers, and something in his eyes, a gentleness or determination, or whatever it was, quieted her doubts. Maybe Jonathan Taylor held a lot more strength than she'd given him credit for.

"I think it's all Teacher's fault." Isom neared, rubbing his eyes, with Butter at his side. "We ought to send him back afore a bear comes callin'."

Mr. Taylor offered a helpless shrug, and Laurel chuckled again, covering her nose from Isom and Butter's nearness. Oh, they'd gotten the worst of it, especially Butter. "No bear in all creation is gonna come after us right now, Isom, especially you."

His frown ground a little deeper. "I don't wanna take another bath in sody water."

Laurel resumed her walk, tossing an explanation to Teacher. "Butter got Isom into trouble last spring the same way." She flipped her gaze back to Isom. "And you're getting the bath first, 'cause ain't none of us gonna stomach breakfast with that kind of stink around."

Teacher's laugh was the sort that made a person grin right along with the sound, all warm and toasty and authentic. "I have never seen such an animal in my life."

"You ain't never seen a polecat afore?" Isom placed his hands on his hips like the grown-up he wanted to be. "Where is it you come frum anyhow?"

"A place without polecats." Laurel tousled her brother's hair and then regretted it, because that simple motion unearthed a stronger whiff of putrid air. "Which sounds close to heaven right now."

"What is . . . sody water?" Teacher asked.

Isom shuddered at the mere mention of the word, but Laurel shook her head at his dramatic tendency. "It's just a good ol' mixture we mountain folks use to help lessen the stink. First off, it was just bakin' soda and peroxide, but when Mrs. Cappy started carryin' Palmolive liquid soap in her store, Mama mixed a good dose of that in with the soda and peroxide to make the smell even better."

"I still don't like it none," Isom groaned, but then his pale gaze flitted to Teacher, lit with his usual rascally-ness. "But ain't no better way to git welcomed into the family than a skunk squirtin' and a sody water bath. Yes siree, what stories you'll have to tell your people back in . . . wherever it is yer frum, Teacher."

Teacher pinched his eyes closed, his grin burgeoning against another laugh. A sweetness clung to him. Maybe it was the fact he was as green as a spring tree when it came to mountain people, or maybe it was the way he'd managed to adjust to their wild world with such a quiet acceptance, but whatever it was, Laurel knew he was in Maple Springs for a reason . . . and she was determined to help him succeed for the good of the children. Her smile twisted up on one side. And maybe for the good of Jonathan Taylor too.

"I expected the McAdamses to take good care of you in my absence, but they've already got you laughing?"

Jonathan turned to see a face he'd missed

for much longer than two days. "Uncle Edward?"

His uncle stood near the front porch of the McAdams cabin wearing clothes much better suited to mountain trekking than those Jonathan wore. Thick brown trousers and a heavy jacket. A satchel crossed him from shoulder to hip, and he'd grown his beard thicker than Jonathan ever remembered, but the twinkle in the man's eyes remained evergreen.

His uncle's face, more creased than eight years ago, held a peace that emulated the tone of his letters. He'd found where he belonged among these people and the rugged mountains. The welcome smile on his face twisted into a look of pure disgust as Jonathan approached, flanked by Laurel and Isom.

"Heaven and earth!" His laughter burst out in a rich rumble. "I see you're becoming acquainted with much more than the McAdamses."

Jonathan paused his advance, but his uncle bridged the gap, despite the horrendous odor and took Jonathan into his arms. "It's good to see you, lad," he whispered into Jonathan's ear and then pulled back, keeping his hands on Jonathan's shoulders. "Not so good to smell you right now, but you're a sight for sore eyes."

"Preacher Anderson."

All eyes turned to the porch where Mr. McAdams stood, surveying the group with his intense gaze.

"Sam. Thank you for taking good care of my nephew."

Mr. McAdams's attention shifted to Jonathan, bringing with it the unnerving feeling of being peeled apart and measured. He nodded and released Jonathan from the hold of his stare.

"Breakfast is 'bout ready. Come on inside."

"I'm gonna go warn Mama and Daddy about the stinker we got with us before they let him too far into the house. I reckon y'all wanna catch up a bit." Laurel gave Isom a little push ahead. "Come on, Isom, let's go around back and find the washtub."

Jonathan released a quiet chuckle as he watched Laurel guide — or push — a disgruntled Isom around the back of the house.

"They're a good family."

Jonathan turned back to his uncle, nearly crying at finding one familiar face in this new world. "They've been very kind to me."

His uncle nodded and gestured for Jonathan to join him in a walk, as they used to do when Jonathan was a youth. Edward Anderson had always taken time to talk to Jonathan, inviting him to his country farm or giving him a sense of acceptance he never received from his father. In fact, Jonathan grew up rarely seeing his father at all.

"I'm sorry I wasn't here when you arrived. In the mountains, I've had to adapt my profession in many directions." He looked up at the sky. "In this case, I was assisting the doctor with a sick visit that turned into a funeral."

"I'm sorry."

"It is a much too common occurrence in these mountains. Dr. Hensley is one man for many communities, and he's not a young man anymore."

His words, the implicit plea, tugged at Jonathan's heart. A physician, the course he'd set for himself before the war had derailed those plans and sent him from his partial degree into medic training for the front lines. Training that was cut short by his inadequate mobility and leg strength.

These mountains afforded little patience with his disability. Surely his uncle wasn't suggesting Jonathan could be useful here . . . as a doctor?

"And he needs my help still." Uncle Edward tipped his head toward the McAdams cabin. "You'll be fine here with the McAdamses for one more night as I travel to Asheville with Dr. Hensley for a meeting regarding this unexplained epidemic which is decimating entire communities."

"I read something in the paper on the train. What are they calling it? Spanish influenza?"

He nodded, rubbing his chin. "It's like nothing I've ever seen. Dr. Hensley wanted me to accompany him in the hopes two minds are better than one, especially since his hearing isn't what it used to be. I've invited him to my cabin for Sunday supper, so you can meet him."

"You'll be back by tomorrow for church?"

His grin perked with an added twinkle in his eyes. "They can't have service without the preacher. I'm leaving on the nine o'clock train this morning and should reach the pulpit tomorrow just in time for service."

Jonathan followed him up the steps to the cabin. At the top of the landing, his uncle turned and placed a palm on Jonathan's shoulder. "I know you've been trying to find your place for a long time, and this may not be exactly what you've wanted, but perhaps Maple Springs is exactly what you've needed."

# CHAPTER FIVE

It wouldn't do any good. Laurel tried to read the next page of *Little Women,* but her thoughts scattered like chickens at supper. For some reason, she'd had the hardest time keeping Jonathan Taylor out of her head. Of course, it made sense to feel a little curious about him. Every new teacher from the outside brought his own mystery, but Mr. Taylor confused her. She'd only met a handful of other men who'd carried themselves with such gentleness as Teacher, all from the mountains, but he brought an added sense of refinement that made him plumb fascinating.

With all the shock he'd had in the past two days, even taking a sody water bath in their metal tub by the fire to get rid of the skunk smell . . .

Laurel covered her laugh at the memory of his wide-eyed reaction as realization dawned. He'd stared a full ten seconds at the tub by the fire in the middle of the open room, Mama reassuring him she'd put up curtains to protect his privacy, and Isom reminding him that there wasn't nothing Teacher had that Isom hadn't seen before, which brought a look of unveiled horror to the man's face.

Yet through it all, he'd held a quiet dignity, even though he probably should've been running for the train station. He had a whole lot of his uncle, Preacher Anderson, in him, she could tell. And she'd always liked Preacher Anderson.

She sighed, tucked her book beneath her arm, and started down the ladder to make quick work of the milking, since the whole polecat situation had stalled the usual workings of the morning. Then she'd take some biscuits down to the men working on the mission house, and most likely take Teacher with her, since he smelled less like a polecat after his bath. He was surefire determined to work, which would make the menfolk like him better.

Mr. Barnard from five years hence barely lifted a piece of chalk to the board. He didn't last more than three months in Maple Springs, and he didn't have near the welcome Jonathan Taylor had.

Mountain lion. Polecat. Danette Simms.

Her chuckle resurrected as her feet hit the barn floor.

"Are you thinking something humorous or reading it?"

She spun around, slipping the book behind her back, searching the barn for a sneaky sibling only to find Mr. Taylor at the door.

"Because I feel fairly certain the circumstances of the morning should leave anyone either laughing or terrified."

Her smile stretched wide. "Well, I'm sure glad you got a good sense of humor, 'cause as far as I can see, you ain't run off yet."

He stood a little taller, his grin still intact. "I'm not afraid of a challenge."

"It seems you're gonna get one whether you're afraid or not . . . and then some."

He attempted to peer around her back, brow tipping ever so slightly, before his attention fixed on the barn loft. "Were you reading up there?"

She wasn't sure why, but her face warmed to hot, and she followed his gaze to keep from looking directly into his eyes. "If I'm gonna get any reading done, I have to find myself a hiding spot or two."

"You hide to read?"

"Come on now, you've seen what a gang lives in this house. If I sit down for any length of time, someone will either give me a chore to do or bother me with a sackful of questions." She shook her head, sending a quick peek up to his face. "If you're the friendly sort, you won't go tellin' my secret."

"Your secret's safe with me." He stuck his hands into his pockets and lowered his voice. "I'm a huge proponent of reading. And I don't know what I'd do without the imagination of books to take me places. They're truly one of the underappreciated treasures in this world."

She tucked her book under her arm. "I feel that way. It's amazing how words can be powerful enough to trick you into thinking you've gone places and experienced things, when you've never even left your . . . barn loft."

His smile softened, and her cheeks flickered back to scorching. Book talking had never caused such a stir in her chest before, so she reckoned the feeling had more to do with Jonathan Taylor than imagination and storybooks. Unless, it was book talkin' with a . . . man.

She cleared her throat and walked over to the barn stall where Maude waited for her milking. Laurel had never conversed about books with any man before, except a few short talks with Preacher Anderson, and those were mostly about the Good Book. Most boys she knew didn't have schoolin' on the mind at all, except Joshua Polk, who loved math about as much as Sally Lawson. Did city folk like to talk about the books they were reading? She pulled out the milking stool and studied on that thought. What a wonder!

Teacher had followed her to the stall. "I know your home is remote, but have you had much variety in your reading choices?"

Not as much as she'd like. "I've read everything in the schoolhouse library and whatever I can get my hands on from Mrs. Cappy or Preacher Anderson." She drew in a deep breath. "I'm hungry for learnin'." She gestured toward the loft and grinned. "Whenever I can."

He shifted his feet, hesitating. "Have you ever considered attending college?"

Her attention shot to the spot where her savings hid. Could she trust this stranger? Her throat went dry, and she turned back to the cow. "You know anything about milking a cow, Teacher?"

He chuckled. "I watched but didn't participate."

"Well now . . ." She raised a brow, determined to get him off the subject of college. "Wanna participate?"

His gaze shot from the cow back to Laurel's face as if he wasn't sure whether she was teasing or serious. "I don't want to hurt the cow."

She grinned and gestured toward the stool. "Oh, you won't hurt ol' Maude here. Besides, having a cow of your own will make life sweeter. Milk, butter, maybe even some cheese. Mmhmm."

He slid a step closer to the cow as if she might reach out and bite him, and then with a pinch of his lips and an unusual twinkle in his eyes, he took a seat on the stool. "I'll try my hand at it on one condition."

Laurel placed a palm to her hip, waiting. "And what's that?"

"You answer my question about college."

Her grin slid right off her face. The rascal. He wasn't quite as green as she thought.

"Aha, I knew I was right. You changed the subject." He turned back to the cow, rubbing his palms along his knees in anticipation. "What do I do first?"

After a pause to grimace at the back of his head, Laurel bent low and began instructing him through the process — warm hands, squeeze-not-jerk. In no time at all, Teacher had the hang of milking like a regular mountain man.

"So?" he asked, keeping his gaze fastened

on his task as the gentle swish and ting of milk in a pail gave rhythm to his words. "Your answer."

A sliver of fear trembled up through her chest, tugging at her to keep quiet, but she'd wanted to shout it from the rooftops for nigh six months, and Mr. Taylor offered an easy opportunity, even encouragement. Only her parents and Mrs. Cappy knew the truth. Surely she could trust him? She drew in a deep breath and watched his hands work the teats. "I've thought about it of course. Hard."

She couldn't unfist that dream to him yet.

"I hope you'll seriously consider it."

She released her hold a little. "I'll tell you a secret. I've already applied."

"That's excellent. I know you'll hear something soon. What does your family think?"

"My parents are for it, but my siblings don't know, so I'd appreciate you keeping it close to your chest for now." She bit back the release of more information and turned the conversation back on him. "Now you get to trade me one secret for another."

The milking rhythm came to an abrupt stop and he turned clean around on the stool, eyes wide as walnuts. "Trade you a secret?"

She wasn't so green either. "I just told you a humdinger of a secret." Even if it wasn't the whole secret. "Now it's your turn."

He grinned and seemed to realize he'd left his post, so he turned back to milking. "Is that how it works then?"

"We're all about trading fair around here. Unless it comes to the Almighty, and He's given us so much more than we can ever trade. But amongst us humans, we can surely try."

"A secret?"

"How about I ask you a question because I have a feeling the answer's a secret?"

His eyes narrowed. "Very well, though I hold the right to decline."

"Fair enough." Her smile responded so quickly it pressed into her cheeks. "You come an awful long way to teach here, farther than any teacher before. I see you want to help, and that's good, but I sense there's somethin' else that would drive you this far from home."

He leaned back as if she'd hit him, and her hope deflated. She'd gone too far. A problem she usually had about being so direct with foreigners. Her curiosity always got the better of her. "Sorry, I was pryin'. I shared a heart secret, but I shouldn't have —"

84

He raised his hand to quiet her ramblings.

"From the sound of a fair trade, I suppose a heart secret deserves one in return." His smile didn't reach his sad eyes. He looked up at the roof of the barn again, waiting? Praying? She wasn't sure, but she almost ended the conversation again.

"I think . . . well, I think I was running away from home, at first."

Running away from home? This was an awful long way to come.

"Ever since I had my injury as a child, I've always felt less than able to accomplish my family's expectations. My father, who was a very poor man in his youth, worked tirelessly to create a living for his family, one that led to a comfortable . . ." He focused on his milking. "No, affluent lifestyle, but such work required dedication, perseverance, and . . . sacrifice." His gaze flickered back to hers. "It also cultivated a mind-set of not accepting less than perfection. He pushed his children to excel in every way. My brothers proved my father's dogmatic expectations valid by meeting every demand, particularly in sports, no matter the cost, but I just couldn't." He gestured toward his leg. "So I pursued excellence through learning, which fueled a natural love to help others, I suppose, particularly those who needed help most. In fact, I was training to become a doctor when the war broke out."

"Did your daddy talk mean to you? It's not like you could help your gimp leg." Laurel knew the sting of words from a father, though hers only used harshness when liquor took his sense.

"It was never so much about what he said as what he didn't say. When I was released from military training as a medic because of my injury, I couldn't bear to face him and all the other families whose sons were out giving their lives in a war in which I couldn't participate. I'd completed two years of medical training at university, and because of this limp" — he slammed a fist against his leg, pausing the swish and ting on tin — "they wouldn't allow me to help soldiers at the front? It made no sense. And it's not as though it's an obvious wound, so when I returned home, the looks, the comments from others, and my father's embarrassment at having such a . . . failure, made home an unbearable place."

"So, your uncle suggested coming here?" All the pieces fell into a clearer picture of Jonathan Taylor. A man wounded clean through.

"I think he saw this as an opportunity for

me to discover my own strengths and help others in the process. He's always understood me." He shrugged. "And perhaps some distance from my father wouldn't hurt either."

She studied him in the silence following his story, his head bent. It hadn't been a fair trade at all. He'd given her much more than she'd given him.

"Laurel, Jonathan. Lunches are ready for the boys," Mama called from the house.

Laurel stepped back and gestured toward the cow. "And I think, Mr. Taylor, you've just milked your first cow like an old hand. Next, I'll teach ya how to catch a chicken for supper."

He laughed, a little nervous like, and stood, pail in hand. "Milking cows and baring souls. Work to make me stronger."

She chuckled. "If you're lookin' to get stronger, then takin' you down to help the menfolk repair the mission house will surely move the process along." She stepped toward the barn door, glancing back over her shoulder and seeing Jonathan Taylor in a little different light than when she'd entered. "Not rightly sure you'll be able to walk in the mornin', but no doubt you'll be heaps stronger."

■ ■ ■ ■

Jonathan crawled onto the bench at the McAdams breakfast table, every muscle in his body screaming in protest. He stifled his groans so as to not show weakness to the patriarch of the McAdams family seated at the head of the table, but his internal lamentations cried out to return to his bed and sleep away his agony. He'd never imagined anything could beat his body worse than training camp, but hauling rocks over uneven terrain uphill, then helping set those stones in place for the walls of his new home, met the mark. And left a mark.

He'd pushed himself to his limit, attempting to keep up with the six mountain men who'd already worked from morning until he'd arrived midday. The men were a diverse crew in their personalities, but similar in their discipline and directness. Sam McAdams brought a gruff levity to the group with his dry sense of humor and boisterous laughter. Another man, Judah Morgan, wore a welcome smile that seemed out of place with the rest of the more solemn men. Strength and pride oozed from them — a type of strength Jonathan had seen before in the more experienced soldiers and officers he'd met. Strength earned from hard trials. Grief, even. Difficult choices.

The word *stalwart* came to mind.

As he took a silent trek with Sam McAdams back up the mountainside to his home, a deeper understanding about the world he'd entered settled over him. These people were bound by both the physical boundaries of the mountains but also a tie of community. Fascinating. The discomfort he'd experienced from the dirty floor and unidentifiable meat in his supper became a little less distasteful. At least potatoes tasted like potatoes and eggs like eggs.

The conversation with Laurel the previous day had fanned a flame of determination in him brighter than the one that had propelled him across an ocean. Something about her dream, her . . . courage, reminded him of the deeper reason behind his trek than a mere lad fleeing the shame of failure.

Service.

"Teacher's made of tough stuff for a flatlander, and a city one besides." Sam McAdams reached across the table for some bread called a biscuit, but it wasn't like any biscuit Jonathan knew. Light, fluffy . . . more like a bread roll than a sweet. "Hard worker."

Though Mr. McAdams didn't look in Jonathan's direction, Jonathan couldn't help sitting a little taller. He'd passed some test — received some stamp of approval. Mrs. McAdams, Caroline as Mr. McAdams referred to her, stood to the side of the room with Laurel, waiting to serve those at table like footmen or maids. Was that the expectation? After they'd prepared the meal, did they wait to eat until everyone else had finished? Then the possibility bloomed into something worse. Were they waiting to ensure enough food lasted before they took the remainders?

Jonathan suddenly felt full, even though the biscuits smothered in some sort of sauce called apple jelly were the best tasting delicacy he'd had since the train dropped him off.

"I'm grateful for the lessons in stonework." He took a smaller bite of his eggs to make them last longer. "And for the generosity of so many men to help prepare my home for living."

Sam's work-worn brow wrinkled. "It ain't fittin' to have the teacher's home in such a state, but it's been a coon's age, it seems, since we had a man teacher. Womenfolk board with Mrs. Cappy since they're unmarried, so we ain't been obliged to keep the mission house up for a man teacher." He raised his tin coffee cup to his mouth, a slight hint of a grin curving as the cup dipped. "Though a pet coon or . . . lion might git you broke right in."

The eggs solidified in Jonathan's throat and he had to force them down with a hard swallow. He never wanted to hear a mountain lion ever again, let alone have one close enough to actually see. "I think I'll be content with students for now, sir."

"Though a few of your students can caterwaul better than any ol' cougar," Laurel snickered from the side of the room. "Maybe bite like 'em too."

The other children never spoke during the meal, unless it was a baby sound from the twins, who took turns being fed in the wooden infant chair in the corner of the room. The only time they talked at all was to ask for something to eat, but he'd noticed that Laurel and Caroline both interjected comments into the conversation with Sam, though Caroline spoke little and with a gentle voice. It was a pleasant sort of idea to have an entire family at table together, though he preferred the women sit with them.

"You startin' school on Monday morn?"

Jonathan turned his attention back to Sam. "Uncle Edward suggested Tuesday, to give me another day to find my bearings and make out my lessons."

Sam nodded and scooped up another forkful of eggs. "You're from good stock, I reckon. Preacher's as hard a worker as they come. Built his own cabin three years ago and only asked for help with the roofin'." Sam tapped his head. "Studies somethin' then knows how to make it. Keen mind."

"Which you're bound to hear this mornin' at church, Teacher." Caroline McAdams warmed up Jonathan's coffee with a touch more. "But I reckon you've heard him preach before in England?"

"Only once."

"You'd like hearing him preach, Daddy. He talks worth listening to." Laurel took her father's cup from the table, her bright eyes hopeful. "Maybe you should give him a try."

Mr. McAdams pushed his palms against the table and stood, broad and thick with strength. "No doubt he is, and I'll listen to him when he comes a callin', but I ain't no churchgoin' sort." He reached for a container in his shirt pocket and drew out the vile black tobacco the men used the day before. It gave off a saccharine sweet scent in contrast to the taste. "But Teacher'll make a scene for shore." His dark eyes twinkled with the mischief he contained behind a more somber veneer. "Give the Preacher some good competition for folks' attention."

"Come on now, Daddy, Preacher's got some good wind in him." Laurel's smile failed to brighten her eyes, but she moved on as if the disappointment wouldn't hinder her steps. "I wouldn't give Teacher too much credit. What was it you said, Daddy?" Laurel wiped at the face of one of the twins with a cloth then tugged the child up on her hip from his chair with the ease of familiarity. How long had she taken care of her siblings as a mother would? "Took awhile for the folks to warm up to the preacher because he didn't yell near enough."

"Yell?"

"The kind of preachin' that shakes the sinner from the edge of hell right into the gates of heaven." Her grin took a mischievous turn. "Didn't you know that the louder a preacher is the more likely a lost soul is gonna hear the good Lord?"

"Laurel." Her mother spoke the gentle reprimand, though her pale eyes glimmered with shared humor. "If God spoke creation into bein' without a bit of yellin', I reckon He can use whatever voice He wants to change a heart now. He made the hearts anyhow, didn't He?"

Jonathan couldn't be sure, but for a moment a look passed between Caroline and her husband. Was it a plea? A gentle prodding? He wasn't sure, but he knew the quiet faith of a wife's desire to influence her reticent spouse. He'd grown up with the very picture.

As his gaze found Laurel's, he recognized the panged expression of longing for a father to know the same faith. Perhaps Laurel McAdams and he weren't as different as he'd imagined.

## Chapter Six

"It's more than you expected, isn't it?"

Jonathan rubbed at the lingering soreness in his neck and looked across the table in his uncle's small cabin. Hand-hewn logs and careful detail outfitted this two-room home, complete with loft and pristine neatness. Two wingbacks stood by the fire, a decorative dining table tucked in one corner near a window, and a wide bed nestled in the back room covered with the most uniquely colorful duvet Jonathan had ever seen.

If his uncle was going to brave the wilds of the North Carolina mountains, he'd ensure a bit of home and hearth came along too. It wasn't impossible, was it? To build a real home here, whether temporarily or, as his uncle had done, more permanently? He rubbed his palms together, taking in a breath before turning his attention back to the light brown eyes in which he'd found such kinship in his childhood. "I should have been prepared by your letters over the years, but . . . but I thought you'd waxed dramatic in your descriptions. I never expected this. It's a culture stopped in time."

Uncle Edward stared over the rim of his teacup, his gaze unrelenting. "So you wish to stay?"

Jonathan nodded. "I know my training is not in teaching, but I've had my share of experience as a teaching assistant at university. The least I can do is try."

"You taught the children on my sheep farm how to read."

A chuckle slipped through Jonathan's lips as he reached for his own cup. "I was an eager youth who needed to prove himself in one way or other."

"And with a heart to help others." Uncle Edward gestured with his cup. "As I see it, not all that much has changed, except the pitch of your voice and your need to shave."

"You're a regular jester, you are." But there was a hint of truth in his uncle's words. Jonathan did feel the need to prove himself . . . to find a purpose beyond the uneven expectations in his home and the framed-in confines of his social status. He'd craved an escape for years, but to what end?

His uncle chuckled and took a sip of his tea, the silence of evening enfolding them. "I'm pleased to have you here, Jonathan. I know it will be more convenient for you to live at the mission house once it's repaired, but for now, I'm happy for your company."

"And I'm eager for your wisdom and guidance." Jonathan set down his cup, holding his uncle's gaze. "There are thousands of things I don't know about the life of Maple Springs, and if it hadn't been for the McAdamses, I'm not sure what would have become of me those first two days."

"I know your interests are more inclined toward medicine, but I can assure you, you'll learn plenty about life and survival here." Uncle Edward stood and stretched out his back then took his cup and placed it in a pail in the kitchen. "And, to keep up your medical training, I can have Dr. Hensley take you with him on some visits. He has a wealth of knowledge on herbal remedies schools won't teach you."

Jonathan stood, following his uncle's lead by placing his own cup in the pail, his steps a little lighter. "Yes, please."

Uncle Edward settled a palm to Jonathan's shoulder. "It's time to put the expectations of home behind you. You've already seen how folks live. On Tuesday, with your first day of school, you'll see many other families, most worse off than the McAdamses. They'll be stubborn, curious, eager, suspicious, and a whole host of other things, but beneath it all are hearts who desire to learn and create. To grow and find joy. A people who love their families with a ferocity that is breathtaking, hold music close to their souls, and survive unspeakable odds without a complaint. What you've known — your understandings will be challenged." He lifted his chin, his smile growing. "But I feel fairly certain you can meet the challenges."

"Fairly certain?"

His uncle chuckled. "You're in the Blue Ridge Mountains." His eyes twinkled. "Anything's possible."

The group of children, though some looked almost the same age as Jonathan, crowded through the schoolroom door in an unorthodox conglomeration of shapes and sizes, but all shared one commonality. Curiosity.

Eyes — dark, pale blue, one or two an interesting shade of gray-green — stared at him as the children entered and found their seats — girls to one side of the room and boys to the other. A few carried a book or two. Most brought pails, which he assumed housed their lunches, but all of them reminded him of some sort of fairytale about lost children. Wisps. Wanderers among the wood.

Or maybe listening to the tales Mr. McAdams recounted by the fire at night and the haunting ballads the family sang in intricate harmonies inspired his mind to tip into the creative.

Some, mostly the girls, walked barefoot, their thin gingham or calico dresses barely suitable for the September air. With the simple collars and line of buttons down the front, the frocks resembled similar styles worn by women of the lower class back home. Many of the boys sported the same blue overalls covering white shirts as he'd seen on Sam and Isom McAdams. Others wore trousers and plaid shirts, all in various states of cleanliness, many threadbare.

A sliver of gratitude pushed through his uncertainty. At least meeting the McAdamses had prepared him for the current state of his students a little. The fresh air slipping through the windows helped circulate the growing scent of dirty bodies, but after an introduction to the skunk, Jonathan had a new definition of unpleasant odors for comparison's sake.

Once the mass entrance died down to a

trickle, Jonathan offered his most welcome smile and clasped his hands together. "Good morning. My name is Mr. Jonathan Taylor, and I am to be your new teacher." He pulled on the ends of his sleeves, a nervous habit, as he attempted to limit his limp. "I'm looking forward to becoming acquainted with each of you."

A snicker erupted from one side of the space, followed by a giggle from the front corner. He searched the room for the culprit or reason, but the expressions stilled. His gaze found Maggie McAdams's smile at the front — his one ally in the room — and he breathed in some confidence.

Jonathan cleared his throat. "I can see many of you have questions, as do I." He pressed his cold palms together in front of him. "I'd like to spend time this morning getting to know you. First, I'm going to show you some magic."

"Magic!" one voice called from the back.

"You can't do no magic," another call resounded from the back.

"My mama says magic is from Satan hisself."

"We can't go to no school that does Satan's work," called another.

Heat seeped from Jonathan's face, and he raised his palms. "I'm sorry, *magic* wasn't the best choice of words. It's a bit of . . . science, really."

"Is it the devil's science?" another voice cried.

Hadn't one of his uncle's letters mentioned the mountain folks' single-mindedness?

"No, it has nothing to do with the devil." Jonathan walked over to his bag and drew out the little concoction he'd made before school. "Science is the study and observation of the world around us. How things work together or how they're made."

One girl stood up from her desk and moved back toward the door. "I ain't gonna get caught in any of your devil's magic."

"No, no." He shook his head. "It's not magic at all. It's a special kind of soap." Before she could retreat, he pulled out an old pipe, poured a little of the mixture into it, and then blew through the pipe. Dozens of bubbles funneled into the air.

A collective gasp followed with a few giggles. Some boy exclaimed, "Ain't it a wonder!"

"Try to catch them," Jonathan encouraged and raised his own hand to the spheres, his finger barely grazing the bubble before it popped.

"How'd you make 'em?" a boy asked from

the middle row. He had a man's body but the bright curiosity of a child in his dark, round eyes. "I ain't never seen lye soap make them."

Jonathan raised a finger. "That is the science part *and* something we're going to do today once I find out more about each one of *you.*" He blew one more round of bubbles and then put the bottle back into his bag, amid a round of protests. His grin stretched. His uncle had been right to recommend a showstopper beginning, even if it nearly backfired into devil's magic. He'd never have thought of it on his own. It seemed too childish for older children, but now, as he watched them stare about the room in awe, he found another reason to adjust his expectations and his heart.

At university, most of his professors thought their vast knowledge and words proved adequately inspirational without the addition of "magic."

Some of them were exceptionally misguided.

His world had been filled with luxuries such as bubbles and indoor plumbing and abundant food, even something as simple as sufficient buttons on his shirt and water for baths. Here, everything blared with need and dirt . . . so much dirt, but even as those thoughts darkened the corners of his mind, his remembrance of the McAdams family singing, or the calming welcome of the forest, or the vast expanse of the horizon — those grander thoughts somehow colored his purpose with hope . . . and a great deal of humility.

"I'd like for each of you to tell me three things. Your name, one piece of information about yourself, and something you'd like to learn in school. For example, as I said, I am Mr. Taylor and I enjoy reading and shooting."

At this, several boys' faces perked with interest. Ah, another good suggestion from his uncle. "And I'd like to learn how to cook squirrel and rabbit from you, because I've never learnt how before."

"You ain't never learnt how to cook rabbit?" a younger boy called out.

Jonathan shook his head. "Where I come from, someone else does all the killing and cooking."

"So, all you have to do is the eatin'?" A redheaded girl in the second row widened her blue eyes.

"Yes. I've only recently learned how to wash my own clothes."

"You lived in one of them fancy houses with servants and all?" This from a boy in the back row, rather gruff looking, with a suspicious glint in his dark eyes.

"We had three servants, yes, which means in some ways you all are going to have to teach *me*. And I've gone to university, so there are other things I can teach you, an exchange of information, so to speak." His grin broadened at the memory of Laurel. "A trade."

"You got a whole lot to learn about livin' in the mountains, Teacher," another boy from the second row said, smile welcome, pale eyes bright.

"He's a fancy sort. He ain't no *real* teacher," the same surly boy from the back added, which caused an explosion of comments.

"Hush now. Just 'cause he ain't old, don't mean he ain't no teacher."

"He don't even know how to cook a rabbit."

"Most teachers don't know that stuff, Claude. They've got book learnin', not life learnin'."

Jonathan almost laughed at the comment.

"He's too pretty to be a teacher."

"Miss Lark was as pretty as a posy if I ever did see one."

"He ain't no girl. Girls is supposed to be prettier than fellers."

Things were beginning to get a little out of hand. "Now, class, let's get back to the questions."

"How come you're teachin' here at such a prime age for marryin', Teacher?" The question no sooner left the redheaded girl's lips than a blond-haired, younger boy answered from the front row. "I reckon it's 'cause of your gimp leg?"

A slender, dark-haired boy from the back corner waved away the question. "Gals don't keer none about no gimp leg if a man knows how to sweet-talk."

"Then I reckon he don't know 'bout how to sweet-talk none," said a girl with long blond hair, whose entire expression took on a dreamy quality as she stared over at Jonathan, " 'cause I ain't seen him with no gal."

"I think we ought to get back —"

"Tate Hawks, you don't know nothin' about what gals want." Quiet Maggie McAdams broke into the conversation with an unexpected fury, her fiery gaze directed to the dark-haired boy in the back corner. "I'd take a feller with sweet manners and words worth sayin' over sweet-talkin' with no sense in his head any ol' day."

"What'd you know 'bout fellers, Maggie McAdams. You ain't keered to talk to none since you actually started lookin' purty."

"Okay, okay." Jonathan raised his palms to the group. "Do you still want to learn how to make these bubbles or not?"

A silence fell over the class, and Jonathan took another deep breath. He'd have to learn how to manage the quick digression of conversation. He turned to the right and gestured toward Maggie, who sat near the window. "Would you mind beginning our introductions, Maggie? State your full name, something you enjoy, and one thing you'd like to learn from school."

She sat up a little straighter and kept her eyes forward. "Front name's Maggie. Back name's McAdams. I . . . ," she faltered and looked down at her desk, a blush rising into her cheeks.

"She likes drawin'." The dark-haired girl beside her said. "Draws like nothin' I've ever seen."

Maggie looked up, the hint of pink in her cheeks darkening. "I do like drawin', Teacher."

"That's wonderful."

Her smile bloomed. "And . . . well, I'd like to learn more about art. Laurel's showed me some of the pictures in a painting book back in the library, and I'd like to learn more 'bout them famous folks who painted."

Jonathan nodded. "I'll make certain to include that sort of information in our history lessons, Maggie."

His attention shifted to the next girl in the row.

"Front name, Edner-Jean. Back name, Boone." The girl's lips twisted like an unruly set of wires, as if she was waiting to order people around. "I like cookin'. I reckon I wanna learn to be a better reader so's I can order some of them recipe books from town and make enough food that the whole hollow will come runnin' for my cookin'."

"That sounds like an excellent idea, Edner-Jean." He nodded. "Perhaps you'll have your own restaurant someday."

One of the boys in the back laughed. "Womenfolk don't own their own shops."

Jonathan shrugged. "Mrs. Cappy does."

The boy puckered his face into a frown. "But Mrs. Cappy is Mrs. Cappy. She ain't like a typified woman."

The red-haired girl was Mary Rippey. "I like pretty dresses. I done made my sister's marryin' dress."

"Prettiest one in the whole holler," another girl, later introduced as Luanne Jacobs, added.

"I'd like to sell 'em in Mrs. Cappy's store. Clothes like Miss Simms wears, with her puffy sleeves, as big and soft as clouds." The girl turned to Luanne. "Luanne here makes some fine clothes too. We could open up our own shop one day and buy our own play pretties, if we want."

The introductions continued. Another girl sobered the daydreams a little. "Front name's Alice. Back name's Combs. I don't rightly know what I like to do. I only come to school 'cause my mama says I need to git on outta the house. Don't reckon there's much I wanna learn nohow."

"Perhaps we'll discover something together, Alice."

Claude Greer said he enjoyed frog giggin', an activity Jonathan would enquire about with his uncle later. "I enjoy lookin' at all the gals to see which one's gonna be my woman."

Several of the girls giggled. Maggie McAdams and Mary Rippey offered him a most impressive eye roll.

"And I only come to the school 'cause my daddy wants me to keep an eye on the new schoolteacher." His dark eyes took on an unveiled look of warning. "And his devil's magic."

Jonathan unleashed a smile despite a sudden inkling of concern. "I expect to have both of your eyes on me, Mr. Greer. You'll learn much faster that way."

The day moved on at a frantic pace with Jonathan attempting to keep his students somewhat engaged while fielding dozens of questions and maintaining a healthy awareness of Claude Greer and his cohort, Allen Carter.

Most of the children didn't have answers for what they wanted to learn in school. Twenty-five children in all, ages ranging from thirteen to nineteen, half the number Miss Simms had next door. His uncle had told him that once the children became old enough to work or marry then they usually were taken out of school. But the bubble activity worked like a charm, allowing Jonathan a chance to weave through the groups of children to hear how they communicated with one another. Some would even hum while they worked, which encouraged Jonathan to brush up on his violin playing.

He had to find a way to be accepted and — he sent a look toward Claude Greer — lessen suspicion.

Jonathan's shoulders slacked as the school day ended, pressing him down into his desk chair. With some kind goodbyes from a few of the students, he glanced out the window toward the mission house. He still had a good two hours of daylight in which to work on his future home, and his body protested the very idea. Couldn't he live with his uncle for the next nine months?

He pinched his lips closed and shook his head. No, he'd never be accepted if he didn't take what the mountain folk offered him.

"Well, look at you!" Laurel McAdams's familiar voice pulled his attention to the front door. She wore the pale green dress he'd seen her in before, and this time her hair swung back in a long plait. Her smile seemed to bring a new rush of energy to his weary limbs. "You lived through your first day and still have enough charm for a smile."

He gave her a nod of welcome. "Despite their best efforts, I think."

She chuckled, a sound as effortless as the birdsong. "Oh Teacher, you can be sure they ain't shown you their *best* efforts yet. I reckon they'll wait until you put down your guard for that."

He sighed back into his chair. "Thank you for nothing, Miss McAdams." He gestured toward the window. "Aren't you supposed to be off somewhere instead of discouraging the new and somewhat ill-prepared schoolteacher?"

Her laugh broke free. "Aw, you'll make it.

I see it in your eyes. You like a good challenge." She studied him. "And that's what you'll get, but I'm on my way to Mrs. Cappy's for the evenin'." She gestured with her head down the hill toward the store. "I promised I'd start coming four evenin's a week since school's back in session and the lumberyard's keeping her busier than a squirrel in a windstorm."

The quaint speech was beginning to grow on him. "I won't hold you up, but . . ." He pulled a book from his bag and walked to the door, grin growing with the idea of her response. "I thought you might like this."

She stared up at him and then down at the book he offered. Her smile faded into surprise. *"Anne of Green Gables?"*

"It was one of my sister's favorites. It reminded me of you."

Her brows shot high. "Well, now you've got me all kinds of curious."

"And if you'd like more, since you've read everything in the school library, perhaps I could offer you others. I brought some of my favorites, along with those my sister sent."

She stared at him for a long time, her lips not seeming to know whether to smile. "That's awfully good of you, Teacher." She ran a palm over the cover of the book and

111

her smile returned. "I'll have this back to you tomorrow."

"You'll read it by tomorrow?"

"If it's a good one." She turned to go and then stopped, facing him. "When I stay with Mrs. Cappy, I got time all my own for writing and reading." She sighed. "And there's nothin' quite like fallin' into the world of a book."

## Chapter Seven

Morning sunlight barely winked over the silhouette of the distant mountains as Laurel finished her climb home from Mrs. Cappy's. She'd left before breakfast, which was a mercy on account of Mrs. Cappy's love for eyeball eggs. Laurel shuddered. She despised those horrible eggs. She couldn't rightly remember what they were called, but she didn't like them at all. Poked?

Off in the distance, along the path, the outline of a man moved forward, a broad outline in the early dawn shadows. Straw hat tilted in a haphazard way, with satchel slung across his shoulder and whistlin' a jolly tune. She grinned.

Daddy.

His frame seemed to take up the whole path, sturdy and strong. She couldn't make out his expression, but from the easy stretch of his pace and the melody of "Jackaro" on his lips, she knew he was in a fine mood.

" 'There was a wealthy merchant. In London he did dwell.' " His deep voice carried the words forward to meet her on the path. " 'He had a lovely daughter the truth to you I'll tell.' "

Laurel laughed as he came to a stop in front of her, his eyes bright.

" 'Oh, the truth to you I'll tell.' "

Laurel took over the verse. " 'Her sweethearts they were plentiful. She courted day and night. Until on Jackie Frasier she placed her heart's delight. Oh, she placed her heart's delight.' "

He chuckled and patted her on the shoulder. "I don't reckon I know why you ain't got sweethearts aplenty, Laurel Loo."

The nickname warmed her through, and she pinched back the rising caution from her mind. He always had a spell of golden days before the dark ones took over. Was this a sign of his change? "I ain't lookin' for no sweethearts, Daddy."

His gaze sobered, and he studied her with eyes the same hue as hers, though his carried a wisdom framed by crinkles. "I got an inklin' your sights are set on other things, and that's a fact." He nodded, his hand slipping off her shoulder. "I've a mind to talk to you while we got this little bit of time."

She stood to attention, focused on his

face. If he took a shine to talk serious, she knew better than to let her mind wander.

"You been workin' hard for nigh a year, keeping a little portion of your money but givin' the most of it to your mama for our family." He placed his satchel down on the ground at his side and tugged his hat off, pushing a thick hand through his oak-colored hair. "And I've studied on it for some time now. How you love books and learnin'. I reckon you should take a little of that money you been givin' to your mama and send off for more of them books you want. Harder ones. Or leastways, ones you've had a hankerin' to hold."

Laurel's jaw slacked. "Really, Daddy?"

"You think I'd tell you a tall tale, girl?"

She raised a brow, and he shook his head before she vaulted into his arms. "I won't buy a lot. Just a few things. There's a history book I've been longin' to read, and a book on geometry, and then there are two Emily Cabot mysteries I can't wait to get my fingers on."

He shook his head and pinched his eyes closed. "With a mind like yourn, ain't no wonder you got your gaze fixed over the mountains." He patted her cheek then crammed his hat back on his head, clearing his throat as he did. "Well now, we done enough jawin' for one mornin'. I need to git on to work, and your mama will appreciate your help at the house with Maggie off to school."

Laurel squeezed her hands together, barely containing the desire to squeal loud enough to carry all the way down to the schoolhouse. "Thank you, Daddy."

"Go on now." He waved her away, nodding in the direction of the house. "And pick some of that mountain gentian to take to your mama. She'd like it to brighten up the house."

Laurel followed her daddy's gaze to the bright violet flower growing a little off the path. "Yes, sir." She moved toward the flowers but glanced back to watch her daddy continue his walk down the path, picking up "Jackaro" where he'd left off. Her mind braced for the shift, the fall, the utter chaos of his dark days — nights when she had to remind herself that underneath the terrifying drunkard lived the man who called her Laurel Loo and sent her mama flowers.

Several children didn't come to school on Wednesday or Thursday. The Greers, Jacobses, and Hawkses. He hadn't grown to know them very well yet, except the youngest, Sarah Hawks, who'd taken a fascination to science from day one. And since the Maple Springs school didn't hold classes on Fridays, he couldn't decide whether those children didn't come on purpose or perhaps a sickness kept them away.

His gut told him the former.

Finding a pair of dead rats on the front porch of the mission house, both with stomachs slit wide to ensure Jonathan didn't miss their very deliberate placement for him to see, confirmed his fears. A response to his presence? A warning?

His uncle had left the day before to make his circuit preaching route, covering his other two churches and their needful congregants until he arrived back in Maple Springs on Saturday, so Jonathan couldn't talk over the situation with him, but he recalled his uncle's letters. The mountain folk held deep-set convictions and offenses, and *this* was no accident. Perhaps he could discuss it with Mr. McAdams later.

Jonathan had made solid progress with most of the students, he'd thought. At least, they were engaging in more conversations, though some of the students drifted off to sleep at various times of day, and some stared at him with red-rimmed eyes. He was certain at least one of the boys needed glasses, and in response to the hunch, he moved the child, Tate Hawks, from the back row to the front. All at once, the child he'd thought was a very quiet, inattentive lad began answering questions and engaging in discussions, particularly when Jonathan asked the children about special animals and plants of the Blue Ridge.

All the children had special things to say about their home. Their proclivity toward "talkin' up" something introduced Jonathan to all sorts of unfamiliar words — such as *slicks* or *heaths, azaleas, jewelweed, huckleberry, sweet gum,* and *hemlock. Wallink, ginseng,* and *cocklebur* were mentioned as possible teas — but they didn't sound like any tea Jonathan knew. Other words, like *witch hazel, bug dust,* and *ratsbane,* he hesitated to even question.

In the challenges of a first week, when some of the children still regarded him with suspicion, he found a fascination with his new pupils and their world. And then there was the view. He couldn't get enough of it.

Although he enjoyed his uncle's house with its refinement — an atmosphere he wanted to replicate in his own place — he couldn't wait to wake up to the view spanning the horizon from the mission house windows. It had been his uncle's first house before he built his current home farther up the mountain at a more central location to the needs of folks all around Maple Springs.

Jonathan walked the final students to the door and leaned against the frame, drinking in the afternoon view from the hillside. Spectacular. Even with a cloudy mass in the distance, the world stretched on to forever, leaving all the little cares from the day in perspective. He'd never seen such a radiant display of colors, woven intimately upon the mountainside until they blended in with the wilds of smoky hues at the horizon.

"They call to you, don't they?"

Laurel waited at the bottom of the schoolhouse steps, her profile turned to examine the view. Her customary braid hung thick down her back, almost to her waistline, reminding him of the fairy-tale Rapunzel. He grinned. She did carry an otherworldliness about her, like many of these mountain folk, though hers shone from some inner glow. An untamed joy.

"I've never seen anything like them. Each morning, each afternoon, they offer a different view." He nodded as she looked up at him. "Yes, I guess they do call to me, but I haven't sorted out what they're saying."

Her grin perched in true fairy-fashion. "Oh, don't you worry 'bout that, Teacher. Your heart'll figure out the language soon enough."

He scanned the horizon again and breathed in the scent of pine with a hint of sweetness. Honeysuckle? His gaze dropped back to Laurel. "The language of the mountains, is it?"

"That's it. Granny used to say it's the call of the mountains. Our ears can't hear it, but our hearts can." She drew a step closer, withdrawing a book from the satchel across her shoulder. "I appreciate the book."

He took the proffered novel. "You finished."

"And here's my question." She narrowed her eyes in a playful way that made his smile a little wider — the kinship deepening between them. "So, I remind you of a short-tempered, dreamy-eyed, red-haired girl who can talk the bark off a tree?"

"Anne of Green Gables is quite the character." He laughed. "But no, you don't talk the bark off a tree. You do express yourself quite colorfully." He held up a finger for her to wait. "I brought a few more books to tempt you, if you're particularly adventurous."

She followed him into the schoolhouse. "More from your sister? What's her name anyhow?"

"Cora," he called as he knelt to retrieve

two more books from his bag. "She's probably fairly close to your age, I think. Nineteen?"

Laurel nodded as he took the books and met her in the middle of the room. "Twenty in the spring. And your sister, does she talk the bark off a tree too?"

He chuckled. "She talks more than me." He scanned the spine of the first book and raised a brow of challenge to Laurel. "I recall you've read *Frankenstein,* yes?"

Her eyes widened. "Whew, fascinatin' story, but I've seen enough horror in real life not to want to read 'bout it too often. I like mysteries though. Can't quite get enough of trying to figure out the ending, if you know what I mean. Emily Cabot mysteries are my favorites."

His gaze dropped back to the book in his hand. *Dracula.* He offered the other book instead. "Perhaps this one will be more to your liking then."

She took the book and flipped to the title page, her wide eyes staring up at him. "*The Return of Sherlock Holmes?* You mean he didn't die after all? Well, shoot fuzzy."

The quaint phrase tipped his smile afresh.

She pointed to him with the book. "And is this the sort of book Cora likes, or you?"

He shrugged. "I must confess, I do prefer

these to *Anne of Green Gables* or *Little Women.*"

"And that sort too?" Her gaze dropped to *Dracula*. "I don't rightly see you as the bloodsucking, coldhearted type, Teacher."

"You've read it already?"

"I told ya. If a book comes by, *any* book, I'm obliged to give it my attention. Even the ones with womenfolk in white who nab young'uns at night." She shuddered. "But . . ." She raised the book he'd just given her. "If I have my druthers, I'd choose this kind or the ones that make me get a little starry-eyed." Her gaze twinkled as example. "Like Miss Anne Shirley."

A sudden movement behind Laurel caught his attention, a figure in the shadow of the woods. From the build and height, Claude Greer's surly expression rose to Jonathan's mind.

"What's turned your thoughts, Teacher?" She followed his gaze to the tree line, but the shadow was no longer there.

"Some of the pupils haven't been back to school since the first day." He drew in a breath through his nose and jammed his hands into his pockets, straightening from his position against the doorframe. "And I think they left me an unwelcome gift on my front porch this morning in protest."

"Rats, frogs, or a polecat?" She raised a golden brow.

"Rats."

Her grimace crinkled her nose. "Well, at least they weren't as all-fired mad as a polecat." She placed a hand on her hip, readying herself for one of her sharp retorts he was beginning to predict. "Let me guess. Would it have been the Greers and Jacobses?"

"And Hawkses."

She groaned. "I was hopin' Larp and Izzie Hawks had kept themselves away from the Greers, but I reckon deep paths are the easiest to follow, and the Hawkses live not a mile from the Greers. Ozaiah Greer's a take-charge sort of man. Stubborn too. Real stuck in the old ways."

"The old ways?"

She nodded. "Before the mission came, before your uncle. Before —"

"Mr. Taylor." Danette Simms stepped from her room and directly into the conversation, bringing her body and lilac scent uncomfortably close. He'd avoided a few evening conversations with her, but not enough to discourage her continual attempts. "I'm so sorry we haven't had much time to talk this week. It seems every after-school opportunity, you've already left for the day."

He offered her a guarded smile. He had the slightest inclination that Miss Simms was very much akin to Olivia Reynolds from back home. The smallest kindness was easily contorted into the most ardent affections. "I find it easier to focus on planning my lessons when I'm alone. My uncle's home is an excellent location for thinking and grading."

"Far too much, if you ask me." She raised her nose and sniffed. "I see the work on the mission house is coming along well enough."

He followed her gaze to the rooftop through the trees. "Indeed. My uncle seems to think it will be ready by the end of next week."

Her golden eyes glimmered. "How excellent to have you so convenient to the store and school."

His smile froze on his face as he searched for a reply.

"Miss Simms, I reckon it's right providential you walked up when you did. Mr. Taylor and I were just trying to work out a problem." Laurel's gaze let him know she recognized his discomfort and swept in to the rescue.

"Well, I'll be happy to help Mr. Taylor in

any way I can." Her wordless message held volumes more.

He drew back and quickly explained the situation, adding in the fact he'd seen Claude Greer outside the school. "Perhaps a visit to their home would be a good idea."

Danette's hand flew to her chest, and Laurel's eyebrows shot to her hairline.

"Ozaiah Greer's home?" Danette shook her head. "I can barely look the man in the face when he enters Mrs. Cappy's store, let alone visit his house. Terrifying man, and to leave mutilated rats on your doorstep." She shook her head so hard her dark curls bounced. "Best to leave him be."

"Law, Miss Simms, you're gonna scare the hair right off Mr. Taylor's head, and that'd be a cryin' shame for sure. Ozaiah Greer ain't as scary as all that, but truth be told, he isn't the friendliest of sorts neither."

"I heard tales of what he did to one of the last teachers he didn't like. Threatened to skin her alive." Miss Simms fanned her hand in front of her face.

Laurel's laugh eased some of the tension. "Now, Miss Simms, no man in this whole mountain is gonna take the time to skin anybody alive when he can shoot 'em a whole lot faster." Laurel turned to Jonathan, her words providing little comfort. "They don't take to strangers too easily around here, Teacher, and the Greers are worse than most folk. You probably did something that set them off, and they're nursing a little grudge to teach you a lesson."

"If that's the case, how will I uncover the problem if I don't go to their house?" He took a much braver stance than he felt. "It's the right thing to do for the children's sakes alone."

Laurel's gaze softened with sweet encouragement. Danette's widened in horror.

"I do not venture into the woods without a well-trained escort, Mr. Taylor, for fear of getting lost, wounded" — she lowered her voice — "or attacked. I haven't the slightest idea where the Greers live except at the ridge of one of these mountains, and I have no intention of finding out."

"If you got your heart set, Teacher, then Isom and I can walk you there tomorrow, midmornin', unless you want to wait for your uncle to get back from his circuit. He knows the way to the Greers' too, but Isom's been friends with their boy, Tucker, for time out of mind, so Isom can get there lickety-split and maybe ease the way a bit."

"Are you certain you don't mind?"

"Naw. It's a good thing to see where your students live." Her gaze softened. "The more you understand, the more you'll be understood too." She grinned. "It's a fair trade."

"Well, if I don't see either of you at church on Sunday, we'll know exactly what happened. Ozaiah Greer or one of his wild dogs let his offense turn into actions."

"Or we got him converted, Miss Simms, and Ozaiah Greer done preached us such a fine sermon we decided Preacher would forgive our absence from pure astonishment." Laurel's lighthearted comment failed to brighten those hazel eyes as she looked back at him. "Because Mr. Greer needs a whole lot of Jesus, so you best prepare yourself, Teacher."

# Chapter Eight

The song floated over the morning breeze as Laurel hung a load of clothes on the line to dry, a hum and tune so familiar she didn't need to hear the words. Her mama's voice, gentle and sweet, carried the melody like a lullaby, the song twisting into Laurel's heart. "The Touch of My Love."

It was the song Mama always sang when she thought of her distant children. Three now. Betsy, married off and living on the other side of the mountain on Patton Ridge; Jeb, fighting on some distant shore; and Kizzie. Laurel's throat tightened at each remembrance of her younger sister, her closest sister. The wild-and-free daydreamer. Always lookin' beyond the horizon for a better life.

Laurel squeezed her eyes closed, hands paused on the wooden pins as she pressed a shirt into place on the laundry line. "Dear Lord, wherever she is, take care of her."

Mama's hum turned into words from the other side of the line.

> "My love will bind your heart and mine
> Though seas and lands divide us
> The warm sun on your face in the morn'
> Will be the touch of my love
> Will be the touch of my love.
> My song will carry my love to you
> O'er fields and forest and rivers,
> And when the wind kisses the curls of
>   your hair
> Twill be the touch of my love.
> Twill be the touch of my love.
> The heart is strong at rememberin'
> The heart holds fast to what's true
> And days may pass, and miles grow long
> But nothin' can keep my love from you.
> No, nothin' can keep my love from you."

Laurel wiped away a tear and retrieved her basket, walking around the hanging clothes to return to her mama, who sat on a stump with the wash bin between her knees. Strips of the silver-tinged golden bun blew in the wind as she scrubbed at a pair of Daddy's overalls, water slapping a rhythmic swish between the washboard and tub.

"You heard from Jeb," Laurel said, knowing the answer.

"We got a letter yester eve." Mama turned the clothes over in the tub and scrubbed some more, her voice low. "It's a hard world over there."

Nothing but the splashing of the water and a hard scrub of cloth filled the silence. Mama wrung out the overalls and gave them to Laurel, picking up a plaid shirt next.

"Each letter is a blessed reminder he's still breathing."

"Aye." Her mama's soft reply blended in with the harsh sound of the scrubbing. "Aye."

The longing in that one word nearly tore open Laurel's heart. A mother's ache for her child, even if her child was a twenty-one-year-old grown man. And surely the pain swelled even greater after Kizzie was sent away. Not even a year ago yet. She'd have had her baby by now, though, if she'd survived this long on her own.

Laurel swallowed back knotted tears and waited, allowing the silence and the steady work to loosen her mama's thoughts into words.

"He's strong, your brother. Strong like your daddy." She handed over the shirt and pulled a dress from the basket. Maggie's pale blue church dress, with a few paint stains at the wrists of the right sleeve. Dark blue. Elderberry mixed with saffron stain. She must've been painting another mountain sky scene.

Laurel pinned the overalls on the line, followed by the shirt, giving her mama ample time to share.

Those piercing blue eyes fastened to Laurel. "You're strong too, girl." Mama gestured toward the water, her worn fingers working over the dress with familiarity. "The Almighty's called you to something different than the rest of us. From your first days, I seen it. You and Maggie and Isom too. The world's a changing place. Y'all got a hunger for learnin'."

"College don't mean I'll be gone forever, Mama." Laurel knelt by her mama's knee. "A few years, mayhap."

Mama smiled, a slight crease forming around her eyes. "I know, but my heart is gettin' ready for whatever the call. I feel it comin' like the smell of rain on the wind or the look of snow round the moon." She pushed the dress into the rinse water and then wrung it out. "Ain't no cause for frettin' though. You'll be as close as a thought, won't ya? Just like Jeb."

Laurel pinched her lips against adding one

more name, but her mama supplied the words.

"And Kizzie."

Laurel nodded, taking the dress. "I wish we knew where she was. Even if we couldn't see her, just to know she's livin'."

"Aye," came the soft answer again, relinquishing control she couldn't take. "Maybe someday, Laurel." Mama drew in a deep breath as if coming up from a dream. "Go on and finish hanging them clothes. You and your brother need to git on down to meeting Teacher."

"Yes, Mama." Laurel started toward the line.

"Laurel?"

She turned. Her mother's gaze fixed on hers.

"Be careful at the Greers'. Some men hold to their dark days all year round."

"Ever seen an autumn-leaf rainbow, Teacher?" Isom bounced up ahead of Jonathan and Laurel, Butter trailing his every move like the faithful hound he was.

Jonathan sent her a curious look and then called back, "No, I don't believe I have."

"Well now. You gotta see one afore the leaves take their fall." He slowed his pace and surveyed the forest on either side of their path, most likely looking for the perfect spot.

Laurel leaned close to the confused teacher. "It's somethin' our mama's done with us every autumn since we were little. She's always stopping the work to admire the Almighty's creation. Paints extra color into life, she says."

His eyes lit with his smile. "I see she's had a profound influence on all of you with her bright outlook."

"What do you mean?"

"Come on, I found a good spot. Right here." Isom waved for them to follow him, as he scuttled up underneath a low-lying oak.

"What is he doing?" Jonathan looked from Isom's disappearing form back to Laurel.

"He's taking you to see an autumn-leaf rainbow." She raised a brow. "You don't wanna miss one of those." Without another word, she ducked beneath the limbs and followed her little brother into the thicket, a giggle waiting in her throat.

Something about introducing city fella Jonathan Taylor to her world brought a funny feeling into her stomach, akin to being tickled. Kind of. But not exactly. Even in the little while she'd come to know him, it was plain as clouds in the sky that he needed some joy in his life, some shine. Most folks did, though.

The crunch of leaves behind alerted her that Teacher followed, but he didn't ask for more clarification. She reckoned he'd learned by now to just follow along for a discovery.

Isom collapsed on the ground up ahead, cozying up beneath a brilliant red maple. The color lashed through the other trees like lightning at midnight. She looked upward and her grin grew. He'd found the perfect place. Butter licked Isom's face before lying down too.

With a glance behind her, she lay back on the pillowed leaves and stared up into the crimson sunlight.

"What are we doing?" Teacher whispered as he settled beside her, shoulders nearly touching.

Isom answered. "Look yonder. An autumn-leaf rainbow."

Laurel looked through the branches of the maple, and the rainbow appeared as the trees of various kinds raised one above the other. A yellow birch, an orange sassafras, a hint of brighter red from the black gum, and a golden oak towering above them all. Each color, filtered with sunlight, complemented the next, like a God-made quilt.

Laurel sighed. Now that would be some kind of quilt to behold.

"It's . . . remarkable." His voice held the appropriate amount of awe.

"Sure is." She breathed in the earth, the scent of pine, and the faintest hints of mint from the dainty dittany nearby. She might dream of seeing the world beyond her mountains, but home would always call her back.

Another scent invaded, less natural. Leathery. Sweet. Jonathan Taylor.

Isom'd had his fill of rainbows and scurried back toward the path, but Laurel turned her face toward the schoolteacher.

He had a strong profile. His thick hair, a mingle of gold and brown, fell back from his forehead giving an unhindered view. He was too handsome to be a backwoods schoolteacher, but there was a comfort in knowing him — a spring blossom–scented sweetness. Like she'd always known him. "What'd you mean back there on the path?"

He turned to face her, gaze to gaze, his brow peaked like a question mark.

"Mama's bright outlook," Laurel reminded. "Her influence."

"Ah, yes." His attention didn't waver from her face. The haven of maple leaves closed in around them, urging her to stay where she was, with Teacher. "There's a difference with your family than most of the others I've met. A light. A joy. I knew it had to come from somewhere, and I saw it in your mother when I stayed at your home. There's something in her countenance that lights the conversation, if I may."

She'd never heard anything so pretty in all her living days, except what came from the Good Book sometimes. It nearly brought her to tears. She looked back up at the leaves. "She'd say it's Jesus. No good without Him."

"I've only seen such a clear indicator of His presence in my uncle, a contentedness despite the situation or circumstances. It's one of the reasons I agreed to come to Maple Springs. I wanted a chance to be near him and understand better what kept his . . ."

"Soul quiet," she finished, knowing the very notion.

"Yes. A quiet soul."

She turned to him again, scrunching up her nose. "I don't reckon it comes easy."

His eyes twinkled to life. "No, I don't reckon it does."

She grinned. "Then maybe I don't want it so bad. You?"

He chuckled. "The result is certainly

enticing, but not the journey to it."

She stared at him a little longer, his eyes a shade of brown-gold that fit the surroundings. Her chest squeezed in a confusing response. "The greater the prize, the harder the journey, Mama says." Laurel slid out from under the maple, waiting for him to join her in a stand before leading the way back to the path. She thought about her daddy, long years of pushing away Jesus and filling his dark days with liquor instead of something to . . . quiet his soul. Would Mama ever see the prize of her loving him long?

They walked on in silence for a piece, listening to Isom's chatter about one critter or another. The mountain path rose higher, leading toward Copperhead Peak.

"I hate you're missing work to help me today."

Teacher's breath came hard, his limp more pronounced, so she slowed her pace. "I don't mind a'tall. It was Maggie's turn and I needed a little break from Mrs. Cappy's breakfasts. Law, she makes the awfulest eggs you ever did see. Every single mornin' it's the same. What does she call 'em?" Laurel looked up at the sky for answers. "Pinched? Naw, that's not right."

"Poached?" he offered, a laugh in his voice.

"Poached." She shuddered at the much too vivid memory. "They look like an eyeball peekin' up from the plate at me. What body wants to eat something like that?"

Teacher's laugh exploded, full and deep. "When you describe it in such terms, I don't think I'll see a poached egg in the same way ever again."

"I'll take scrambled or fried any day of the week, but poached?" She shuddered again.

"And you must stay the night with Mrs. Cappy?"

"Well, that's one of the reasons we go to work for her in the first place. Mrs. Cappy's scared of bein' by herself at night. My granny had a friendship with her, since Granny was the wife of the blacksmith, and they lived just a stone's throw from each other's houses. Mrs. Cappy was like Granny in the sense they both was used to strangers, and thinkin' outside the mountains, and seeing different sorts of people pass through and all that. It's why Mama's a little different than some of the other mountain folk, like you were sayin'. And since Daddy works outside Maple Springs, in town, he knows about things beyond too. Doesn't mean he likes those things, but he knows about 'em." She sighed. "But Mrs. Cappy pays us for afternoon work and a full night's stay, so that's what we do. I work more often than Maggie, since she's still in school and all, but the pay's nice, in spite of them poached eggs."

"And what do you do with all of this income you're accumulating?"

She shifted her attention away from him, to the trail ahead. "We help out with family costs and such. Ever once in a while I buy a book or two that I've been longing to read." She opened her mouth to continue and then snapped her lips closed. Could she trust him with the truth? "How's teaching going? Maggie yammers on about your bein' the best science and math teacher she ever laid ears on."

"I am more proficient in those — and enjoy them more."

"Well, she's always been fascinated with science, but not math, so if she's sayin' good things, it means you must be fair to middlin' on the subject."

"I can tell the students aren't as engaged with my English and history lessons. And though many of them look tired during the other lessons, I actually catch some of them falling asleep during history."

She grinned over at him, feeling a kinship to this stranger from beyond the mountains. "Yeah, I hear'd ya a few times. You just read the words from the book."

"I wanted to ensure they had the facts, understood the specifics. There are a lot of dates in history."

She chuckled. "But you grab 'em with the story. That's where you gotta start. Heads can only hold so much talkin', so they're gonna hold what matters more than what doesn't, right? You can still tell history, but maybe something like . . . this." She looked up at the sky. "He was a southern boy. Born in South Carolina but traipsed the mountains between there and Tennessee, learning the wild wilderness and the love of the land. They called him Andrew, and as a young'un, life wasn't easy for him at all. His daddy died early, and his mama had a hard time making ends meet. The mountains taught him a lot, but so did the rowdy mountain folk etchin' out their lives in places that didn't even have roads or houses yet."

Her grin shifted to him. "And bein' the rowdy bunch of folks we was, and King George bein' the hoity-toity sort he was, a war broke out. A war agin' the people who lived on the Continent, as America was called then, and the ones in England. Andrew was only a boy of thirteen, but you know what?"

Teacher's eyes lit with the power of the story. Laurel loved this fire, this spark of sharing one imagination with another. It was one of the reasons why teaching called to her. Stories breathed through her. She felt them. Drank them. Dreamed them.

"What?"

"He joined right up in the war. Only thirteen. Crazy young'un, but a spitfire, for truth. When he was captured by the British at the battle of Hanging Rock, he thought he was done in for sure. After the war, he traveled on to Tennessee to live a spell and took up lawyerin'. Why, he got so good at it, he even helped Tennessee become a state instead of just a no-named piece of wild land. The folks there was real grateful. And since Andrew had gotten the taste of warrin' so well, he got right back into the thick of it in the War of 1812. You know what? Folks seemed to like what he was all about. His fightin' spirit and determination. He got so good at talkin' to folk and learnin' and figurin' out the politics and such, well . . . they made him president."

"Andrew Jackson."

Her grin spread wide. "Sure enough."

"That was remarkable."

"And I figure you can tell me back a whole heap of facts about that story, if I was to ask you."

"You didn't tell the part where he got hit in the face by the gun of one of them rotten, no-good British soldiers, just 'cause he wouldn't shine the soldier's boots," said Isom.

A hint of pink rose in Laurel's cheeks. "Well, I was trying to keep the war from startin' back up between Teacher and us, Isom."

Isom let out a loud laugh and ran on ahead, Butter on his heels.

"I don't know if I can tell stories like that, Laurel." He hesitated and shook his head. "It seems so easy for you."

"I think you have it in you. If you enjoy reading all these books you keep handin' off to me, I already *know* you can. You just got to see things in pictures instead of only in words." She tapped her lips and looked up at the sky. "What's your house like?"

His brows shot wide at the sudden change in topic. "My house?"

"Right. The one you growed . . . grew up in. Is it big? Small? Brick, wood, or stone?" She winked. "Did you grow up in a hollow tree?"

He chuckled and drew in a deep breath. "No, I did not grow up in a hollow tree, though I'm fairly convinced you did."

She laughed and then waved toward him. "Come on now, your house."

"It's made of stone."

"All right." She drew out the words, urging him forward. "Brown? Black?"

"Gray."

"Gray?" She stopped walking altogether and pierced him with a look. "Okay now, Teacher. Don't stop there. You ain't done nothing to paint a picture in my head. Come on. Is it gray like the rock cliffs standing guard over the view at Devil's Hold, or is it dark gray like a storm's getting ready to rage from the sky?"

He grew quiet, and she decided he needed a little rescuing. Besides, the Greer house was just around the bend in the creek and there wouldn't be any talk about imaginations and fancy houses in such company as the Greers. "That's your homework, Mr. Taylor. Next time we meet, I want you to tell me the story of your house." She pointed a finger at him. "And if you want a good grade, you'll be prepared."

He offered a dutiful nod. "Yes, teacher."

"The Greer house, yonder." She gestured with her chin up the hill.

## Chapter Nine

The house barely looked livable. Smaller by half than the mission house, the log cabin sat back against the mountain so closely it appeared a part of the forest. Jonathan wouldn't have noticed it at all, had it not been for Laurel's gesture toward the nearly hidden structure. The woods even darkened around the entrance, obscuring the narrow doorway with shadows. Isom rushed ahead, not a care in the world, but Laurel reached down and scooped up a handful of some delicate purple flower. She crushed it in her hands then rubbed her palms together. With a quick sweep, she took up another handful and gave it to Jonathan.

"Purple aster." As if that explained everything. "Crush it, so the scent's strong on your hands."

He took the flowers without question. The petals released a warm scent, like sage, as he rubbed them between his palms. Before he could question Laurel's motives, she turned toward the cabin and shouted, "Hellooooo."

A howl and bark gave warning as four dogs charged from somewhere near the house directly toward them. Isom opened his arms wide as one of the dogs, a hound, jumped into his chest and knocked him to the ground.

The other three forged ahead, not unfriendly, exactly, but not entirely welcoming either.

"Don't you even think about it, dogs," Laurel said, stepping in front of Jonathan, her voice firm.

"Down." A low voice boomed from the direction of the house, a thunderclap of bass and power. The dogs' tails dipped between their legs and they turned back toward the house with slower strides.

A shadow moved into the open doorway of the cabin, a man with shoulders thick from hard work and hard life. Darkness and distance obscured the man's face, but Jonathan felt his gaze boring down on them from his height on the porch as they approached. He'd experienced intimidation back home in England, but it failed to compare to the untamed rawness of these mountain men.

Laurel held out her hand to stop Isom from running up the uncertain wooden steps and then covered her eyes from the cloud-cloaked sunlight. "Hidee there, Mr. Greer." The man didn't move. "It's Laurel and Isom McAdams, and we've come by with the new schoolteacher, Mr. Taylor."

"State yer business."

Jonathan stepped forward, taking the conversation in hand. "Mr. Greer, I have missed your children in school the past few days and was anxious for their health. Are they well?"

As if in answer, Claude appeared at the man's side.

"Good to see you are well, Claude."

The boy gave no acknowledgment of Jonathan's greeting.

"May we come up to speak to you, sir?" Jonathan continued, taking a few steps forward.

"I won't have my young'uns going to no devil school."

Jonathan released a long sigh. "Mr. Greer, there's been a misunderstanding."

"We don't abide our young'uns going to no devil school." The man's voice grew louder, echoing off the rock facing to the right of his cabin. "Don't need religion myself, but I won't have my young'uns taught witchcraft. I's right not to trust the likes of you."

Jonathan blinked and looked over at Laurel for interpretation. She shrugged and turned toward the house. "Mr. Greer, I can tell you true, our schoolteacher isn't leading no devil school."

The man moved from the shadows to the edge of the porch. Deep lines etched around his dark eyes, and his chiseled features disappeared behind a heavy beard. He stared down from his perch, an almost Zeus-like aura of command. Jonathan straightened his shoulders and refused to look away from the fierce expression.

"You callin' my young'uns liars?" His attention focused solely on Jonathan.

Jonathan braced himself, somehow feeling that the strength in this confrontation held a much greater bearing than he fully understood. "No, sir, of course not. But I do believe there is some mistake. I've come to teach children in these mountains. Teach them good things, and if I've somehow spoken out of turn, I'd like to set things right."

Silence passed between them, but Jonathan refused to break his eye contact with the man. After what seemed like a full minute, Ozaiah Greer narrowed his eyes and gestured toward the steps. "We'll talk on the porch."

He took the encouragement in Laurel's small smile and climbed the rickety stairs, keeping his limp as steady as possible as he reached the top. Tucker Greer darted out the door and down the steps to greet Isom, leaving Ozaiah and Claude remaining on the porch — and a small, thin woman in the doorway. An odor, more potent and vile than any he'd come in contact with thus far — even the skunk — radiated from the house.

Jonathan looked to Laurel. She held his gaze and slowly rubbed her hand against her nose, as if giving it a light scratch. Recognition dawned. The flowers. A combatant to the smell! He followed Laurel's example and breathed in the sage scent with a nod to the woman in the doorway.

He waited for an introduction, but none came.

Ozaiah wasn't as tall as he'd appeared from below, meeting Jonathan eye to eye, but the strength in his arms doubled Jonathan's. He wore the staple overalls with a dirty plaid shirt beneath, and his sturdy arms crossed an equally robust chest.

Jonathan offered his hand. "A pleasure to meet you, Mr. Greer."

Nothing moved on the man except his gaze, which measured Jonathan from head to foot. He turned his head to the right and let out a long spittle of tobacco juice, another staple of the mountain men . . . and many of the boys.

Laurel folded her own arms, her look of disapproval as evident as Mr. Greer's. At least she was on his side. A little of the apprehension dissipated with that knowledge, and he lowered his hand. "What did you mean by the devil's school?"

Whether Mr. Greer was trying to use silence as a weapon or it was the natural reticence of the mountaineers, Jonathan wasn't certain, but he waited.

"My boy here, told me you was teachin' black magic."

Jonathan blinked and tilted his head closer. "Pardon?"

"That you was teachin' magic with floatin' circles in the air. Then you talked about a herd of folks flyin' in the sky together in a box? And you said it wasn't a tall tale but true?" His countenance darkened. "I ain't no churchgoin' man, but I won't have you lyin' to my young'uns then foolin' them with your sinful ways. They be better off here learnin' how to make their way instead of listenin' to that fool talk anyhow."

The bubbles! Jonathan sighed out his tension. "Mr. Greer, those floating circles were not magic at all. They were science — a simple combination of soap and a few other ingredients." His gaze landed on Claude. "And if Claude had been paying attention to the lesson, he'd have understood how it was formed."

"I ain't never seen nothin' like floating bubbles from any soap," the man grumbled, the tension creasing his squint tightening.

"That's because we use lye soap, Mr. Greer." This from Laurel. "It don't lather none. Mr. Taylor brought the store-bought kind."

He sniffed. "Store-bought or witch-made?"

Jonathan drew from every ounce of self-control not to drop his mouth wide at the utter disconnect to the outside world and broader thinking. Laurel and her family were progressive compared to the likes of Ozaiah Greer. "I can show you in magazines in Mrs. Cappy's store, if you'd like. In fact, Mrs. Cappy has a few bottles for sale and you could try it for yourself. There is no magic involved." Jonathan drew in a breath. "And as far as people flying goes, men have been in single-occupant aeroplanes for over ten years now. I know you must have read about it in the newspaper at some point."

"Don't believe in hearin' from lowlanders and their citified ways. I ain't got no cause for it."

"Well, sir, should you ever wish to confirm the truth of what I'm saying, Mrs. Cappy also has newspapers to support my claims. A passenger plane hasn't taken off successfully yet, which is what I told the students during science." He sent a look to Claude and then fixed his gaze back on Ozaiah. "But the likelihood of it is very close."

Mr. Greer shook his head, frown deepening, if possible. "What is any of that gonna do to help my kin? They're gonna be clearing out land and huntin' for food and raisin' young'uns. They ain't got no need for floatin' soap and aeroplanes." He sliced a palm through the air, the most movement he'd made since he spat. "I ain't liked folks comin' in from outside the mountain to teach, and I still don't like it."

Well, how could you reason with such a mind-set? His mind went completely blank.

"You hear about the phone lines going up from Sparta this way, Mr. Greer?" Laurel said, her lips in an uncustomary firm line. "And them loggers felling trees on land some city worker bought not ten miles from the bottom of the mountain?"

The man ground his teeth but gave a nod.

"The outside is comin' to us, whether we want it or not. Claude's generation" — she pointed to the boy still standing, rather pale, behind his father — "and those younger need to be prepared for changes those outsiders are gonna bring."

Mr. Greer reached around the corner of the doorframe and pulled out a rifle. "I know how to prepare."

Laurel's temper flared again before Jonathan had the chance to interrupt. "You want a fatherless family?" she continued. " 'Cause there are a lot more flatlanders than there are of us, so you ought to think about that."

His eyes widened and he flipped his gaze back to Jonathan, his grip on the gun firm. Jonathan eased his stance, hoping to convey appeal. "I have no intention to quell the traditions, beliefs, and beauties of your home, and I can only imagine you want to protect your children from harm, as any good parent wishes."

The creases around the man's face relaxed a little.

"I'm also certain you want to see them have as good a life as possible." He drew in a deep breath, praying, hoping for a breach in the stone demeanor. "I'd love to be part of helping your children have a good life, whether it be here in the mountains or, if by their choosing, beyond. And if they choose that, don't you want them to be as ready for such an —" *Opportunity* would not be the best word at this time. "Choice, as they can?"

The quiet stare from Ozaiah Greer lasted longer than the last before he turned and gave another spit off the porch. "I ain't got no cause for flatlanders and their ways." With those words, he gave Claude a shove in the door of the cabin and followed, without one look back.

Laurel glared at the closed door as if her gaze had the power to burn it down. "Thickheaded, brigity ol' polecat," she whispered, before turning and marching down the cabin steps.

When they were out of earshot, Isom trailing behind to say his goodbyes to Tucker Greer, the joyful Laurel released her fury. "It's thinkin' like that back yonder that makes the situation here in the mountains worse for the young'uns." Her accent thickened with her anger, became edgier. She walked so fast, he almost jogged to keep up, sending uncomfortable tinges up his leg. "Can't he see these young'uns need to be ready? Need more? It's clear as . . ." She waved her hand toward the trees. "Scarlet on a black gum."

"We can hope that once he considers things, he'll change his mind."

She stopped and faced him a moment, hands on her hips. "Mountain men don't change their minds, Teacher. They got heads of rock, especially ones like Ozaiah Greer. It's this mountain way. Don't think 'bout tomorra until tomorra. Stuck in the way it's always been."

The motto made sense from what Jonathan had seen. Poverty. Isolation. Lack of vision beyond their small community.

"And you're not living by that way?"

Laurel shook her head, resuming her race-paced walk. "No siree. Daddy and Mama are a mite bit different than some folks round here. They peek into the future and try to figure out how to prepare for it. Some other folks is like that too, but not enough." She kicked a pile of leaves in the path, sending them floating around them, a few getting caught on the breeze. "That's why we got to go out and learn about the world beyond then bring it back to our mountain folk. I gotta help the twins understand." Her gaze focused forward, determined. "And it won't be much longer now."

"You're leaving Maple Springs?"

She skidded to a stop, face forward, and

her mouth dropped open. Ah, she hadn't meant to speak of it. He rounded her to stand in front of her.

"Where are you going?"

She pinched her lips closed and stared up at him, her forehead wrinkling with some inward struggle. His smile grew. "You're going to have to tell me now, you know? I overheard your confession. Do you have a job in town?"

She shook her head, eyes still wide, lips still pinched.

He tilted his head, studying her. "A . . . suitor?"

This unlocked her lips. "A suitor? With the likes of Isom and Daddy, the whole mountain would've already known whether I was sparkin' somebody or not." She sighed and looked over her shoulder. Isom hadn't followed them down the path yet. Her gaze fastened back on his, alive with life and intelligence. "I've owed you the truth since last week in the barn. You didn't get a fair trade." She sighed out whatever fight paused her confession. "I got a full scholarship to Greensboro Women's College."

"What?"

Her index finger shot out. "But you can't go talkin' about it. Nobody but Mama, Daddy, and Mrs. Cappy knows."

"That's fantastic news, Laurel. Why would you hide it?"

She gestured with her chin back down the path. "For folks like Mr. Greer who won't understand and will see it as a slight to our mountain ways. For the little'uns, who are still gettin' used to Jeb not being home." She shrugged and looked away. "And . . . well, I reckon I don't want everybody to know, just in case . . . I can't go. I don't want to fail 'em."

"Them?"

She looked back over her shoulder and then faced him, her expression so earnest, so pleading, he had the urge to take her in his arms. "Well, I went to figuring about it and here's what I know. We've had teachers come to the mountains to teach for a while. None of them stay longer than a year, which means every year all the young'uns have to get used to a new teacher with new ways. Same for the teacher. I'm going to school to be a teacher, to come back here and teach. I know this life. I know these people. If anybody's going to help them get ready for the changes ahead, maybe . . . maybe it's somebody from inside. That's why I work at Mrs. Cappy's — to save money for room, board, and transportation, until I can get to Greensboro."

"So, you're trying to take my job."

She laughed, enjoying his banter, judging by the glint in her eyes. "I don't reckon it's your plan to stay in Maple Springs forever, Teacher. You're passin' through like most other folks from outside the mountains, and there's nothin' wrong with that, but I see the need."

"And you're brave enough to fill that need."

Color bloomed in her cheeks, drawing him a step closer. What a heart!

She took a step back and fiddled with the corner of her apron. "To most folks around here, college is a fool notion. And a girl besides?" She shook her head. "But . . . but I know it's right. I can't really explain it, but I've always had a hankerin' to go over those mountains. These people, the people you're teachin', they don't see beyond the mountains, beyond tomorrow. I want to help them, if I can. Have you ever felt that way?"

"I have. In fact, I'll trade you one revelation for another. My heart is more into medicine than teaching. I'm here to learn and grow and make a difference, but my ultimate goal isn't teaching."

"You wanna be a doctor?"

"I'm halfway there, actually. The war

changed things, but I still plan to do my training for it." He placed his hands into his pockets. "But, in the meantime, what if I read some of your papers, your writings? Or give you assignments to prepare you for college?"

Her eyes brightened, tightening the bond between them. "For true? You'd help me?"

"Of course. Share some of your writing with me to start, and I'll make suggestions, then we can move on from there. One . . . friend helping another."

The word *friend* sounded so fitting paired with her.

She studied him, her smile finally winning over her doubt. "All right, Teacher." She grinned. "But only if I can help you in return."

"You've already helped me more than I can say."

She began walking again, a slower pace, her gaze fixed to the sky in thought. "I know what we're gonna do. I'll teach you about mountain ways in return. Things like cooking, living, and thick-headed rascals." She thumbed back over her shoulder toward the Greer cabin, before stopping and offering him her hand. "Sounds like a fair trade to me."

He took her hand into his, the simple action inciting a deeper rush of connection he didn't quite understand. Friends, indeed. "Agreed."

"Good." She said, slowly pulling her hand from his. "And I know just the way to start with *your* training. We're gonna prove to these mountain men that even if you're an English flatlander, you still have some worthy skills."

They resumed their walk, their narrow path hemmed in on both sides by a delightful array of autumn rainbows. "I'm glad you think so."

"But we have to show them you do. The mountain men measure skills different than city folk. As far as I can see, city folk appreciate book learnin', ways a body might use their mind, *and* dressin' high on the hog." Her gaze slipped down him, but he still wasn't quite certain what the hog had to do with dressing.

"But you played the fiddle like a house afire when you stayed at our place. There isn't one man on the mountain who wouldn't appreciate your good music."

An idea sparked from a previous conversation he'd had with his uncle. "I'm a good shot too."

She leaned her head back and gave him a steady look with those large, curious eyes.

"Are you now?"

His face warmed under her playful perusal. "Indeed I am."

"Well Teacher, you show off some of those skills tomorrow at the church get-together and you'll start making the right impression. A good trade for sure." She raised a golden brow. "*If* you're talkin' true."

He placed his palm over his chest, almost in pledge. "Miss McAdams, you can trust that I always talk true."

## Chapter Ten

Jonathan hadn't been certain what a "get-together" was, but it proved to bring in almost everybody in Maple Springs.

His uncle had said the church usually ran about half-full on a regular Sunday, but this day it burgeoned beneath the weight of the packed crowd. Even with his uncle's loquacious explanation of the "jollifications" involved in a mountain get-together, after visiting the bleak and unwelcome Greer home, Jonathan didn't hold out hope for anything particularly jolly.

He'd been wrong.

His uncle's sermons held a welcome, fireside-chat quality without losing their depth. He'd never been privy to such sermons, such clarity of scripture in plain speech. The only other time he'd heard his uncle preach was in a small village outside London. He'd lectured as most of the clergy of the time did, high-handed, distant — but now, after years holed up in these mountains, not only had his uncle's personality relaxed to fit into this rural atmosphere, but his sermons had altered.

Jonathan sat on a pew beside Mr. Hawes, the current blacksmith of Maple Springs, and Mr. Morgan, who had one child in Jonathan's class and two in Miss Simms's. Despite the welcomeness and general friendliness of both men, Jonathan couldn't get the Greers out of his thoughts. After the visit to the Greers, he'd spent hours contemplating how to make a difference in the mountains with these people. Something to allay the fears, yet celebrate the uniqueness. Opportunities to educate in ways beyond books, but means that touched even the coldest hearts, but how?

His mind whirled through prayers as he looked around the church. How could he make a difference here?

The cramped space crowded people and their scents all together, distracting him a little from the swell of the music, but not much. Like last time, the men sat to one side of the church and the women to the other, with infant sounds and shuffling children noises scattered throughout. Jonathan's only other service had proved as eye-opening as this one. Tunes he'd never heard before, sung with the gusto of the Scots and such repetition they were easy to learn. Songs such as "Bringing in the Sheaves," which had an upbeat tempo, to slower balladlike tunes such as "A Poor Pilgrim of Sorrow" repeated verses until the people thought the song was finished, he supposed. One he found particularly memorable was "What a Friend We Have in Jesus," a song noting the importance of prayer to find peace because of the closeness of a relationship with Jesus.

His gaze immediately sifted through the crowd to the other side of the church. Laurel stood, head lifted, eyes closed, singing with the same passion as the other voices around her. She stood in between her mother and Maggie, both more demure in their worship than Laurel's expressive nature. She held a simple beauty. Nothing like the glitzy gowns of his father's friends' daughters. Her beauty flowed from the inside. He grinned. Maybe it wasn't so simple after all.

He forced his attention away from her face and back to the front of the church.

Isom McAdams caught Jonathan's attention next as he stood up front, trying to lean over and read a page of a book on Jonathan's desk, which had been pushed back against the wall to bring the pulpit forward for service. It was one of Jonathan's map books he'd brought from home and left open from their final class on Thursday. Isom leaned in, squinted, and looked again. He blinked, rubbed his eyes, made another attempt.

Jonathan stopped singing and studied the boy, his previous training spiking concern. Symptoms. He'd read about them, seen them before as he assisted one of the doctors back home. Did Isom need glasses? His continued observation burned with more certainty. Many of the young people in his class had tired, weary eyes. This was more than tired.

As soon as the final *amen* sounded from the pulpit, the entire atmosphere changed. Though people sounded out "amen" and "preach it" during the sermon, the noise and laughter level took a decided turn. Men carried tables and pews out into the churchyard. Women placed rows upon rows of food out for the taking. All sorts of folks came to wish him well and welcome him to the mountain. Most seemed to mean it.

And then the music began. Three men and two women sat up on the church's porch and began playing some of the faster-paced "mountain music," as the McAdamses called it. Two of the men played banjos and the other took the fiddle. One of the women held what the mountain folk called a dulcimer, and the other tapped a pair of spoons with even more skill than Isom.

They started with a lively tune his uncle told him was called "Young Men and Maids." He'd heard a few of these ballad-like melodies at the McAdamses', and a similar pattern continued in this tune. Longing. Every song seemed to hold a yearning — whether for someone or some place, dead, alive, or far away.

He looked around the crowd, an odd collection of young, old, and all those in between, laughing, tapping toes to the music, and filling the afternoon air with pleasure he hadn't seen since his introduction to the McAdamses.

Life. Joy. More than the gloom and resistance of Mr. Ozaiah Greer.

Some of his students that he'd never seen smile clapped their hands and laughed with ease.

A man, Mopy Larson, stepped onto the porch, bringing a rousing whoop from the crowd. He raised a palm, his grin showing a dingy whiteness from beneath his dark mustache. " 'Birdie in the Cage,' Darrell."

A whole crowd of those gathered moved

from being scattered across the churchyard to forming a large circle with a pattern of man-woman, man-woman. Then the fiddle started off a lively tune with the other instrumentalists joining in. Mopy clapped his hands to the beat and called out, "Swing your partner round and round."

The pairs, like some courtly dance from a Regency era, turned together, keeping their larger circle intact until they split apart into squares of four couples each.

"Birdie in the cage and three hands round," Mopy said, more spoken than singing.

The dancers responded to the call, and a woman from each square of dancers moved to the middle of their little circles.

"Chase a rabbit, chase a squirrel, chase a pretty girl round the world."

One of the men, the woman in the center's partner, circled around the other partners until he caught up with his "gal" in the center and then . . .

"Circle round. Do-si-do. One more time now don't you know."

On it went. Song after song. Some required Mopy's calling and others, slower melodies, looked more like a familiar waltz, except the ballroom was an autumn churchyard and the skylight was a blue mountain horizon. He stood by the food table watching the festivities, drinking sun tea, and fighting the urge to eat another slice of Mrs. McAdams's strawberry stack cake. His uncle's cooking was fine for his young bachelor nephew who knew very little about making his own food, but this? His gaze went back to the stack cake on the long makeshift table beside him. This was much better.

His uncle made his rounds, engaging in easy conversation with young and old, even taking ten-year-old Ellie Hawes for a turn at the mountain-style waltz. Jonathan was struck again by the simple joy radiating from people who had so little.

Danette Simms sidled up to him and held out her hand. "You ought to be dancing, Mr. Taylor."

Jonathan stared at her, allowing her words and intentions to settle like an uncomfortable lump in his stomach. Dancing had never been his forte, especially with his weak leg in tow. "I'm afraid I'm not the best dancer, Miss Simms." He gestured with his chin toward the couples in motion. "And I'm not certain of this style."

"No better way to learn than in step." She grabbed his hands and pulled him into the circle of dancers.

His protests fell on deaf ears. Miss Simms put his hands in waltz position and guided him through the dance even though he stumbled through enough clumsy dance steps to heat his face from neck to forehead.

"I think it's going to take at least another dance for you to get comfortable, Mr. Taylor." She blinked up at him. "But I can see you have a natural grace about you."

*Liar, liar.* "Thank you, Miss Simms, but I'm not certain dancing is my talent, no matter the practices."

"Nonsense." She raised her brow, her most coy performance on full display. "All you need is the right partner."

He stumbled again, scanning the crowd for his uncle or anyone who might rescue him from humiliation should his leg twist in an unexpected direction. The last thing any teacher needed on a day in which he was being celebrated was to fall headfirst onto the ground during a dance.

"My lack of adequate skill has very little to do with such a partner." He pushed up a smile. "I can see you are quite gifted in this area."

The compliment darkened her rouge-pinkened cheeks even more. "It's a miracle I can still dance a step after having been in this forsaken place since August. You arrived just in time. I doubt I would have made it to Christmas without a real peer coming to the rescue."

He barely missed stepping on her foot. "I would imagine some of the women here could count as peers."

Her upper lip curled.

"They aren't trained as you have been of course," he said, "but several of the women are excellent conversationalists, and seem curious to learn, and intelligent."

She sighed. "I'm only grateful we have a three-day break from school in two weeks."

"We do?"

"You didn't know? There's always a long break in early October for apple harvests with, from what I understand, an entire two days of apple butter making. And then we get another set of days off in November for a corn harvest before the end of the session first of December."

"And what do we do during the breaks?"

Her smile spread in unvoiced welcome. "*I'm* planning to go to Asheville and be as frivolous as my tiny salary will allow. I've already decided to visit the illustrious Grove Park Inn for one night, even if it takes everything I've saved. Oh, to drown in such luxury." She sighed, and then her grimace resurfaced. "Especially after . . . this." She stared back up at him, doe-eyed. "But I wouldn't mind some company on my trip, if you're interested."

He cleared his throat, and his foot twisted enough to force another stumble. "It sounds like a pleasant trip, but I believe I'll need to take that time to continue improvements to the mission house for winter. I do appreciate your thoughtfulness to include me, Miss Simms."

The song came to a glorious close, but Miss Simms didn't release her hold on him. "There'll be another song up next, and you need to practice, Mr. Taylor."

"Actually, Miss Simms, I was hoping I could get Mr. Taylor's help." Sam McAdams appeared like a plaid shirt–wearing knight, his grin all but announcing his intended rescue.

"Whatever for?" Miss Simms squeaked.

"Avery's been asked to take a turn with his woman and we're in need of a fiddler." His gaze landed on Jonathan. "I heard tell the new teacher's got a hand for it."

Jonathan's temporary relief dissipated. Miss Simms seemed to share the shock.

"Mr. Taylor does not play the fiddle."

Mr. McAdams shifted his attention to Jonathan, brow raised. "If I recollect correctly, you sure did cut a fine tune or two at my house last week."

Just over Sam's shoulder, he caught a glimpse of Laurel. She stood, hand on hip, her saucy grin challenging him with the question *Do you want to be rescued or not?* He almost returned her smile. She'd put her daddy up to it . . . and Sam was enjoying the sport.

"I certainly wouldn't wish for Mr. Combs to miss dancing with his wife, but I can't promise I'll rise to the occasion, Mr. McAdams."

"Sam." Sam slammed a palm on Jonathan's shoulder. "Call me Sam, boy."

"Sam." Jonathan coughed from the impact of Sam's hand, embracing the sense of belonging Sam's rescue and familiarity inspired. Jonathan turned to Miss Simms. "Excuse me, Miss Simms. Thank you for the dance."

She gave a practiced attempt at looking offended, but it disappeared as soon as Todd Hawes, the blacksmith's son, stepped up to take her for a turn.

"Thank you, Sam."

He laughed, deep and resonant. "Don't thank me yet. You ain't played with Darrell, Coon, and Lacey before." He tipped his head toward the trio on the porch of the church. "They might be a whole lot scarier than Miss Simms."

Jonathan drew in a deep breath and stepped forward. "I'll take my chances."

Law mercy, Jonathan Taylor could fiddle.

Laurel grinned as she walked with her mama up the trail back home. Daddy and the other young'uns had left the church hours ago, but Mama and Laurel had stayed behind with some of the other womenfolk to straighten up for the next school day.

The look on those familiar faces around her when Jonathan got comfortable and began to light into the music, well, it was a sight to behold. They were surprised. Impressed. He'd broken through that initial barrier her people placed between outsiders and themselves.

She'd heard him play a few tunes up at her house, but watching him let loose on "Cripple Creek," once he heard Darrell play it through a few times, or "Sally Ann"? Have mercy, he'd made those strings sing!

And from the way he closed his eyes and tapped his toe, she knew he liked it too.

He was such a puzzle. Learned and gentlemanly, yet willing to step into a world so different from what he'd known. A gentleness and compassion shone through him and built a bridge between their different worlds. He proved as much a student as teacher.

*"Kindness is as universal as music,"* her granny used to say.

And Laurel had seen the truth of it.

The idea that thoughtful, kind men like Jonathan Taylor fought alongside her brother gave a heap of comfort. If he shot a rifle as clean as he played the fiddle, then woowee, not a highlander alive could argue his skill. Even Ozaiah Greer might crack a smile or two.

Mama hummed a little tune as they walked up the trail, the smoke from their cabin coming into view above the pines at the top of the hill. Apples tanged the autumn air with a hint to their ripeness. The trees lined their path in rows of gold, red, orange, and green. Everything glowed with life and home.

No matter how wonderful college proved, she'd always come back home. The thought reminded her of her trade with Jonathan, and she sent a look to Mama from her periphery. "It's a fine afternoon for a walk, ain't . . . isn't it?"

Her mama's humming stopped, and she smiled up to the sky. "Sure is. Just enough coolness to make the fire welcome."

Laurel chewed the inside of her cheek,

working up the confession. "Your stack cake was mighty good today, Mama. Not a crumb left behind."

Mama tipped her brow and looked over at Laurel, her gaze urging the truth right out of Laurel's mouth. "Teacher knows about college."

Mama's other brow rose to meet the first one, but she didn't say a word.

"I got all-fired up about Ozaiah Greer and his thick-headed ways that the words just slipped right out before I could catch 'em."

Her mother's grin encouraged further confession.

"So, we made a pact."

"Did you now? About your schoolin'?"

"He says he'll help me with my writing for college." Laurel hurried on, hoping her mama understood the importance. "He'll even give me ideas for papers to write and help correct my words so that I'll be more prepared."

Her mother stopped and turned, basket poised in hand. "That's mighty nice of him."

Laurel nodded. "And since he's moving to the mission house tomorrow and doesn't have a wife, I reckoned his first needs would be stomach needs. 'Cause you've always said, a man with a satisfied stomach has a clear head."

A look of pure confusion wrinkled up her mama's brow as they resumed their walk. "You plan to cook for him?"

Laurel laughed. "I ain't his wife. I aim to teach him how to cook for hisself, but I thought that was a good trade. And I know I can help him with mountain learning, because he's doesn't have no idea about most everything around here. You can be sure, he hasn't ever made butter or even gathered eggs." Laurel came to another stop in the path. "Mama, you reckon we could give him a chicken or two as a welcome gift? That's a good place to start, don't you think? Chickens aren't so hard to tend to, and then he can save up for a cow."

Mama chuckled. "Heaven sakes, girl, you're gonna keep him busy, that's for sure."

Laurel quieted, another thought filtering in through the others. She studied her mama and then took a deep breath. "Do you think I talk the bark off a tree, Mama?"

Mama's eyes widened, and her lips quirked to one side. "Not to my thinkin'."

"What about the hind legs off a mule?"

Mama's chuckle turned into a full-fledged laugh, not near as frequent a sound as it ought to be. "Law girl, where did you take such a notion?"

"A book." Laurel frowned, studying her

mama's glowing face, eyes sparkling like sunlight on water. "I talk a whole lot more than you or Maggie, at any rate. Suppose I'll grow quieter as I get older?"

"I hope you don't." Her mama started walking again, the sound of logs splitting breaking through the woodland noises. Daddy was preparing.

Laurel's stomach tightened. He'd chopped logs for two days straight, missing work on Friday.

"Why's that?"

Mama paused right before the path opened to their cabin's clearing. "Laurel, you see these leaves?" She gestured overhead at the collaged display of color. "Which tree you think is better?"

"I can't pick a favorite. They're all pretty."

"And that view." Mama pointed just over the tree line to a hint of blue mountains, fading into late afternoon. "Which do you think God likes better? The sun arisin' or the sun settin'?"

"What sort of question is that?" She shrugged. "Seems He likes 'em both the same."

"They're both beautiful in their own ways, ain't they?"

Laurel caught the lesson. "So, God made me to talk the hind legs off a mule and He made you to keep the mule's legs on, did He?"

Her mama's gaze softened. "He's called you to a path only you can go, just the same as He's called Maggie, or Isom, or Suzie, or the twins. The only one who can take the trail for your life is you, and make no mistake, He's already been workin' in you the strength and wisdom you'll need. Seems Teacher is a part of your path for now, and you're a part of his."

Laurel's grin grew so wide it pinched into her cheeks. "And I'm nearly saved up enough to take that path, Mama."

"I thought I heard you womenfolk gabbin' over here." Daddy pushed through the rhododendron bushes and filled up the gap between them with his sturdy frame. "Ain't no bird alive that makes the sounds of such a ruckus."

"Our sounds are so much sweeter, right, Daddy?" Laurel hoped the signs were wrong this time. Just this once.

"I do have a particular fondness for the sounds of these gabbin' womenfolk of mine." His grin laced with good humor, and he placed his arm around Laurel's shoulder.

"Did you come out to greet us like courtiers from the old country, Daddy?"

He chuckled. "I thought you was Isom at

first. I sent him on an errand for me, but I reckon it's still too soon for him to be back."

"And what sort of errand did you send him off to?" Mama asked, her tone giving nothing away.

Daddy ran his thumbs down the straps of his overalls, up and down, nervous like. Laurel's skull prickled with a warning chill that traveled plumb down her back. "Nothin' much. I sent him down to Hezekiah Cane's for a favor."

Mama's eyes drifted closed for a brief moment and then opened again, resolution and resignation tightening her features.

Hezekiah Cane was the best moonshiner in Maple Springs.

Winter was on the way.

# Chapter Eleven

One home visit with Dr. Hensley secured Jonathan's growing concern about the knowledge and welfare of the mountain people. He'd accompanied the doctor to Mercy Lindsay's house, a widow with two children. Dr. Hensley, as kind and respected as he was throughout the mountains, had known younger times. Nearing eighty, his eyes failed to give him a clear understanding of symptoms as they probably once did, or at least Jonathan hoped.

Dr. Hensley diagnosed her chest pain as stress related, giving her some sort of homemade tonic that had the strong scent of liquor, but, based on a few simple questions he'd gleaned from his studies, Jonathan wondered if Mrs. Combs suffered more from anemia than stress.

In the next visit, a man had a particularly nasty-looking infection on his arm. After applying an ill-smelling poultice, the doctor again administered liquor and said he'd return to check on the wound in a few days. The conditions of the homes reeked with uncleanliness, and yet the doctor used cloths from the home without sterilizing them. Why? This was not the front lines of war, where there was no time to disinfect the operation area. Dr. Hensley had the time but didn't take it.

Had he lost hope? Grown indifferent?

*God, they need someone who can help them.*

Uncle Edward later explained that Dr. Hensley, a native of nearby Boone, had only completed a few courses in medicine before practicing, and since he knew more than most folks in the area, they called him a doctor. So, not even a proper education in medicine? Good intentions carried a limited amount of weight.

"He's a fount of knowledge on mountain remedies and sewing up gunshot wounds, but as far as a great medical understanding" — his uncle had frowned, shaking his head — "there isn't much more available to these people."

And the glimmer in his uncle's eyes asked an unspoken question, one which bled clearer and clearer as the week progressed.

The vision Laurel inspired by her desire

to bring education back into these mountains caught fire inside of him — her purpose, contagious. He'd wandered into this world, half as a runaway and half as a man searching for a purpose, and in over two weeks, he'd seen more passion in a mountain girl with barely anything worldly than he'd seen in anyone.

The knowledge clicked inside of him the way a tune wound its melody beneath his skin, bringing his fingers to life on the strings of his violin. Was this what his uncle felt as his vision for Maple Springs swelled to reality? One tiny mountain church became two, then three. One school was planted, then two? One mountain-trained doctor, then a college-trained one?

His uncle had started all of that. Had God called Jonathan to a similar mission? Surely not. He wasn't as charismatic as his uncle. He didn't know the people or culture like Laurel. How could God use him with his quiet demeanor and gnawing limp?

The mountains, cold blue and vast in their expanse, seemed to bolster his heart with possibilities as endless as their reach. Could this world truly offer him something he'd never known . . . a place to belong?

After school, Jonathan made his way to Mrs. Cappy's store, in desperate need of some "sweet milk," as the mountain folk called it, and anything else besides eggs. He'd had eggs for nearly every meal since moving to the mission house. Thankfully, apples were in season, but even those had lost a little of their appeal. He'd even resorted to some long-lost skills he'd learned as a child on his grandfather's farm, by killing, field dressing, and subsequently burning rabbit on one occasion. But . . . even burnt rabbit tasted better than another meal of eggs.

The jingle of bells announced his entrance into the eclectic store. Over two weeks ago, Jonathan had looked humorously at the simple offerings on the shop shelves, but today, Mrs. Cappy's mountain store seemed a treasure trove of options. Beef and deer jerky waited on the shelves for purchase, along with some homemade-looking pastries and cakes of various styles. There were even a few candies in jars waiting for his taste buds.

A potbelly stove stood in the middle of the room with a long L-shaped white shelf to the left and two rows of various items to the right. Barrels lined the way to the counter, each filled with a different article for purchase — one full of potatoes, another of boxed crackers. Jars and cans of foods lined the shelves on the wall, and Jonathan stepped directly toward a few canned fruits and vegetables.

The door's bells jingled again and in walked a tall man, built like a mountain himself. He had to bend slightly to fit through the door, his rolled-up shirtsleeves pinching against glistening dark skin on his massive arms. He made an imposing figure in the little store. An impressive specimen of humanity, and one of the only negros Jonathan had seen since arriving in North Carolina, they'd crossed paths at the train depot when Jonathan needed directions to find his way to Maple Springs. What had his name been? Harris?

The man's dark eyes widened, and then his white smile split his face with welcome. "Well now, I see they ain't run you off yet."

The jovial welcome eased Jonathan into conversation. He stepped forward and offered his hand, bridging the short distance. "It's good to see you again, Mr. Harris. What brings you up the mountainside?"

"Mrs. Cappy knows I come once a week for some of the sweets she fixes for sale." He nodded toward the showcase at the end of the L-shaped shelf. "Right now, she's got some apple fritters that my men can't get enough of."

Jonathan flipped his gaze from the glass case back to Mr. Harris. "Fritters?"

The man's smile creased at the corners of his eyes. "They ain't no need to talk when you can taste, Teacher. Come on."

Laurel emerged from a back room, her thick blond hair pinned back into a bun, and a white apron making her look like a server from a French pastry shop. She patted her hands together and grinned. "You men look awful hungry. What can I get for you?"

Mr. Harris sidled forward and leaned his elbows on the shelf. "Mr. Taylor ain't never had no apple fritter before, Miss Laurel. You reckon we ought to remedy that?"

She raised a brow and studied Jonathan from head to toe. "If that ain't about criminal, I don't know what is." She dusted her hands against her apron and stepped to the showcase, keeping her attention on his face. "But Elias is right as rain. You can't go another day without one of Mrs. Cappy's fritters."

Laurel placed one of the crescent-shaped pastries onto a piece of brown paper and set it on the counter, the customary glint in her eyes in full sparkle.

"I'm trusting you, Miss McAdams."

"Shows you're a smart man."

Mr. Harris's deep laugh rumbled through the room as Laurel handed him one of the fritters too. "I trust you to cause a little mischief every once in a while."

Her grin broadened, capturing Jonathan's attention again. "Well now, Elias, that shows you're a smart man too," she replied, turning her attention, with all its pixie-glint, back to Jonathan.

"Go on, Teacher. Give that fritter a taste. It might not be change-your-life good like Mama's strawberry stack cake, but it's close enough to leave a memory."

Jonathan bit into the pastry and closed his eyes. A wonderful combination of sugar, butter, maybe cinnamon, and some other type of sweetness poured over his tongue, reviving his appreciation for apples. And the apples! They held a tangy flavor to complement the sweet in a most tantalizing way, with the entire bite wrapped in soft bread.

*Bread! He'd missed bread.*

"Looks to me like Teacher doesn't mind that fritter one bit." Laurel's voice broke into his appreciation.

He opened his eyes and wiped his mouth with the corner of the paper. "Did you make these?"

"I know how to make them, but not as fine as Mrs. Cappy." Laurel closed the showcase and proceeded to wipe down the countertop she stood behind.

"Miss Laurel's cobbler is the best in these parts," Mr. Harris said. "Ain't tasted better this side of Asheville anywhere."

Her face bloomed from the compliment, enhancing the natural beauty she wore so well. Jonathan's gaze caught for a second before he turned back to Mr. Harris. "I look forward to trying cobbler then too."

"You won't regret it." Mr. Harris waved his fritter toward Jonathan as he spoke. "You been here, what, nearly three weeks now, Mr. Taylor?"

Jonathan nodded, savoring another bite.

"How's school teachin' been going?"

"Call me Jonathan, please."

Mr. Harris's face took on a curious expression, surprise turned to pensive, before he offered a small smile. "Elias."

"I have a great deal to learn about Appalachia and the people, but I certainly hope I can bring a lot to them as well. For the most part, the students are eager and curious. The greatest challenge is their range of needs, from early readers all the way to more advanced."

Elias nodded, his gaze roaming the store. "Like any place, you have the hard people and the good ones." He tipped his head toward Laurel.

Laurel planted her palms on her hips and raised a playful brow. "If you think sweet talkin' gets you another free fritter, you ain't never lived 'neath the wrath of Mrs. Cappy."

Elias chuckled and placed the last bite into his mouth, his expression sobering. "Good or bad, them young'uns are lucky, that's for sure. They wasn't no schoolin' for me. Workhouse was all we had."

Jonathan recollected little about his studies on America's war between the North and South. The conflict appeared a massive tangle of politics, states' rights, human rights, and a great deal of unfettered anger, but certainly over half a century made a difference in educating whites and blacks.

"It's never too late to learn, Elias." Jonathan tried the name on his tongue. Different, but a smooth path of vowels and consonants. "Learning is a lifetime pleasure, and reading can be taught at any age."

Elias rubbed the back of his head and shrugged. "That's all good, but I'm more in need of cypherin' than readin'."

"Cyphering?" He looked to Laurel.

"Math." She mouthed the word.

"Well, that can be taught as well, if you're interested."

Elias looked around the room as if waiting for someone to object. "I know my young'uns would love more schoolin' than what me or the boys can teach 'em. They barely know their alphabet nor nothin' about their numbers."

Jonathan swallowed another bite of the delicious fried pastry. "You have children?"

The man's face softened with a gentleness Jonathan didn't know in a father. "Hank and Dolly. Ain't big enough for your part of the school yet, but they's smart. Dolly's learnin' to cook 'bout anything she tastes, and Hank's gonna be a fine builder one day. Good with his hands."

"And they live with you at the mill?"

" 'At's right. Me and the boys. Their mama took sick a few years ago with typhoid, so it's been the three of us since. We had a man stop in once in a while to teach 'em a little, but they only got so far on their readin' and cypherin'."

"Why not bring them to the school?" Jonathan gestured toward Laurel. "The sawmill isn't even as far as the Dawsons' house, and they walk the distance every day. It would be an opportunity to get some consistent teaching."

Elias stared at Jonathan for a long silence, measuring, then glanced over at Laurel as if she had the answer for whatever caused his sudden seriousness.

"My children? In your school?"

The quiet bound with a sudden tension. Had Jonathan stepped into one of the feuds he'd heard about in these mountains? Was there a conflict between Elias and Jonathan's uncle? Neither possibility seemed to fit. "Of course," he answered, slowly looking from Elias to Laurel for clarification.

Elias narrowed his eyes and then seemed to find whatever answer he was looking for. His smile softened, almost sad. "That's awful kind of you, Mr. . . . Jonathan," he corrected, nodding slowly. "Awful kind. Maybe for another time. But I best be gettin' back to the mill." He turned to Laurel. "I believe you know what I come for, Miss Laurel."

She was already taking out a few more of the apple fritters and wrapping them for travel. Then she added some deer jerky to the bag. Jonathan watched, attempting to make sense of Elias's response, but Laurel's voice pealed into his thoughts.

"You ain't missed a week yet, Elias. Sure you don't want to take a slice of raspberry cake with you too. I bet Dolly'd figure out how to make one in no time at all."

He whistled low and rubbed his palms down his flat stomach, the previous levity returning. "Well now." He released a long breath. "If you add one of them jars of raspberry jam to the order, then I reckon she can."

Laurel's light laugh met his remark and returned the sunshine to the room. Jonathan could only imagine the mischief and fun Laurel and his sister, Cora, could get into. Both exuded an inner delight, though Cora's came with a less mature bent. Laurel held an undercurrent of depth and knowledge that gave her eyes a wisdom, a strength, he didn't quite understand, but . . . he wanted to.

Elias paid for his goods and turned, bag in hand. "Pleasure to see you, Jonathan. Good luck with the school."

Jonathan wasn't certain what to say, so he wished the man a good day as he left.

"I've been meanin' to come talk with you, Teacher, since the deal we made, but Mrs. Cappy's been gone to town for supplies the past two days, so I've been full-up here at the store. She just got back about an hour ago, so I'll have some time to teach you."

Jonathan pulled his attention away from the door and approached the counter. "Teach me?"

"You haven't forgot our deal already, have you?"

He placed his palms on the counter and

leaned forward. "A fair trade, I believe you called it."

"I did for sure, though I was half hoping you'd forgotten about our deal." She reached down behind the counter and pulled out a satchel. With halting movements and a wary glance in his direction, she finally succeeded in drawing out some papers from the bag and placing them on the counter. "I ain't . . . haven't had anyone read my writing except my old teacher. Sometimes I'll read things out to Mama or Maggie, but I'm a lot more skittish about giving you my words than about teaching you mountain ways."

He shot her a look. "Why?"

"Sharing my words? My thoughts?" She shrugged. "I don't know. It feels like you're seein' inside of me, to the core."

At her sweet confession, something in their kinship deepened. "I feel certain there's only good things to see."

Her gaze flickered to his and held before her grin tipped with a twist of one brow. "You remember when I wanted to light into Ozaiah Greer like a wind-throwed tree? There wasn't nothing good to see in my heart then."

He tapped the papers against his other hand. "Well, those were extreme circumstances."

"And trying to teach Avis Morgan to read this week? That boy stuck a frog right down the front of my apron. You can be sure as shootin' my thoughts took a murky turn."

Jonathan laughed and glanced down at the pages. "Will I find deep-felt essays about the evils of boys and frogs in this set of papers then?"

Her smile took a nervous turn, and she looked down at the pages in his hands, in uncustomary seriousness. "Well, I figured if you were serious about helping me . . ." Her voice dropped to a whisper, "I'd give you a few things to look over. Different styles, as my teacher called it. There's an essay on the theme of working for your dreams from the book *Little Women*. And then there's a fiction piece I wrote, a tall tale for the young'uns. I put a poem in there too."

"That's excellent." He held her gaze, attempting to reassure her. "I'm excited to read these."

Every crinkle from her puckered brow to her pinched lips screamed doubt.

"I'm serious, Laurel. If your natural flair for colorful speech comes out in your writing, I feel certain I'm to enjoy the discovery."

She shrugged off the compliment with

another sideways glance and then tapped the counter. "And after school tomorrow, if you'll come on down here to the store, I'll give you your first cookin' lesson."

His jaw came unhinged. "Cooking lesson?"

The signature impish grin returned. "I'll teach you how to make pone bread. Mrs. Cappy has a newer cookstove like yours in the mission house, and she's said we can practice on it after school."

As if she'd heard her name, Mrs. Cappy came out of the back room, her wiry gray hair pinned into a tight knot at the base of her neck and her dark eyes sending anything but welcome in Jonathan's direction.

"Mrs. Cappy." He nodded a greeting.

She sniffed, gathered up a few scoops of flour into a bag, and then returned to the back room. Every time he saw the storekeeper, images of the witch from Hansel and Gretel crowded his mind. Perhaps he should stay clear of Mrs. Cappy and her cookstove.

"Don't let Mrs. Cappy bother you none." Laurel leaned forward, whisper low and close. "She's always got the mullygrubs, but down deep she's soft as fresh biscuits."

Jonathan felt fairly certain he could listen to Laurel and her lyrical phrasing all day long. "She is a little terrifying."

"Only her eggs." Laurel winked and then reached to the shelf behind her and brought a small cloth bag around to the counter. "I went ahead and baked some pone bread for you to take home with you tonight." She lowered the cloth to reveal a circle of golden bread. "Pone is one of the most important foods you can make for these parts, and since you're living on your own without a wife, I reckon it's a fittin' idea to learn first. This is corn pone."

The scent of warm butter and corn rose to his nostrils and made his mouth water. He sighed and took the offering. "You're wonderful."

"And you're a hungry man. Take some more of the jerky with you when you leave. It'll taste fine with the corn pone for now. I'll teach you gravy too, but that can be tricky. And since you took such a shine to sun tea at the get-together Sunday, I figured I oughta teach you how to make it too."

"I think we need to renegotiate our deal. I am, by far, the better recipient of it."

"I wouldn't go countin' my chickens yet, Teacher. You ain't started the hard work, but I reckon you can live off of sun tea, pone bread, a few eggs, and some side meat for a while without getting sallow-faced." The glint in her eyes teased out his grin. If she'd been a woman back home, he'd have taken her forwardness as flirting, but he knew Laurel well enough now. In fact, it seemed to be ingrained in most of the mountain folks he'd met, a forthrightness. Manipulation appeared to be a waste of time and words. No, she was refreshingly authentic. And somehow, her existence in his world made everything a little better.

The poor man didn't know anything about cooking a'tall. Laurel held back her giggle at every turn, especially the first time he lifted the iron skillet and nearly dropped it on his toe. After a few attempts, they finally had success, and the proud beam on his face nearly had Laurel wanting to go through all the trial again.

He had such a good heart. Did he see himself that way?

While the corn pone baked in the oven, Laurel suggested they look for some elderberry leaves to make a few jugs of sun tea. She'd been cooped up inside the store too long without a breath of afternoon air, and the sky called for a visit. They followed a path behind the store that led toward an outcropping called Lady Hawk's Roost, a place with a view clean to Wilkesboro and beyond. The autumn day teamed with life and color and the tangy scent of wild grapes and fresh pine.

"You smell that sweet scent in the air?" She looked over at Jonathan as he walked by her side, the wind tousling his hair with such force, he removed his hat.

He drew in a deep breath, a smile spreading across his face. "Yes. A flower? Fruit?"

"Wild grapes." Her feet followed the scent as she searched the woods for the familiar vines. "We ought to pick some before they're finished for the season, and we can make you some jam to tide you through winter."

"I need to work much harder on my end of this bargain, Laurel."

She chuckled and stepped off the path, pushing through the brush to a place where a rocky ledge opened to an endless horizon. The late-afternoon light hazed the distant mountains into the sky, as if the colors had smudged from deep blue to white by a careless thumb. Her eyes, her skin, drank in the view, every shade of blue, every hue of afternoon auburn sinking into her skin. Strength, peace, a sweet belonging.

"I wish I had the words to describe a view like this to Hazel Spencer." The wind blew her hair in a wild tangle around her head, but she paid it no mind. "She's been blind since anyone can remember, but I can't rustle up the right way to show her this view through words."

"That reminds me." Jonathan turned to her, breaking her focus on the view. "I think Isom may need glasses."

"Glasses? How do you know?"

"He was showing all the signs when I observed him during church on Sunday. Rubbing his eyes, squinting. With your parents' permission, I'd like to come to your house to examine him."

Cold splashed over Laurel's skin as if winter had already come blowing through. Visit home? She released the hold on her breath and gave an internal prayer of gratitude to God. Her daddy's attempts to get liquor from Hezekiah had temporarily failed because of the moonshiner's being abed with the miseries. Maybe that bought Laurel's family another week at least. Maybe two.

"You can examine eyes?"

"It's one of the things I learned before my medical training was interrupted." He shrugged. "I'm fairly adept at sutures and some infection treatment too."

She stepped toward a nearby vine that twisted from one tree to the other. The dark purple grapes hung in healthy clusters from their places, as if requesting relief from the heaviness. Reaching into her pocket, she pulled out her pocket knife and then crimped her apron into a basket to catch the clusters as they dropped. Jonathan rushed beside her to help, slowly taking the knife from her hands.

"I see you are *adept*" — she tried the word — "at picking grapes too."

He chuckled, his shoulder brushing hers in his attempt to relieve the cluster from the vine. "A skill honed more on my grandfather's farm than in the halls of university."

Jonathan needed to get to their house sooner rather than later. "How about tomorrow for supper?"

"Your parents wouldn't mind?"

She shook her head. "They'd be obliged to you. Mama's wrestled with Isom's learnin' for years. Maybe this is the answer. He's struggled somethin' fierce to read."

"That reminds me of another question I have for you, if you won't find me impertinent."

She shot him a grin. "Impertinent?"

His face relaxed with a smile. "Rude. Intrusive."

She gave a slow shake of her head and opened up her apron wider to accommodate another bunch of grapes. "I think your definition of . . . impertinent and mine are different. Go ahead."

"Elias Harris. Why wouldn't he bring his children to the school?"

Jonathan Taylor really did have one of the kindest hearts in all creation. What on earth was he doing in Maple Springs? "Elias doesn't want to cause a ruckus at school. He's too good for that."

He peered down at her, arms raised to grip the vine. "A ruckus?"

"Them being colored and all. Some folks ain't too keen on coloreds learning or worshipping among white folks." She looked down at the bounty in her apron, a sadness she couldn't name weighting her shoulders. "Why, you hear most folks still talk about the war among the states like it was yesterday 'cause their daddies or granddaddies are still livin' and talkin' about it."

"So, if Elias's children came to school, it may cause trouble?"

"For some folks."

Jonathan sliced a few smaller bunches from the vine and then paused to look back down at her. "How does your family feel about people of various skin colors learning together?"

She met his gaze, thinking, wondering. "Before your uncle came to be preacher, we had a heap of preachers come through that spent a whole lot of time shouting about God's wrath and judgment. About bad blood and some folks deserving one way of life while others deserve another. None of it ever sat right with my granny or mama, who'd come from a tradition of teaching that paired God's wrath with God's love. If that makes sense."

His brow puckered.

"I know wrath and judgment has its place, else God wouldn't have put it in the Bible, but your uncle came and preached God's love and beauty too. He brought a new kind of preachin'. Though some folks said he didn't have enough wind for them, he spoke in a way that makes a body want to pull up a chair and stay awhile. Like God had more to say with gentle talk than hard. More about beauty and love and kindness than hate and vengeance and war."

Jonathan was staring at her in a strange way. His gaze never left hers, intense and nearly causing her thoughts to stumble around in her head.

"I haven't seen schools with all colors of folks in them before. But that doesn't mean it can't be so. God's truth is in His Word, but He's also been kind enough to spill His answers into the whole world around us."

She waved her hand toward the view. "Not one single tree as far as you can see, not one, is exactly the same as another, but they all work together to create this kind of beauty. God uses them all. Studyin' on that sure helps make big things big and small things small." She pushed her hair back from her face to have a clearer view of his face, his expression. "He made all sorts of critters too, even polecats." Her grin twitched. "Why wouldn't He want variety in His people? Makes a heap of sense, don't you think?"

He stared back at her with those round, dark eyes of his, and suddenly the cool breeze turned almost springlike. She liked his eyes. Kind eyes. Intelligent ones.

"It does, Laurel."

Her name somehow sounded sweet. Different. Almost magical.

"Indeed, it does."

# CHAPTER TWELVE

*September 26, 1918*

Brother dearest,

I was so delighted to receive your letter yesterday, but to think it will take almost two weeks for correspondence to reach you! All news will be old news. I miss you terribly. The house is intolerably silent, so, as you can imagine, I've been forced to seek occupation elsewhere. Believe it or not, I have volunteered my services at Endell Street Military Hospital. Do you remember it? A hospital run entirely by women. Even the doctors are women. It's a fascinating place and terribly efficient. Mother beams with pride, even when I return home with an apron stained with all sorts of horrible things, but Father remains positively horrified. I feel certain he believes all of my marriage prospects will wane at the idea of a working woman, but I told him all of my marriage prospects were fighting the war, so he needn't worry too much on that front.

However, he is quite dedicated to marrying all of my brothers off, and has secured a lucky heiress for both you and Charles so far. I thought you ought to know, so when you return home you won't be surprised to find a bride waiting. Her name is Eleanor Hollingsworth, second daughter to a man who recently received his fortune in the salt mines. I suppose she could add seasoning to your life! As if you needed any additional spice with the many adventures you're experiencing in the wilds of North Carolina. Did you say there is not a streetlamp in sight? Nor even a road? I hope you will not be lost forever in some cave or hollow.

Are there any young women there? Do they still have their teeth? I've heard stories of the mountain women having no teeth or hair and living pitifully. I suppose Miss Hollingsworth will have no competition for her hand. Please keep me abreast of all of your adventures. I will have more to write of my adventures in my next letter.

Mother sends her love. Father sends his . . . well, Father sends a stern nod in acknowledgment that I am writing you a letter. I do believe he's softening in your absence.

With love to bound the ocean,<br>Cora

Of course his sister would work in a hospital filled to the brim with suffragettes. Jonathan stared at the return letter he'd composed to his sister, his chuckle resurfacing at the very idea. He couldn't imagine his father's disdain, but he'd always been softer on Cora, allowing her liberties none of the boys ever knew.

And a bride for Jonathan? His smile faded. Always the expectation. Always the forced decision waiting for acknowledgment. In the time since he'd arrived in Maple Springs, he'd felt freedom he'd never known. Even if his own decisions resulted in sleepless nights or burnt rabbit, they were his own, without the echoes of his father's disapproval in his head. He sat a little straighter in the school desk chair and released a long breath.

A breath of liberty.

He was determined to make his own way, whatever way that might be. And in the end, his father would see the results and be proud. Surely. He'd always touted the values of hard work and strength. Jonathan would show him. Prove to him that he was as worthy of acceptance as either of his brothers.

And as far as the mountain women? Jonathan's grin returned, and Laurel McAdams's image floated through his mind. Her white smile. Her wealth of golden hair. No, his sister was quite wrong on her thoughts about mountain women.

He finished his letter and tucked the envelope into his jacket pocket, snatching his satchel from the floor and his hat from the hook by the schoolhouse door on his way out. Laurel, Maggie, and Isom waited in the field beside the church, a large space that separated the church-school from Mrs. Cappy's store and the blacksmith's shop.

He hadn't expected the two younger children. After staying up the night before, reading through Laurel's work, all he wanted to do was encourage her. He shouldn't have underestimated her, but he'd expected something less than the quality she'd given him. She'd surprised him once again.

"It looks as though I have an entire entourage escorting me up the mountain today."

"A what?" Isom scratched his head and

crinkled his nose. "You talkin' some different language again, Teacher?"

Jonathan reached out and ruffled the child's hair, an action he'd noticed his uncle gave to many of the younger boys. Isom's grin grew, the touch adding a connection. Jonathan wanted to understand, to connect with the students, and with a little help from his uncle, he'd gleaned a few ideas.

"*Entourage* is a word that means a group following a person."

Isom's brows pinched together. "Then you're my entor . . . whatever 'cause you're gonna be followin' me." He shoved his thumb into his chest and marched up the trail, sending one look behind him to make sure they were all paying attention.

Laurel shook her head as she laughed. "We'd better get movin' before the king there, leaves his entourage in the dust."

Maggie moved to the far side of her sister, leaving Laurel at Jonathan's right up the path. They stepped from the field into the forest, goldenrod, russet, and orange leaves framing their way. "Maggie's coming back to stay with Mrs. Cappy, but she's running some groceries to Mama first and picking up a change of clothes for the night."

"And I can eat Mama's cookin' instead of Mrs. Cappy's for supper," Maggie added, sending a shy grin his way.

"She doesn't like the eyeball eggs either," Laurel explained.

"Or the liver pudding," Maggie added.

It seemed the wrong time to share his enjoyment of kidney pie. "After your sister's tutelage yesterday, I feel a bit more prepared in my eating options than only store-bought food and my limited knowledge of cooking eggs."

"Don't worry that head of yours, Teacher. When I teach you how to make beans, cake, and then cobbler" — Laurel whistled, an unexpected sound from a woman — "you'll be set for a long time. And as long as there's salat growin' around your house, or taters, or rhubarb, then you'll be fit for sure."

Maggie nodded her dark head. "Rhubarb pie is something else, Teacher."

He grinned. "You are all full of ideas."

"Daddy says Laurel's too full of ideas for anyone's peace of mind," Isom parroted from up ahead. "Says it's scary how many thangs she thinks up in a day."

Jonathan's laugh joined in with Laurel's, the thoughts within the papers confirming what Jonathan had already begun to decipher about his new friend. Clever, kind, *and* talented. "I'd like to use both of your quick minds regarding an idea of my own, if you will."

"Well, I'm not sure I want my peace of mind disrupted. What about you, Maggie?"

Maggie responded with a wrinkle-nosed grin.

"I'll attempt to share only *two* ideas."

Laurel looked skyward, as if considering, and then back to him. "Well, I reckon if it's only two, Teacher."

"I'd like to begin skill classes, for anyone who wants to come." He rubbed his palms together, readying for his declaration. "Maybe start with a woodworking or carving class after school led by students like Enoch Spencer, Guy Sharpe, and Bent Morgan. I've seen their excellent skills and believe others would like to learn from them."

Laurel's eyes brightened. "That's a wonderful notion. And they're good boys too. It's a great way to help them learn about teaching and leading."

"That's what I thought too. And, if they decide they want to try and sell some of their creations, I could teach them about managing money for a business."

The look of complete admiration on Laurel's face expanded his chest two sizes. "Why, that's the cleverest thing I've ever heard."

"Is it just for boys?" Maggie asked.

"Of course girls can come, but I'd thought about asking your mother, Sarah Anne Larson, who is always sewing something, and Granny Morgan if they'd be willing to offer quilting classes for those interested."

"And flatlanders would snatch up those quilts for high prices. Daddy says they sell like hotcakes anytime he's seen them in stores." Laurel clapped her hands. "And this could be the start of lots of choices. We could do a cooking class and smeltin' class and dressmaking."

"And painting," Maggie added.

"Exactly." Jonathan's pace quickened in excitement. "And a gardening class to teach about what can be planted when and how to use those plants for cooking or medicine."

"What do you need us to do?" Laurel kept by his side, encouraging him.

"I'm going to talk it over with my uncle, since the school is part of the mission *he* began, and I thought I'd discuss it with your father, as a leader in the community, maybe with Mr. Morgan as well, to ensure I've thought through everything."

"I reckon Daddy's peace of mind is about to be disrupted."

His laugh burst out. "Hopefully, he'll bear it well."

The notebook in Maggie's hand caught his eye. "And Maggie, I've heard about your paintings. I saw one in class yesterday. Do you have some with you?"

Her dark eyes grew wide, and she loosened her hold on her notebook, lowering it a little. "You want to see my paintings?"

"I'd love to."

"Come on, Maggie. Mr. Taylor knows about paintings and such in his world." Laurel turned to him. "They're like them photographs you see in newspapers, except with colors. Our teacher two years ago taught Maggie how to make paints from berries and flowers and all sorts of other things."

With a little more encouragement, Maggie opened her notebook and held two pages out for Jonathan to take. The first painting showed a forest brook framed on either side with autumn colors. A ray of sunlight split through the foliage, bathing a burst of violet flowers at the water's edge in a spotlight.

Jonathan looked over at Maggie, only then realizing he'd stopped walking. "This is remarkable, Maggie."

A rush of pink filled her cheeks. She smiled and looked down at her notebook.

"Truly. You have a gift." He quickly turned

to the second page and his jaw dropped at the likeness. A view of those mountains outside the church doorway, her colors capturing the varied hues of blue blending into a golden sunrise. "How did you learn this?"

"She's always had an eye for it, but Miss Leonard, our teacher two years ago, moved up here and took such a shine to Maggie's natural talent that she started givin' Maggie lessons."

"Maggie, I've ordered some additional items for my house. A larger bed, a reading chair, some rugs, and things to make the house more a home. Are you willing to sell your paintings?"

Maggie looked up, wide eyes blinking. "Sell 'em? Who'd buy 'em?"

"Well, I would. I'd love to frame them and place them in my house." He grinned at her widening eyes. "But I can only imagine how many other people would be interested in this type of scenic representation of these Blue Ridge Mountains. If we can take wood carvings and quilts to sell in Wilkesboro or Sparta, why not paintings?"

Maggie looked to Laurel, who patted her little sister on the shoulder. "Sounds like some excellent peace-rattlin' ideas to me."

■ ■ ■ ■

Jonathan Taylor was a surprising person. As Isom led the way up the last leg of the path, Laurel watched him draw Maggie out of her quiet self and engage in conversation about her paintings. Menfolk in the mountains weren't known for their gentleness. In fact, she only knew a handful who carried themselves with the same sweetness as Preacher Anderson and Jonathan. She knew a lot of good men. Kind, even. But something in the way Jonathan showed his interest held a mesmerizing sort of tenderness.

Just before they reached the cabin, with Maggie and Isom rushing on ahead, Jonathan stopped her with a touch to the arm.

"I wanted to speak to you alone about your papers."

Her stomach tightened like a banjo string.

"Laurel, your pages . . ." He drew them from his satchel. "They're excellent. I made some notes about your grammar and a few suggestions regarding the organization of your work, but the information you have here —" He was almost breathless. "The descriptions. Your way with words. It's very good. No wonder the college wanted you."

She shrugged off the words, her stomach

unwinding a bit. "That's awful nice of you to say."

She reached for the papers, but he wouldn't let go. "It's not a void compliment. I'm serious. Have you ever thought about becoming a writer?"

He was bloomin' crazy. "A writer?"

His palms came up. "There's talent and beauty hidden here in these mountains. My uncle wrote to me about it, but I never imagined. Crafts, paintings." He looked at her. "Stories. You really do have the makings of a writer, a storyteller. It's in your blood, your culture, and you have the ability to capture it on paper."

He released his hold on her pages, and she tucked them under her arm, tilting her head to study him. A writer? The title reached into some shadowed spot in her heart and shone a light. A writer? She shook her head free from the thought. "Teacher, Miss Simms won't be back next year. I'd be surprised if she lasts another month or two. My people don't need a writer — they need a teacher, and that's what I mean to do."

His shoulder sank a little. "Maybe you could do both."

She laughed. "I can't hardly get one dream to come true. It'd seem greedy to hope for two."

"Laurel," Maggie's voice called from beyond the shrubbery.

She turned back to Jonathan and raised the papers. "But I look forward to seeing what you wrote."

"You'll share more of your writings?"

She drew in a deep breath and nodded. "We have a deal, remember?"

He followed her around the thick bushes. Her cabin emerged through the thicket, perched toward the morning sky. Afternoon shadows hung over the yard now, but sunlight brought out the colors of surrounding trees. Maggie waited on the front porch, her expression stalling Laurel's forward momentum.

"What is it?"

Maggie's face paled by the second. "It's Daddy. He's gone to Hezekiah Cane's house."

No, no, no. The fall colors had barely ripened on the trees. It was too early.

"Is everything all right?"

She prepared her answer before turning to face him. The truth would certainly take a little of the shine off his ideas. "Daddy isn't going to be able to join us for supper."

He hesitated, his hand going to his satchel. "Should I wait to examine Isom's eyes?"

"We'll ask Mama, but I imagine she'll

want to go on ahead with the examination."

Mama greeted Teacher as if there wasn't one thing wrong. She had a way of staying calm that Laurel hoped and prayed she'd learn as she grew up, because her stomach buzzed like the bees in Daddy's hives out back, waiting for the sting. Would he come home soon? Tonight? Next week?

Would he rejoin the family in a friendly mood or much worse?

She watched the shifting afternoon light and listened for the sound of footsteps on the porch as Jonathan examined Isom's eyes. Her brother basked in the attention, even as he squinted through looking at the pictures and letters Teacher placed on the table before him. Everyone gathered around the table to watch. How had none of them noticed Isom's struggle? His repetitive blinking? The way he rubbed his eyes over and over, as if trying to clear the view.

Curiosity was the only excuse for Daddy entering the house without anyone seeing him, but his scent reached the kitchen long before his body ever filled the doorway.

"The boy sick?"

They all turned, except Isom, who was dutifully sitting painfully still for his examination. Mama stepped forward, her voice as smooth as honey. "Teacher come to check

Isom's eyes. Says it seems he's having a hard time with seein' up close."

Daddy peered down at Mama, her words taking longer to make sense through his bleary-eyed haze of drink, then he stepped around her to the kitchen. Jonathan rose, his smile unaffected by Daddy's altered state. Most likely, he didn't know the signs.

"That's a fact, Mr. McAdams. But it's nothing glasses won't fix. I'd imagine that's why he was struggling so much with learning to read."

"Some folks just can't read," Daddy grumbled, his words sluggish. "I ain't never been good at it myself. Cypherin', yes, but not readin'."

"Thankfully, it's something that can be easily remedied. I can send the specifications to the doctor my uncle knows in Wilkesboro, and then he will ship the glasses here."

Daddy scoffed and narrowed his eyes, a warning Jonathan didn't understand. "What do you get out of this?"

Jonathan blinked. "Pardon?"

"You come all this way to teach in some country school that can't pay you in nothin' much but hard work." He stepped closer, and Mama angled her body to stay between the two men. "What did you really come here for, boy? We've had your kind here before."

Jonathan looked to Laurel, then Mama, and back to Daddy. "Mr. McAdams, I'm here to teach and help in any way I can. If you're concerned about the cost for the glasses, my uncle's mission has funds set aside to —"

"We can pay." Daddy's face tightened, and Jonathan took a step back.

Laurel began nudging him toward the door.

"Of . . . of course you can." Jonathan stumbled ever so slightly. "I'm sorry if I offended you, sir. I'm fond of your family and would never —"

"I know what you flatlanders are like. All the same." His voice firmed, darkened. Laurel gently turned Jonathan one way as Mama nudged Daddy away from the door, without him realizing it. "You think you can come into our mountain and push your money on us. I know your kind. Come to steal our stories and our liquor and our daughters."

"Teacher, it's time you got on back home. Sam ain't fit for visits right now," Mama said, jerking her head toward the doorway. "Laurel."

Laurel pulled Jonathan by the arm

through the sitting room and out onto the porch, Daddy's voice rising. "He can't have our young'uns. His kind already took one. They already took one."

She gave him a little push toward the steps, breathless. "You need to get home."

"He's . . . he's drunk."

The concern in Jonathan's searching gaze paused her frantic movements. "The likes you ain't never seen before."

Daddy's voice roused again, and Laurel edged Jonathan down the steps.

Jonathan turned and searched her face. "Are you sure you're going to be all right?"

Something inside of her softened to jelly. Such sweet concern. She inwardly groaned, and faced him, hating to soften the truth for his sake. "We'll be better if you get away from the house for a spell till he's calmed down."

Jonathan moved toward the steps and looked back to her, almost as if he wanted to ask another question. Her father's booming voice roared some unintelligible fury from inside, heaving steps coming toward the door.

"Go, Jonathan. Go now."

## Chapter Thirteen

Laurel hadn't left the house in three days. Neither had anyone else.

Staying close to Daddy during the first few days of his drunk kept him calm, and everybody wanted him to keep as calm as possible. The calmer a drunk, the nicer. But on Thursday morning, he'd disappeared from the house, most likely going for more mountain dew, so Mama urged Laurel to pack some things and stay at Mrs. Cappy's for a few days.

"Ain't no use for Mrs. Cappy to suffer on her own no more, and you need to keep savin' your money," Mama had said, and despite Laurel's hesitation, her mama wouldn't hear of any different.

Jonathan showing up at the store after school came as no surprise, but the rush of pleasure at seeing him emerge through the door did. Mrs. Cappy had said he'd shown up each day after school, asking about her.

Her? Surely, it was just simple kindness, but a piece of her wished his interest leaned a little more toward sparks than not.

She shook off the thought. She'd stopped daydreaming about weddings when she'd set her mind to go to college, making sure to gently turn down any boy interested in sparkin' her, but Jonathan Taylor, with his oakmoss scent and tender gaze, had her mind jumping in all sorts of unexpected directions. Silly. He'd leave Maple Springs like every other teacher. He'd get his time of mission work, serving the poor mountain folks, and then return to a world she couldn't even imagine.

No need to ponder romances, no matter how sweet the man.

She was going to college.

That was that.

"Laurel, I've been anxious as to how —"

Laurel raised a hand to stay his approach and then peeked her head into the back room of the store. "Mrs. Cappy, I'm going to gather some more witch hazel for your itch cream concoction. Be back shortly."

The older woman waved a dismissive hand from the cookstove where she was mixing who-knew-what to sell in her store.

Jonathan opened the door for her to exit and fell into step beside her.

"Witch Hazel?"

His humorous initiation to the conversation stole Laurel's wariness of the topic she knew he'd come to discuss. She chuckled and attempted to keep the wind from brushing her loose hair across her face.

"You're going to gather a witch?"

"Maybe more than one." She waved her basket down the hillside toward the creek. "Want to tag along and see?"

He pushed his hands into his pockets, his head free of his usual hat. Most likely because of the strength in the breeze today. She liked his hair, especially when it looked a little untidy, as it did today.

"I've been anxious for your family."

She looked ahead, trying to figure out a way to explain something she didn't fully understand. It was life. All she'd known. But she knew how outsiders would respond. Preacher tried to save her daddy, but when he was drunk there was no reasoning with him, and when he was sober he could easily turn the conversation with humor and wit. Preacher gave up trying and just went to praying.

Like the rest of the McAdams family did.

"Don't worry about us, Teacher. We'll be all right." She lowered her head, not wishing to brush off his concern. "It happens about this time every year."

"His drinking?"

She nodded. "Daddy goes on a drunk during winter. There are a whole clan of menfolk who do. There ain't no stoppin' it as far as any of us can tell."

"He did this last winter?"

She sighed, feeling the judgment rising in Jonathan's voice. "He does it every winter. Has for years. Plans for it, even. In fact, he cut enough firewood to last us for three months, somehow knowing the time was getting close."

Jonathan touched her arm, stopping her, his gaze locked to hers. "He planned for it? For three months?"

She pulled her gaze out of his and resumed the walk. It never made sense, no matter how many times she tried to explain it. "We can't never tell if he'll make it to November or start down the dark path early. Mama was hoping he'd make it through the corn shuckin' this year, but it just wasn't meant to be."

Their footsteps crunched against some of the newly fallen leaves, the colors painting a carpeted path before them through the trees.

"How does he complete his work in that state?"

"He doesn't go to work." More silence.

Most likely Jonathan was trying to sort it all out, but there was no making sense of it. "He doesn't leave us wanting. He saves up for it every year, even stocks up on some store-bought canned food just in case we run out of what we canned ourselves."

"I can't even fathom how . . ." Jonathan's words trailed off, but then he seemed to find them. "Do you mean to say he, and other men like him, perform perfectly normal for three-quarters of the year, and the last quarter during these dark days of winter, they remain drunk for the entire time? Why? How?"

"Preacher asked the same things when he came. I don't have all the answers." She stopped by the creek, looking just across the stream at a row of bright yellow bushes. With careful steps, she moved from one rock to the other across the easy-flowing water. "Some folks say it's a battle against the weariness of winter, like a sickness in their heads that they can't figure out. Others say it was born in them from their daddies before them." She stopped on the other side of the creek and turned. Jonathan followed her, less sure of his steps on the rocks.

"But . . . but your father wasn't an angry man at all when I met him. Or any other time I've seen him." Jonathan wobbled on the last rock.

Laurel grabbed his flailing hand and pulled him to the other side of the creek. "He *ain't* an angry man. He's a good man. The liquor makes him a different person."

"But why would he do this? It doesn't make sense." He looked down at her, sunlight showing a bit of gold in his brown eyes.

She realized she still held his hands and gently tugged free. "No, it doesn't make sense." How could she take the anger from Jonathan's eyes? "You remember working with Daddy on the mission house? And playing the fiddle with him by the fire at our cabin?"

He tilted his head, those eyes searching hers with intensity, but something else too. Something that pooled over her skin like a honeysuckle breeze on a hot day. Compassion. Sweet compassion. Oh heavens, she'd never wondered how a person could drown in eyes before.

"Yes, I remember."

"Then keep those thoughts in your head. Someday I'll tell you the heartbreaking story of my daddy's life, of the hard childhood he shouldn't have survived. Of all the ways love and kindness was stripped from him at a tender age. It ain't no excuse for lawlessness, but it might help you understand better." She cleared the gathering emotions from her throat and drew in a steadying breath. "Maggie will be back to school next week, because then we'll have gotten through adjusting to him, but even if you hear hard stories about him through the mountain" — she drew in a deep breath — "and there's a good chance you will, remember the good. Hold fast to it."

She spoke as much to herself as to him and turned, stepping toward the bush, not wishing to see Jonathan's response. He wouldn't understand. Couldn't. She plucked a few of the golden leaves and placed them in her basket. The breeze created a *shhhh* overhead, tickling the silence.

"What happened to your sister?"

Laurel's fingers paused on a branch, her breath suddenly shallow. She plucked off the leaves and lowered her head as she placed them into the basket. "Her name's Kizzie. She turned seventeen last month."

"She's alive?"

She rubbed the smooth leaves between her fingers, her throat tightening with uncertainty. "As far as we know." She dropped the leaves into her basket, and Jonathan came to stand beside her, mimicking her movements and dropping more leaves into her basket. "We heard tell of a young tenant farmer outside of Parsonville who was looking to hire some workers for inside his house. Womenfolk who could clean and such. Kizzie took such a shine to the idea that with her winsome way of negotiatin', Daddy and Mama said she could go interview."

"She got the job," he said, dropping another layer of leaves into her basket.

Laurel nodded. "And it didn't take long to catch the eye of the farmer, a widow-woman's son and heir to the farm. Kizzie had a way 'bout her. Fiery and confident. With a little wooing and a whole lot of promises of fancy things and a rich life, I reckon, he got her in the family way in no time."

"But he wouldn't marry her."

Laurel nailed him with a look. "A rich, school-learned heir marryin' a nobody country girl? When Kizzie showed up to tell her tale to Daddy and Mama, she said the son would lose his inheritance if he married the likes of her. So she came home, but . . . but she'd brought such shame on the family, Daddy . . ." Tears closed around the words, the memory of her sister's pleas echoing in her ears. *"Please, Daddy. I ain't got nowhere else to go. Don't cast me off, Daddy."*

"He sent her away?" The phrase came on a whisper.

"He was at the end of his drunk. The worst time." Laurel looked up, Jonathan so close his shoulder almost touched hers. "We ain't seen her since that day. I pray for her every night, hoping she's safe out in the big world somewhere. There are rules in these mountains, laws that have been made by generations of people who've had to carve out a hard life." She pushed a smile in place, the quivering hope in her chest flickering to life. "But your uncle's preaching and his mission has already started changing things, and I hope I can be a part of that too. Compassion is going to win over more folks than anger ever can. That's why we have to remember the good, and hold on to hope."

True to Laurel's words, Maggie arrived back in school the following Monday, not more worse for the wear than when he'd last seen her at her cabin. As another week passed, then another — with Jonathan learning his place among the children, editing Laurel's work, burning enough biscuits to build a fence out of them, and finally beginning the boys' after-school woodworking class — Jonathan found his rhythm.

The news of taking homemade items to sell for "cash money" at the open market in Wilkesboro brought a wide variety of interest from the young people in his class. Before he knew it, he had carvings from the boys, along with a few excellent horseshoes and handcrafted garden tools.

A few of the girls supplied some items for him, especially Luanne Jacobs. She had a knack for sewing girl's dresses, from mostly feed and flour sacks. Though you'd never know it from the detailed embroideries on the smocks. After some coaxing, Maggie added a few paintings, two of which Jonathan purchased on the spot and had the woodworking boys teach him how to make frames for them. With the addition of the items Jonathan had ordered from town, his mission house was becoming as cozy as his uncle's.

Enoch Spencer and Bent Morgan had become Jonathan's right-hand men, staying after school almost every day to help him with packaging items or asking for extended lessons. Enoch especially wanted to know how to manage money for running his own business. Jonathan even won Mrs. Cappy over enough to have her come answer questions from the older students who wanted to learn more about owning a business. He made a mental note to ask Elias to come speak too on his way to Wilkesboro on Friday.

After speaking with Mr. Spencer to gain permission, Jonathan asked Enoch to accompany him to market and help keep accounts. The boy shook Jonathan's hand for so long, his fingers became numb, but there was such a joy in sharing opportunities with these children. And Jonathan was quickly learning that "smarts" came in a variety of shapes and sizes. Being compared to athletic and socially apt brothers his entire life, it was an easy segue for Jonathan to search for all sorts of ways people showed their talents. Not just book learnin', but also in music and debating and crafting. Once he began to have the students show their specific smarts to the class, an amazing reciprocity occurred. They became more invested in the lessons.

Jonathan even started a class after school on simple medical care, allowing Dr. Hensley to speak about certain mountain herbal remedies while Jonathan touched on various procedures he'd learned in school, even adding a few simple hygiene options.

On the way to Wilkesboro on Friday, Jonathan made certain to leave early enough to stop in at the sawmill. Enoch waited outside with the wagon as Jonathan walked through the open door, a host of high-pitched grating sounds coming from all around. The massive room looked like the inside workings of a clock. Gears moved in careful, repetitive motion, grinding through a massive log in the center of the room. Voices rose over the sounds, shouting unintelligible commands.

A fizzy noise, like the exhale of a train, hissed from below, followed by a shrill whistle burst. The grinding halted, and Elias walked into view from behind the machinery. "Edger's ready, Moses. Get on back to work."

He started to disappear behind the gears but caught sight of Jonathan, as the grating noises began again. His surprise took a quick detour to welcome, and he turned to motion for the other men to continue work before approaching Jonathan and gesturing to the doorway.

"There's no use trying to talk with the saws a'runnin'," he explained once they were outside. "And we got a big order to run, so they're going to be screamin' for a good while yet."

Jonathan grinned, taking Elias's outstretched hand. "I won't keep you for long, as I'm on my way to Wilkesboro this morning." He tipped his head toward the wagon. Enoch watched from his perched seat. "I only wanted to stop by long enough to make an offer."

"You in need of some lumber, Teacher?" The tall man's brow rose to his close-cut hairline.

Jonathan laughed. "Perhaps in the future, if I build on to the mission house, but for now I'm more interested in offering you something."

Elias rested his large palms on his hips and peered down from his lofty height. "I'm listenin'."

"Are you planning to visit Mrs. Cappy's store tomorrow, as is your usual Saturday custom?"

The man crooked a grin, taking pleasure in Jonathan's unusual speech, most likely. He was getting used to the well-humored glint. "I am."

"Would you have an extra hour before returning to the mill?"

Elias's gaze shifted to the left, where a little girl, perhaps seven or eight, and a boy, a few years older, played around a large oak near the side of the mill. "I can't be gone too long. Why are you askin'?"

Jonathan stood taller, attempting to com-

231

municate confidence. "If you're still interested in learning math." He shrugged. "Cyphering. I'd like to teach you."

The man stared with those large dark eyes of his, jaw slack. Jonathan rushed ahead. "You could walk over to the school before or after visiting Mrs. Cappy's." He gestured toward the children. "Bring them with you, if you need to. They can play or look at picture books while we work together."

Elias cleared his throat. "What'll it cost me?"

"Cost?" Jonathan hadn't considered a cost. "There's no cost."

The tall brow furrowed into deep grooves, and he folded his thick arms across his chest. "I won't abide no charity."

Ah! Yes, Jonathan had heard of the fierce pride of the mountain folk. He sifted through options, prices. "What would you suggest?"

The man seemed equally as unprepared as Jonathan. "I could build you a nice room onto your house. A bedroom, maybe, with some windows lookin' out over that view out your back."

"That seems a bit extreme for math lessons."

"You're gonna give me the best of your learnin'. I can give you the best of mine."

Jonathan's smile spread. He'd been using the small separate room in the mission house for a bedroom, cramped as it was, but if he had a separate bedroom, he could convert the small room into a study. A library, perhaps. He was certainly beginning to live high on the hog around here, as Laurel would say. "If you're certain about the price, then let's begin tomorrow."

Elias's massive hand wrapped around Jonathan's. "See you tomorrow."

# Chapter Fourteen

Daddy had been gone three days. Nobody knew where for sure, but his absence left a strange combination of nervousness and relief in the house. Laurel helped set the table for supper, relieved to have a night back home from Mrs. Cappy's store, as much as Maggie was relieved to go. The younger children resumed their usual antics of playing with blocks and toys on the floor, while the older ones worked. Isom kept the fire stocked with wood, but all the while, any noise outside sent Laurel to the door, checking for Daddy's return so his presence wouldn't come unexpectedly.

No one knew what sort of mood would bring him home.

She turned to the oven and pulled out an apple cobbler, her grin peeling wide at a sudden memory. "You ought to have seen Teacher taste his first bite of apple butter. The man fell in love-and-marriage with the stuff. I think it's encouraged his desire to master biscuit baking."

Her mother's smile smoothed away some of the worry lines crinkling her brow. "Did you teach him about cobbler yet?"

Laurel carried a bowl of beans to the table. "Not yet. That's next on our list, once he gets the hang of biscuits and gravy. The poor man gets to talkin' about a book he's readin', or some new idea he has, and then the biscuits burn, or the gravy does. Or both." She squeezed her eyes closed as she chuckled. Three times. He'd burned them three times because of his talking excitement. And he'd suggested that *she* could talk the bark off a tree!

Mama studied Laurel with one of those long looks that paused everything else around them. Quiet. Intense. She finally turned back to mashing the potatoes. "It's good, him comin' here."

"I think he'll make a real difference." Laurel sprinkled a little brown sugar over the top of the cobbler, her smile resurrecting. "He cares about teaching and learning about the children and our ways."

"It's been good for you that he's come too." Her mama's accent came with soft touches on her words, which always added a calm to the conversation. "You've needed somebody to talk to about all these books you read and these dreams in your head."

Laurel took a towel and covered her hands so she could carry the cobbler to the table. "I talk to you and Maggie about those things, Mama."

Mama ground the masher into the potatoes. "That's a truth, and I don't want you to stop talkin' to me about them, but you've needed somebody who dreamed those sky-sized dreams, same as you. He's a quieter sort."

Laurel almost snickered considering her experience with the gabbing man.

"But you can see in his eyes the same kind of dreams and ideas in his head as you got." Mama looked up, gaze soft, and . . . a little sad?

Laurel only knew enough about Mama's past to know she'd married young after a childhood that wasn't as remote as where she lived now. Mama still had heirlooms of pretty things passed down from her granny from the old country. Jonathan's country. Laurel stepped around Suzie, who was banging a bowl and wooden spoon together in the middle of the floor, and stood beside her mama, gazing at her profile. She'd always thought her mama a pretty lady. Regal like. A long, slender neckline and eyes as pale as a summer sky. Had Daddy thought those things about her? Had he told her?

"Did you have dreams, Mama?"

The mashing paused and then resumed. "I reckon most folks do."

Laurel looked around the kitchen with fresh eyes. It was a small room, almost a lean-to on the backside of the house, but her mama had found ways to pretty it up. A flower box outside the window. A careful shelf to showcase the only remaining salad plates her great-granny carried all the way from England. An heirloom bowl in the center of the table, always filled with some sort of roots or berries or the like. Curtains sewn from feed sacks to soften the windows. Cleaner than any other house on the mountain, except maybe the Spencers' cabin, and it always smelled like her. Honeysuckles, from the scented water she created for them to wash in.

A skill brought down through the generations.

She looked back at her mama, unsure what was worse — having no dreams at all or knowing the dreams you did have would never come true.

Laurel leaned close, keeping her voice low. "Do you regret marryin' Daddy?"

Mama tilted her head, not one hint of surprise in those eyes, as if she'd expected the question. "Regret don't do nothin' but steal your joy and cloud your eyes from seein' the blessings. Your daddy has given me as good a life as he knows how. He's given me you young'uns, which is God's best gift to this mama's heart." She looked out the window. "When I was a young girl, I thought about things that were bigger than this mountain. Like you do. But I got married and started a family and those dreams had to change along with my life. Were the new dreams worse or better than the first dreams?" She smiled at Laurel. "No, they were different. They met my life where I was. And I still dream bigger than these mountains, through you — and you readin' those books to me. Through the excitement I see in your eyes or the pictures in Maggie's paintings or the wonder Isom has in the world all around him. A hopeful heart never stops dreamin'. God made dreamin' and imaginin' because without those, how could we even believe in all He's brought and done and made. How could we even have a mind's eye for heaven?"

"Don't you ever wish for a nicer house with pretty things in it?"

Mama's brow shot high, and she deliberately looked at each child in the room. "I got plenty of pretty things in my house."

Laurel breathed out her argument on a sigh. "Oh Mama."

"My hands" — she took Laurel's fingers in hers — "your hands, are only meant to carry today. They ain't big enough for yesterday or tomorrow. Only God's hands are big enough. We can dream and imagine, but grasping hold of tomorrow as if we know what goes on there, well, that can lead to a heap of heartache or a whole lot of pride." She squeezed Laurel's fingers and then touched her cheek, her mama's gaze as sweet as any caress Laurel had ever known. "Dream, girl, but trust God to take better care of your dreams than you ever could."

Laurel rounded up the twins and Isom for supper, making sure they washed up before runnin' at the table like coon dogs on a trail, then Mama took a seat and braided her fingers together for prayer.

"Dear Lord, for this food we're grateful, for Your love we're thankful, and for the folks around this table we are abundantly blessed. Protect the ones who are not with us this night and bring 'em home safe and sound."

A crash sounded from outside, pulling everyone's heads up. Laurel met Mama's eyes and ran to the window. The barn door stood ajar.

"Take the rifle, just in case it's some critter," Mama said, standing and wiping her hands on her apron. "Isom, go with your sister."

"Mama . . ." Laurel's argument died on her tongue at the steely look from her mama.

"Pairs is always better than alone."

Like Laurel had done with Jeb. They'd been the pair to go off in search of Daddy, but this was her first winter without Jeb — the first time she'd have to stand as eldest for the younger children in the aftermath of her daddy's drunkenness. She'd be the one who distracted him from the other children or attempted to turn him away from his madness.

She walked toward the barn, Isom close at her heels, the cool metal of the rifle tight in her grip. Another crash sounded, as if someone was searching for something. Her pulse jumped into a gallop for a whole other reason. Her money! Daddy knew she hid it in the barn.

She took off at a run and pushed the barn door wide, the pungent smell of body odor mixed with liquor meeting her senses before the sound of her father's grumbles.

He stood in the middle of the barn, lantern in hand as he shoved aside first one thing then another. Dirt covered his white shirt and jean overalls. Who knew where he'd slept the past few nights? What company he'd kept.

"Daddy!" Isom called from the doorway. "You come home."

Laurel turned to her brother to silence him, but it was too late. Their daddy looked up, his wild eyes barely showing any recognition as he stared at Isom.

"Why don't you come on inside for supper, Daddy? Mama's made some fried chicken," Laurel coaxed, blocking Isom's body with her free arm. "You know how much you love Mama's chicken."

He focused on Laurel's face, and a flicker of something glinted to life in his eyes. "Where is it?" He swung the lantern around like a sword. "I know you got it here somewhere."

Her attention followed the lantern. She turned to Isom. "Go fetch a pail of water, just in case, Isom. You remember the last time." The boy's pale eyes shot wide, and off he sprinted, out of harm's way, leastways.

"Now Daddy, lookie there. Maude's in her pen waiting for her next milkin' and there's no tellin' where the cat's gone to. Probably mousing." Laurel kept her voice gentle, taking another step closer. "Let's get you washed up for sup —"

"Don't talk back to me, girl." He took two steps toward her, one hand fisted at his side. "You want me to tan your hide a good 'un? Where's the money?"

Laurel drew a step back at his approach, but with his next swing of the lantern, he hit one of the barn posts and the light crashed into pieces. Mercifully, half the fire hit directly into Maude's water basin, but the other half produced a growing flame on the dry barn floor.

The fire pulled his attention away long enough for her to grab her jar from beneath the post and twist open the top. She dug into the cash money and pulled out a few bills before hiding the rest behind her back. "You want some cash money, Daddy? You need some?"

He looked over at her, and she waved the bills in the air. "You can have it. Here." She stepped outside the barn door and threw the papers into the air. "They're all yours."

Daddy pushed past her, nearly knocking her over, and then she rushed into the barn, grabbing the cow's water and tossing it onto the growing flame. Isom rushed in behind her and took the rest of the flames with what he brought from the springhouse.

"He won't be distracted for long, Isom, and then he'll come at us hard." She grabbed her brother's hand and pulled him through the other side of the barn. "Go to the corncrib and stay there, quiet as the dead, all right. I'm going to fetch the little 'uns before Daddy can get to the house. Go on and start a fire in the stove so it'll be warmin' up."

He ran off up the hillside to the corncrib, and Laurel edged around the barn. Thank the good Lord Jeb had built a stove into the corncrib three years ago for nights just like this.

She peeked around the front of the barn. Daddy still scraped around on the ground, searching for whatever she'd thrown. With a deep breath, she took off at a full run toward the house.

"Get back here, girl." His voice chased her. She didn't know whether his feet did or not, but she wouldn't look back. Without breaking stride, she bounded up the porch steps and closed the front door behind her, bolting it to gain some time.

Mama already had the little ones by the back door, a sack of provisions ready for a night in the corncrib. Laurel saw her childhood self reflected in the eyes of the twins. *Oh Lord, please protect their hearts.*

Fists banged into the door.

"Go now," Mama whispered. "I'll keep him here, so y'all will be safe. Go on."

And with that, Laurel handed the sack to Suzie, took a twin in each arm, and they all ran for the corncrib. Again. For another night.

Enoch Spencer's news from the sale on Friday had spread through the mountain like wildfire. Every student showed up for school on Monday morning, even Claude Greer, along with a few curious parents too.

Jonathan started the morning off as usual, with scripture reading, prayer, and a song, but didn't leave the crowd in suspense for long.

"We sold almost all of our items at the market, folks." He gestured toward a crate at the front of the room. "These were the only things that didn't sell, which proves what you all have to offer is something the flatlanders want to buy." He turned toward Enoch and signaled him to the front of the room. "Enoch has created a report of all of our sales and the amount owed to each person who provided items for the market. I've also asked him to share his observations of Wilkesboro, since most of you have never been to town."

Jonathan stepped aside and Enoch took his place. The tall, lean boy, with carefully smoothed blond hair, looked every bit of his part as herald to this new endeavor for his class. Cade Spencer, father of three, stood in the back of the room, arms across his chest, a proud tilt to his chin as he listened to his son. Jonathan hadn't made friends with many of the mountain men yet, but Cade Spencer held the same quiet openness to outsiders as Laurel's mother. Instead of the suspicion-laced looks, he asked thoughtful questions, even if he didn't like the answer.

Enoch wanted to go to college.

And Jonathan held out every hope that Mr. Spencer would eventually see the good of that choice, but Jonathan had already learned the idea of college carried an almost threatening connotation to the mountain folks. They saw higher education as vicious thieves waiting to steal their children away and corrupt them with the world's evils — and though there were bad things to be learned outside these mountains, evil was no respecter of place.

The vision of Sam McAdams swelled in Jonathan's mind. What story of his life led him to such a path? Such an addiction?

No, evil came from within as much as without.

Jonathan's attention focused back on Cade. Like Laurel, there were people in these mountains who weren't afraid. Who saw the changing world and knew they needed to ready for it.

"You mean to say some of the girlfolk is workin' jobs in the factories?"

The question pulled Jonathan's mind back into the schoolroom.

Luanne Jacobs stood from her desk. "Making cash money?"

Enoch nodded. "In factories and businesses. There were shops like you never did see. Ready-made clothes, fancy tools for doing 'bout anything you could set your mind to. Rows and rows of buildings piled high on each other like a giant stack cake."

Jonathan stepped up. "Because the war has taken so many of the young men, the women have had to move into the men's places to keep things running. So they've been hired and trained to do all sorts of jobs, and quite skillfully too. Some work in munitions, some in clothes making. There are even some girls who are working as mechanics."

"And drivers too. We saw a girl taxi driver

going around in one of them automobiles, carting folks from one place to another," Enoch added, his grin growing. "It was a sight to behold."

"Did women run their own dress shops?" Mary Rippey asked from the front.

"I'm certain there were some shops owned by women," Jonathan answered.

"There ain't no way I'd let a gal drive me around in anything, especially one them automobiles," Allen Carter called from his reclined position in the back of the room. " 'Sides, you ain't said nothin' about what sort of cash money we made from sending our things to market. That's what I wanna know about."

Enoch looked down at his paper, his excitement so evident he nearly quaked in his shoes as he rattled off what sold and for how much. The children sat up in their seats, craning to hear. Even Claude Greer and Allen Carter sobered their smirks to take in the fair amount.

"As we all agreed from the start" — Jonathan took a jar from his desk — "ten percent of the proceeds will go as tithe to the mission. Another ten percent will be kept to help with extra school costs, whether in the form of field trips or special items to purchase, or even what's needed to prepare for taking items to market. The rest will be distributed according to who participated and what he or she sold."

Despite Jonathan's best attempt at reining in the students for lessons, the excitement never quieted. During recess, he stayed at his desk to grade papers, with the sounds of the younger children in the room next door keeping him company.

Laurel's familiar voice slipped into his thoughts. He stood and walked to the sound, peeking through a crack in the partition that separated the two rooms during the school week. As Miss Simms worked with a larger and older group of children on one side of the room, Laurel sat in a circle on the floor with a younger group.

What was she saying? A double belly?

"You see here? *B* has a double belly 'cause he's been eating too many beans." She held up a card with a letter *B* on it. "Hear the sound. Belly, beans. What's something else that starts with that sound?"

Hands went up with answers coming as fast. "Bones." "Butter."

"Good job." She pulled out another card. "*C* is a sneaky sound, 'cause it ain't satisfied with stayin' the same. No siree. Depending on its mood, it will change its sound. Sometimes it makes the sound for its shape, like a cave." She traced the letter with her finger and made the hard "k" sound. "But other times, it will take the sound of its thickness, so ssssskinny. But most days, the 'cave' sound is bigger and stronger than the 'ss' sound. So you'd be right to guess the 'cave' sound first when you read."

She was a natural-born teacher, painting the ideas in pictures for the children so they could hold on to the concept. He'd found that technique helpful even when teaching Elias on Saturday. Using real-life examples to create meaning behind the abstract concepts.

It was a shame Elias's children couldn't come to school and learn from Laurel and Miss Simms. His gaze shifted back to Laurel. They didn't have to come to school during school days to learn from Laurel. If he worked up some particularly convincing sweet talk, Laurel might be willing to go to them.

# Chapter Fifteen

"Good afternoon, Miss McAdams." Jonathan entered the store, glancing around the empty space before crossing to the counter. Good, they were alone. That would make things easier.

Laurel glanced up from stacking cans on a lower shelf behind the cabinet, her smile as sweet as ever, but a weariness dimmed those bright eyes. "Afternoon, Teacher."

"How are you . . . and all your family?"

She stood, stretching out her back as she did. "We're makin' do." Her answer told him she wouldn't share more, so he derailed his curiosity for another time. His morning prayers had been full of her, with a solid battle between fury at Sam McAdams and the recollection of Laurel's plea to remember who her father truly was. How many years had her family dealt with this drunkenness? How could she keep such luminescent joy and such love for her father in the face of her circumstances?

"You're looking well . . ." His gaze scanned her from head to toe, brain fumbling for words. "In your blue frock today."

"You had to cast your line a far piece to fish up that compliment, didn't you?" Her smile took a crooked turn, and she rested her palms on her hips, surveying him. "I declare, you look like you're up to a sizable amount of trouble, Teacher."

His face warmed from her teasing, but he'd missed their banter over the weekend, so he wasn't about to let it pass. "Nothing more than fractions and geometry, I assure you."

"Now you had to go and mention fractions, didn't you?" She shook her head and added a few more cans to the stack she'd made on the counter. "I'm sure to have nightmares for days now."

He hesitantly took another step forward. "We have another cooking session tomorrow, don't we?"

She paused and tilted her gaze to his. "Every Tuesday, as I recollect."

He nodded, working up another compliment. "You are an excellent cook."

She leaned back and studied him, searching. "You might as well spit it out, 'cause you're chokin' all over it anyway."

"What?"

Her brow peaked again. "Whatever it is you've come here to say."

He planted his palms on the counter separating them. "All right, here it is. I've learned how to describe the pictures and stories in my head by the way you write things in your papers. You've taught me how to make pone bread and sun tea and grape jam and" — he waved a hand toward the back of the store — "someday, biscuits."

Her smile spread so wide, the warmth of it hit him square in the chest.

"And . . . and I've heard you through the partition in the schoolhouse wall teach everything from history to writing to reading, and you're very good at it."

"You sound an awful lot like you're sellin' something, Mr. Taylor."

He leaned his elbows on the counter, closer to her, and lowered his voice. "What would you think of teaching his children to read?"

She placed her cloth back in a tin of water and wrung it out. "Whose children?"

"Elias's."

Her attention swung to him, so he forged ahead. "I gave him his first math lesson on Saturday and his children tagged along. It was only for an hour. Not long. And the

252

children are already here, and Miss Simms won't teach them. It would be excellent practice for you as an aspiring teacher."

She approached the counter. "You started lessons with Elias? At the school?"

He nodded. "He's a quick learner and highly motivated. I feel his children will be too."

"You get fixed on a notion, don't ya?"

"I think we have that in common." He grinned. "What do you say, Laurel? I'd pay you a nickel a lesson."

She opened her mouth to respond then snapped those pink lips closed.

"It would be more money toward college and excellent practice."

She shook her head. "I can't do that."

He deflated, pinching his eyes closed. "You can't?" But he'd been so sure of her.

"A child shouldn't have to pay to learn to read. It's a gift."

Her words sunk in, and his gaze flipped back to hers. "You . . . you'll teach them?"

She laughed, the sound brightening up the room and inspiring his smile. "As long as I can get away and am not needed at home, I'll be happy to. It's a whirlwind keeping up with all of your ideas."

"I think we inspire each other." He patted the counter and backed away, his steps lighter. After the market on Friday, lessons with Elias on Saturday, and this new development today, his father's criticism sank beneath the unexpected pleasure of success — the good kind of success. Helping others.

"Whoa there, Teacher." Her voice brought him to a stop halfway to the door. "You wouldn't know who dropped this off with my name so nicely written at the top, would you?"

She waved a piece of paper, gaze expectant.

He fought the grin tugging at his lips. "What is it?"

She raised a brow, clearly not fooled by his feigned innocence. With a snap of the paper between her hands, she cleared her throat to read. " 'Calling all writers. Do you have a story to tell? The *People's Daily* wants to hear from you. Send us your best fiction piece for a chance to win a fifty-dollar grand prize and publication in our circulation.' "

He shoved his hands into his pockets and continued his back-stepping escape toward the door. "Sounds like someone really knows talent when he sees it."

She crossed her arms over her chest and

narrowed her eyes. "You're persistent, aren't ya?"

He pushed open the door and tipped his hat toward her. "Only helping out a friend."

*Friend.* The word had somehow taken on a new sheen since Jonathan spoke it to her last week. The notion, paired with his playful grin, spiraled a thrill through her like hiding away with a favorite book.

She grinned. He gave her such a nice distraction from going home to the uncertainty about whether she'd sleep in the corncrib with her siblings again, or inside the house. Daddy had pulled a knife on Isom three nights earlier, and Laurel was grateful beyond words that Maggie hadn't been there to witness it. The fewer memories of that side of their father, the better.

She felt for the paper in her apron pocket — another writing opportunity he'd uncovered in a local newspaper on his most recent excursion to Wilkesboro. After their shared tutoring lessons for the Harrises on Saturday, Jonathan had given her the latest account of his students' involvement in the after-school classes and selling at market. After the first week, participation had doubled.

And so had the gossip throughout the

mountain. Good and bad. Mrs. Cappy's store gave her ample opportunity to hear the latest.

"That's what happens when outsiders come in." She heard the semi-whispered voices outside the store kitchen window as she emptied scraps from Mrs. Cappy's latest medicinal concoction. "They bring in ideas that ain't fittin' for nobody."

"Ezra came home tellin' about how they cut open a frog to talk about its innards."

"What on earth reason would anyone have to tear open an animal like that?" came the other voice.

Laurel growled. What did they think cooking chicken was?

"I heard tell he was teaching that God didn't make nothin'. That everything came to be by surprise."

Laurel squeezed her eyes closed and slid down the wall next to the window. The two previous teachers had discussed the various scientific theories being shared in most schools too, but they taught them as *theories,* just as she knew Jonathan was doing. She needed to have a sit-down with Jonathan and prepare him for the attack. Maybe they could come up with a way to diffuse the frustrations of some of the parents by calling a parent meeting.

"My Isaac ain't gonna abide by none of that teachin'. No siree." Another woman joined in. "He's done talked to some of the other menfolk, and they don't like it a'tall. Ozaiah Greer took his young'uns out 'cause he called it a devil school, and I've a mind to think he's right."

"I saw some of them books he brought into school. Monty says they got pictures of naked statues in 'em and drawings too. Ain't no tellin' what else he has in them books he brought over from wherever he's from."

Laurel lowered her face into her hands. Art books! That's all they were.

"Colt read one of them sin-filled novels with the most lustful words I ever heard in all my livin' days. I'm ashamed to even think about 'em right now. Vampires and child killin's and . . ." her voice trailed off into a shudder.

"Rebecca's been askin' about college. She's got an itch for the city too. I reckon it's them books that's got her thinkin' dark thoughts." That from Imogene Carter, if Laurel knew her voices aright, and the Carter family, along with the Greers, had done nothing to hide their distrust of Jonathan from the very beginning. In fact, Ozaiah Greer had kept up the rumbles of discontent ever since Jonathan's first confrontation, and the grumbling had only gotten louder with each passing week. "And he's even started bringing coloreds into the school."

Laurel's head came up.

"You don't mean it."

"Saw them leaving the school on Saturday with my own two eyes."

Laurel jumped to her feet, hitting her head on the cabinet above.

"Next they'll be sittin' next to our young'uns in school. Drinkin' from the same water well, and there's no tellin' what sort of diseases they'll bring to us."

Still a little dizzy from her collision, she poked her head out the window and offered her most dazzling smile. Maybe. Either that or it was a snarl poorly hidden by a smile. "I happen to know for a fact that Mr. Taylor made up some remedy that soothed Lolly Morgan's baby's cough." She turned her gaze to the wide-eyed Imogene Carter. "And he set your very own Amos's broken arm 'cause the doctor was over on Patton Ridge and couldn't be found."

Mrs. Carter had the decency to at least avoid eye contact.

"*And* if you don't want folks thinking we mountain folks are even more addled than they already do, I'd advise you not to go spouting off about your theories on colored folks. There ain't one piece of evidence that proves a person's color — eye, skin, hair, or tongue — will make a hill-of-beans difference on whether they carry diseases or not." She eyed each woman, daring them to contradict her. "Compassion and kindness only sees people, and that's what we've been called to see. God looks at the heart." She pulled from something she thought Preacher might have said, maybe. At some point. "Wonder what color those would be for each one of us."

She slammed the window closed and breathed out shivered air, before sliding right back down the wall into a puddle on the floor. Dear Lord, she couldn't even hold her tongue, let alone the worries for yesterday, today, or tomorrow, and that was the truth. She pinched her eyes closed. *Don't let me have caused a bigger problem for Jonathan than the storm already brewing around him.*

Laurel had warned Jonathan and Preacher about the conversation she overheard at the store, and she held out hope her words of fiery wisdom had caused some miraculous breach in the hardheaded minority. To her surprise, Sunday service went on without a hitch, though the Carter family was noticeably absent, as well as a few others of Ozaiah Greer's posse. An unsettled feeling added a chill to the late-autumn day, though. Like the hint of a coming storm. Laurel walked Maggie and Isom up the mountainside, since Mama had stayed home to ensure Daddy was all right, then she gathered her things and trekked back to Mrs. Cappy's for the night.

Smoke rose from the fireplace at the mission house, the new addition on the back beginning to take shape. My oh my, Laurel wondered what the inside of that house looked like with all the pretty things Jonathan had ordered from town. And where had he hung Maggie's paintings? What did a man's house look like on the inside anyhow? Was it different from one with a woman's touch, as Mrs. Cappy called it?

Two figures sat on the front steps of the cabin as Laurel approached. In the fading sunset gold, she made out Jonathan's lean, relaxed frame and Preacher with his pipe at full smoke. "Hello there, Laurel. Nice evenin' for a walk." Preacher's clear voice called her forward. She redirected her steps, following not only his greeting but her curiosity to the cabin steps.

Jonathan stood at her approach, a dainty teacup and saucer in his hand. She stared at it for a full three seconds, trying to sort out why a man would have such a fancy cup. The coffee she was used to serving would ruin something that pretty.

"Good evening, Laurel." His soft welcome lit her spirit like the summer glow of a lightning bug. In fact, she liked hearing his voice so much, she wanted to hear it more and more, almost waiting for him to stop by the store. She'd even started reading her books quicker so she could return to the school for another. It didn't make sense to feel so close to someone she'd only known for a little over a month, did it?

And she'd never had a male friend before. In fact, her best friends in life were family members, so maybe the sweet glow of comradery came as a sign of new friendship. If that was the case, she was going to invest in making a whole lot more new friends.

"Good evenin', Preacher." She looked to Jonathan, her gaze catching in his. "Teacher."

"Seems all of the grumblers weren't interested in attending church today."

She pulled her attention away from Jonathan and chuckled. "I reckon if you stirred up enough wind to yell those sinners off the brink of hell, like the old-timers did, you might find a whole different set of listeners."

He grinned and blew out a stream of smoke, the sweet scent drawing her in a little closer. "Talk of grace and love doesn't sit too well with the hard-hearted, does it now?"

"About as well as sense and reason sits with the hardheaded."

"Well said," came Jonathan's response, and he gestured toward the step. "Care to sit? Would you like some tea?"

She walked to the place he gestured to and took a seat. "Sun tea?"

His grin rewarded her, and the lightning bugs went off in her head again. "Not exactly. It's tea from home."

From England? "I'd like that. Thank you kindly."

His smile spread, and he slipped up the steps between Laurel and his uncle to move inside the cabin. The song of crickets and chirps of toads filled the evening quiet with their duet, a melody as much a part of the mountains as the ballads from long ago.

"If they could see how much he cares, how much he wants to help, all those naysayers would be ashamed of themselves," Laurel whispered, staring off into the fading sunset.

"They're not interested in seeing."

She leaned back against the step post and looked over at the preacher. "Then how do we get them to see? Make them see?"

He blew out another stream of smoke. "You know your father's drunks, Laurel?"

She didn't need to answer.

"Your mother's tried to reason with him, like many other wives have attempted to do with their husbands all over the mountain ranges here. The arguments are solid. Reasonable. If you love your family, you'll keep the mountain brew out of your home."

Laurel hugged herself against the truth in his words. "He can't."

"No, not on his own. We can't reach into his hard heart, no matter how much we wish to. We haven't the power."

Laurel rubbed her palms against her arms. "No, we don't."

"So what do we do then? Are we hopeless? Despairing?"

She slid him a look, knowing the preacher's mind-set after hearing him preach for almost eight years. "You wouldn't be a very good preacher if you believed that."

His growing smile reminded her of his nephew. "When we are powerless to exact change, we must trust in the One who holds the power. The ultimate power. And the One we know isn't a tyrant king but a loving Father. Even His disciples, who sat beneath His teaching for years, were confused and wounded by the idea that their Savior, their Rescuer, was going to die. The very man who'd raised the dead, would die? Not reign? It made no sense to them because they didn't see the bigger plan beyond the pain. And He said to them, 'What I do thou knowest not now; but thou shalt know hereafter.' Somehow, He's using every situation not only for our good, but to turn our eyes, our hearts to Him."

The truth pressed in on her mind, too big to grasp. Too hard to understand. How could her daddy's terrifying drunks turn her family's eyes to God? All she recalled was the look of fear on her little brother's face and the grief in her mother's eyes. Why couldn't God just make it plain?

"Here we go." Jonathan emerged from the house, another teacup and saucer in hand, bending to offer Laurel the tea.

Gently, she took the offering, her fingers brushing over Jonathan's in the process. He pulled back and tipped his chin toward the tea. "I added milk and honey since you're fond of sweets."

She blinked from his gaze and looked

down at the fragile and beautiful cup in her hands. "You put milk in your tea?"

Preacher chuckled. "Jonathan's had to get used to an entire world different from his own. Surely you can try his English tea."

"Of course I can." She smiled up at Jonathan. "I like the idea of trying new things. Grows the imagination. Don't it, Teacher?"

"Without a doubt."

She took a sip, and the thick, warm liquid flowed over her tongue, strong yet fragile — like nothing she'd ever tasted before. Her eyes fluttered closed to savor the new and familiar flavors combined.

"I think she approves." Preacher's exclamation invaded her experience.

She opened her eyes and nodded. "It's real good." She looked up at Jonathan. "A whole lot better than Mrs. Cappy's coffee and real different than the one time Mama and I had English tea. We didn't know to sweeten it with milk and honey."

Jonathan crouched down, closer to her eye level. "Then I'll have to invite you to tea again. Books and tea are a perfect combination."

"That does sound perfect. Especially on a day when there's snow or rain falling outside the windows." She took another long sip of the creamy liquid.

"And a warm fire crackling alive," he added.

"With a molasses cookie or two," she whispered.

Their gazes locked over the rim of her cup, his softening, golden in the last rays of sunset. He had such nice ideas for the perfect evening. Laurel shook the sudden fogginess from her head and turned, taking a few more sips of tea before standing. "I better get over to Mrs. Cappy before she starts to fret." She handed the cup and saucer back to Jonathan. "Thank you for the tea."

"My pleasure." He took the cup. "Something I actually knew how to make without you teaching me."

She backed down the porch steps and sent a grin to Preacher. "And thank you for the talk, as always, Preacher."

He raised his empty pipe to her in salute.

Laurel pushed her satchel up on her shoulder and headed through the thin row of trees toward Mrs. Cappy's store. On the other side of the trees, a large field separated the mission house from the store, and up to her right, on the hill, stood the church-school luminescent in the moon's swelling glow.

Her steps faltered to a stop. Light flickered

in one of the back windows of the school.

The upper-school section.

Who would be at the school so late on a Sunday evening? She'd left the two most likely culprits behind her at the mission house.

Three shadows ran out the side door of the church and disappeared into the blackness of the forest. Laurel's breath seized in her throat. Her face went cold. She rushed up the hillside, the ebb and flow of the golden light through the windows becoming painfully clear.

Fire.

## Chapter Sixteen

Jonathan's attention followed Laurel as she walked away from his cabin, the skin on his fingers still alive from her touch. He stared, the unidentified feeling fading to clear. He *cared* about her. But, of course he cared about her. She was a kind friend, but another awareness rose up against his mental justification. No, his affections warmed with more than friendship.

But it couldn't be. He still had at least two years of university left, and Maple Springs was an opportunity, not a lifestyle. His pulse beat into his rib cage. His breaths as halted and jagged as his thoughts. But she was like no other woman he'd ever known, a kindred soul. She spoke to him without words, and he understood.

He blinked out of his stare and settled down on the step next to his uncle, placing the cup and saucer on the porch.

"Evangeline was very much like her." His

uncle's voice smoothed into the evening, into Jonathan's bewilderment. "A heart as fierce as her strength."

His uncle's profile turned pensive, sad even. He rarely spoke of his wife, the woman who'd entered Maple Springs with him eight years ago and became the spine of his mission, his love for these people.

"I would give everything I own to" — he grinned down at the cup between them — "share a spot of tea with her. See her smile." His gaze met Jonathan's. "Real love, like hers, was worth every sacrifice. I only wish . . . I wish I had more time."

His uncle couldn't have known Jonathan's thoughts about Laurel, and yet, he seemed to speak to them. No, he was only reminiscing because of Laurel and Evangeline's similarities, surely. Jonathan pulled his attention back to Laurel, her pale silhouette highlighted by the moonlight and cutting a fascinating figure in the middle of the empty field through the tree line. His chest squeezed with a deep longing, new and intense. What was he to do with it?

Suddenly, Laurel started at a run up the hillside, away from Mrs. Cappy's store and toward the school. Jonathan stood. Her voice rang out. One word. What had she said?

He rushed forward. The word came again. "Fire!"

He turned back to his uncle. "There's a fire." Jonathan didn't wait for a response but set off in a run, his pulse hammering in his ears. He made it to the clearing in time to see Laurel round the corner of the school. Flames flickered through the middle window of his section of the school. *No!*

He crested the hill, and Laurel nearly collided with him as she exited the building, two pails in her hands, her face already smudged with gray.

"We need water." She shoved a pail into his chest and rushed past him toward the water pump at the side of the school. He followed.

"They've piled them all," she said, setting the pail down and pushing the pump as hard as she could. "All the books are in the middle of the floor."

Jonathan placed his hands next to hers on the handle, adding pressure. "What?"

Her gaze met his, desperate, sad. "And the maps."

He stared, unable to comprehend, but she wasted no time. Grabbing the full bucket, she raced back into the school. He followed with his own, and the scene inside ripped through him in agonizing reality.

The desks had been pushed back against the wall, and a circle of dirt formed in the center of the room. Every book, map, and piece of paper piled in the center, lit with wild flames.

A very deliberate message, directed at Jonathan.

*"We don't want you or your world in ours."*

Laurel's water crashed over the burning debris, then she ran past him to the door for another. A copy of *Great Expectations* lay at the edge of the flames, as if to taunt him. He rescued it from the rest and placed it on his desk. He caught sight of another book, his grandmother's copy of *Sense and Sensibility,* and he jerked it from the flames, heat scalding his hand. Laurel reentered with another pail of water, setting him back into motion. On their third run for water, his uncle came into the room with a large, heavy blanket dripping wet. Laurel rushed to him and took two edges of the blanket, carrying the dripping cloth to cover the last flames, leaving them in darkness. The white glow of moonlight shone into the windows, giving the scene a much nicer powdering of light than dawn would reveal.

The three of them stood staring at the blackened debris in the center of the room, their heavy breaths the only sound in the darkness. Laurel stepped to the shelf where he kept the oil lantern, and after a few moments, the soft glow of the light filled the room, highlighting the devastation.

The barren walls and bookshelves. The empty desks. And the black, charred remains of Jonathan's intentions.

A new fire shot up through his chest. He fisted his hands at his sides, ignoring the sting on his skin.

"How . . . how could they do this?" His own voice sounded unrecognizable in his ears. Low. Deep. Menacing. It fueled the fury even more. "Many of these books were my own collection. Maps and supplies I purchased with *my* money to make a difference to *these* people, and this is what they do? Here is how they show gratitude?"

He shoved a desk back and stomped around the pitiful conglomeration of charred papers and curled bindings.

"Jonathan, it's the minority who've taken this path." His uncle's words only stoked the flame in Jonathan's chest. "Don't lump them all together."

"Nothing's going to happen because of this, is it?" He waved a hand toward the ashes. "The clan leaders, Ozaiah Greer and his miscreants, will have their good laugh at my failure, and we'll all be expected to go on as if nothing happened. As if they hadn't destroyed years of book collecting and planning. And then I'll still be expected to teach? To give my energies to this? As if I have the power to make bricks with no straw." He kicked the ashes and growled, turning his full fury on his uncle. "How have you worked with these people for all these years? Stubborn, superstitious, bound to their own way of life, their own traditions, and no one is allowed in or they're cut down."

"You're speaking from anger now." The gentleness in his uncle's voice only spiked his agitation.

"Of course I'm angry. Look what they did! I came here to do good. To make a difference. To bring help."

Laurel stepped forward and set the lantern down on a desk near him, her ash-smudged face pale, round eyes glossy. Her look peered into him, hurt, angry, asking him questions he wouldn't answer. With a deep breath, she turned and fled from the building into the night.

A gaping emptiness gouged through his middle. He stumbled back until he collapsed against his desk, weary, wounded.

"You may have come here, in part, to make a difference, but you were also running away, trying to prove yourself. Don't lay your wounded pride on these people's heads too. Be angry about the burning of your books, but also see it for what it is, a clear sign of the changes you *are* making here, that you will make."

Jonathan shot his uncle a withering look. "My plans are in ashes, quite literally, Uncle. It's another glowing example of my good intentions falling short as usual."

His uncle surged forward, eyes glinting in the lantern light. "Are they? Were your intentions only made of paper after all? You came to me as a young man running away from disappointment and the failures of living with a man whose lofty expectations you'd never meet. You're not a failure, but you must answer the question, Jonathan. Why are you really here?"

The words pierced through his fury. He winced and turned away, but his uncle continued, unrelenting.

"Did you come for them, those young people who need a vision of hope? Because if you came for them, then what happened tonight shouldn't change your plans, but if you came for you. . . ."

Jonathan looked up, his breaths shallow, his eyes stinging. "I . . . I don't know if I'm strong enough."

The lines on his uncle's face softened. "You're not, on your own, but the God within you is well equipped for the fight." Laurel emerged in the doorway, satchel in hand, and his uncle tilted his head. "And He's brought other fighters to stand beside you." He cupped Jonathan's shoulders, drawing his attention back to his face. "You were judged by what you did before tonight. You'll be defined by what you do hereafter."

The scene hadn't changed since she'd run from the church-school to Mrs. Cappy's. If anything, the damp, scorched pages and blackened floor looked even worse. Laurel pressed her palm to her stomach, pushing down the rising nausea.

Jonathan's words echoed in her head. Many of the things he said were true — painfully true. Superstitious, stubborn. But not all. She stepped forward into the lantern light, the two men turning to look at her. Preacher bore the least brunt from the fire, wet clothes and a few ash stains, but Teacher's white shirt wore the gray battle scars most. His face smeared with soot, his hair erratic, and, worst of all, those eyes, hard and distant from her.

Tears blurred her vision, stinging. "I'm so sorry, Jonathan." His name slipped from her lips, almost like an unintentional attempt to close the distance she read in his eyes. *Jonathan.* Her friend. "I'm sorry they took your wonderful books," she whispered and crossed the room to him, reaching into her satchel and tugging out the most recent book he'd loaned her. A hardbound and beautifully illustrated copy of *Pilgrim's Progress.* "But they didn't get this one."

He sucked in an audible breath and reached for the cool, sturdy binding. It slipped from her hold. He stared down at the book, blinking and shaking his head. Her heart broke and the burning tears escaped her eyes. With a quick push of her hand to wipe them away, she reached back into her satchel, fingers wrapping around the jar of money she'd kept there since the barn incident. Daddy had gotten ten dollars from the savings, but there was still plenty more. Enough, she hoped.

College would have to wait another year. She pinched her lips together against the searing disappointment and shoved the jar into his free hand. "I don't know how much it would cost for you to replace everything that was lost, but this can help."

He looked down at the jar in his hands as if it were some sort of confusing puzzle, then his gaze came up to hers. Those eyes, so familiar to her she could see them in her sleep, stared back, searching, seeking, uncertain. "This . . . this is . . ." His whisper rasped. His vision seemed to clear. His eyes widened, softened, but his gaze wouldn't release hers. "I'm not going to take your money, Laurel."

She pushed the proffered jar back to him. "My people did this because they're stuck and scared and they think they're protecting their way of life. They can't see that they're hurting more than they're helpin'."

He dropped his head, shaking it, and pressed his lips into a firm line.

"Listen to me." She took his face in her hands, forcing his attention to her, her words. "I believe in you. What you're doing. What you're gonna do. Who you are." The intimacy in her touch shot a tremble through her, so she released her hold, stepping back, fighting for breath. She shrugged and offered a smile through her uncertainty. "And if you use my money, I'll be here for at least another six months to try and earn it back, so I'll get to witness more of what you do to change people's lives for the better. To help them see beyond just today. To give them something to believe in for the future."

His watery gaze searched hers, shifting

through more emotions than there were sounds in the English alphabet. For a moment, his palm came up as if to touch her cheek but then dropped back to the jar in his hands. The tiniest grin pulled at his lips. "It will probably take me that long to master making biscuits and gravy."

She released her breath on a sob and, without thinking, wrapped her arms around him, allowing her tears freedom to flow against his neck. After a moment's hesitation, his hands came around her, and she felt the most beautiful sense of rightness. She'd never been the sort to fall victim to her emotions, and certainly not the kind of girl to go weeping on a man's shoulder, but here she was, holding on to him and mighty grateful to have the chance.

She pushed herself back. "I'm sorry 'bout that." She wiped at her eyes and offered a helpless shrug to the preacher. "I'm not one to fall on a man in an emotional heap. I'm just so . . ."

"Thankful?" Preacher offered, the word strangely surprising in the middle of the circumstances but fitting for the tangled-up feelings in her heart.

How could she feel thankfulness? She'd given away her college money, and Jonathan's books were in ashes on the school floor. Yet, he was staying, and everything else could be replaced.

Laurel grinned from the preacher back to Jonathan, his eyes much clearer and brighter than before. She nodded. "Yeah. I'm thankful."

# Chapter Seventeen

It took three days for Jonathan to get the schoolroom fit for classes, but with Elias replacing the burned floorboards, by Thursday Jonathan was able to offer the upper-grades students a real day of classes.

He'd met with a few of the boys in the woodworking class on Wednesday in his house, refusing to go too long without securing in their minds that he planned to stay, and with each admittance of the fact, his own confidence strengthened.

Ringing the bell for school on Thursday morning, the sound echoing across the mountainside, sealed his choice and somehow battled back all the ache of loss he'd struggled with over the past few days. He'd made his choice. He wasn't teaching these students as a reaction to his father anymore. He was doing it for himself, and for the greater reward of touching the people who needed him.

And the students responded to his choice. Two or three brought threadbare books from home to donate to the empty bookshelves. One student made curtains to replace the smoke-stained ones. Maggie had spent two days recreating one of his maps using six sheets of paper and then pasting them all together.

"I think your version is much better than the store-bought copy I had," Jonathan told her, as he, Enoch, and Bent hung the paper on the wall where the old map used to go.

Maggie blushed but grinned up with pride in her work. "I've started workin' on a copy of one of your other maps too."

"You remember what they looked like?" Bent asked. "I can't hold how all those places looked in my head. There had to have been a hundred or more."

"She remembers anything she sees." Enoch nodded toward her. "Always has been that way. Top-notch brain," he added, echoing Jonathan's words. "Right, Teacher?"

Jonathan didn't miss the look of admiration Enoch sent in Maggie's direction, and from the deepening color of her cheeks, Maggie didn't either. But he also realized how much his words mattered to the children. The positive influence. The need for affirmation. "I have an entire classroom filled with top-notch brains."

"But we ain't all good at math or reading or science," Edna-Jean pointed out, the fire in her challenge as bright as the red in her hair. "So we all can't have top-notch brains."

Jonathan scanned the class. "But smarts, as we've seen in our after-school classes as well as our in-school ones, come in all types. I have very good book smarts, but my building smarts?"

Enoch snickered. "Fair to middlin'."

"Exactly." Jonathan grinned. "I think a C at best."

Several of the kids laughed, deepening Jonathan's sense of belonging. "But Mary Rippey and Luanne Jacobs" — he stepped nearer the girls, happy to see that Luanne had shown up for school despite the fact her father was most likely one of the instigators of the fire — "they have top-notch brains for dressmaking. A-plus, no less, and *my* dressmaking skills?"

"Menfolks don't make dresses, Teacher," one of the boys shouted from the back.

"Not true, actually. Some of the richest and most renowned fashion designers of the day are men."

"Bet those dressmaking menfolk don't know how to swing an ax." Luke Hart chuckled.

Jonathan walked to him. "Which is one of your top-notch smarts, isn't it, Luke?"

The boy grinned and nodded. "Ain't a faster wood splitter in all the mountain."

After a little longer, the lesson shifted into another modification to his plans. He'd use *Pilgrim's Progress* as a book to teach history, literature, and Bible concurrently, while reading it aloud. The plan worked very well, and Jonathan decided that if this synchronous teaching using one book continued to work next week, he'd incorporate it into his lesson plans for the remainder of the year.

With a long weekend for the corn shucking coming up, he'd have time to take a few days to ride into Wilkesboro, maybe even Asheville, to purchase new supplies for the school. If he felt the loss of those empty shelves, he knew the children did too.

After school, he marched over to the store to see if any mail had arrived and — to be perfectly honest — to look in on Laurel. Since the night of the fire, he couldn't shake her from his mind. She filled up his thoughts with her smile and her faith in him. Even with the smoke-smeared face, tangled hair, and stained dress, beauty radiated off her, from her.

He paused at the door of the store, redirecting his mind. He couldn't encourage this interest in her. No. She longed for college. He had to return home to England. It was an impossible option, for now . . . if ever.

But . . . he swallowed down the disappointment grating against his soul, as if peeling away a layer of his heart that belonged. He'd encourage her, buoy her dreams. She'd already delayed her future to make up for the work of angry men; he wouldn't delay her aspirations any longer. Her dreams included college and teaching, not him.

Maggie greeted him with a smile from behind the counter. "I was just gettin' ready to send Enoch over to the school with your package, and here you are."

Jonathan nodded to Enoch, who straightened from his position leaning against the counter. A book lay open between him and Maggie.

"What's this?"

Maggie's cheeks pinkened. "I was just showin' Enoch this book Laurel bought for me. Came in the mail today with my name on it and everything. She told me she ordered me a surprise 'bout three weeks ago, but I never imagined this." She pushed the book closer to him. "It must have cost her a heap of cash money. Some of the pictures are in color."

Jonathan peered down at the hardbound book, open, interestingly enough, to a scene of London. A Monet, giving off the hazy view of parliament as the backdrop to the Thames. *Home.* Though the word didn't quite attach itself to the place as readily as he'd expected. "That's where I grew up."

Both faces turned to him. "With all them roads and tall buildings?" Enoch asked.

He nodded. "Fog and smoke and traffic and a whole host of noises all through the night. And lots of rain."

Maggie crinkled up her nose. "That don't sound as pretty as the picture."

"It also has museums and restaurants and culture and concerts. For many people, it's the perfect place to call home."

Enoch pushed back from the counter and whistled low. "I don't mind the idea of a small town, but I'm not too keen on a city, for sure."

"Do you miss it?"

He paused at Maggie's question. "There are things I miss about it, namely indoor plumbing, and concert halls filled with some of the most exquisite music." He touched the paper. "And I miss my family of course. But I don't necessarily miss the place." He tapped the page and looked up. "This is a very kind gift, Maggie."

So much like the giver.

She pulled the book into her chest and squeezed it close. "There ain't nobody in the whole world with as big a heart as Laurel, 'cept maybe Mama."

Enoch grinned over at Maggie in her delight, his eyes sparkling with a budding interest. Sweet. And much more believable than an upper-middle class Brit and a Blue Ridge mountain girl on her way to college. "You said I had a package?"

"That's right." She turned to retrieve a rectangular box. "From Wilkesboro. Dr. Randolph Donovan?"

Jonathan took the box. "It's . . . it's Isom's glasses." He peeled open the box to reveal a carefully packaged set of wire-rimmed spectacles.

"Ain't that a sight!" Maggie gasped.

Jonathan wrapped the glasses back into the packaging. "Would it be fine to take them up today?" He searched her face for any hidden message about her father's state.

She thought a moment. "All's been peaceable the past few days, and Isom will be plumb over the moon for sure, Teacher." She nodded to add emphasis. "I'd just advise you not to stay long and make sure you got on your fastest runnin' shoes in case winds change."

And everything had been so peaceable.

All it took was one word. One action, and her father's mood turned from quiet oblivion to raving madman.

Isom had been too slow getting Daddy's dram to him. Only a few seconds too slow.

Laurel turned from the cookstove in time to see Daddy barrel into the room, eyes blazing with wildness and rage. Uncontrolled. With no time to prepare, he picked Isom up by the shirt and gave him a sound shake.

"I said bring me a dram, boy."

Isom hung like a rag doll in midair for a second, before he started pulling at Daddy's fingers to let go. "Mama had to go to the cellar to bring some more upstairs."

And she was still searching, Laurel thought, leaning down to whisper for Suzie to grab James and walk with him to the corncrib. "I'll bring along some molasses cookies." The little girl must have felt the urgency, and like a child years older, she not only took James by the hand but John too and led them out the back.

"Daddy, we'll get you a drink as soon as Mama's back," Laurel said, sliding over to the table to grab a handful of cookies and place them in her apron pocket.

His dark eyes met hers, unseeing. "I said now." He gave Isom another shake, this time inciting a pained whimper from her brother.

Her hand settled on a thick wooden bowl filled with flour. "Why don't you put Isom down for a second so he can get that drink for you?" She kept her voice calm and wrapped her fingers around the edge of the bowl, stepping closer to her daddy as Isom wiggled to get free.

"Be still, boy, or I'll make you still." His fist tightened against Isom's shirt, stirring another pained yelp.

A movement at the front door caught her eye. Jonathan? She blinked. The vision didn't change. There he stood, box in hand, wide eyes staring at the scene in front of him. Her throat clamped closed. If her daddy saw him . . .

Laurel calculated her next movements, and with a flip of her wrist, the contents of the bowl flew into her daddy's face. He shouted a round of obscenities but dropped his hold on Isom.

"Run," she screamed, heading for the door.

Jonathan hadn't moved, frozen in place, face as pale as magnolias. Without a hitch in her stride, she grabbed Jonathan's arm and pulled him behind her. Through the doorway in the kitchen, her daddy had wiped away the flour and started toward them, rage contorting his features into something out of *Dracula*. His booming voice rattled the house with some slurred demand that no one could really meet, or half the time understand. She looked down at Jonathan's leg, and with one fluid motion, she turned the rocking chair on the porch over in front of the door to slow her daddy down. Without another pause, she grabbed Jonathan's hand and half pulled, half stumbled through the dusk toward the corncrib.

A yell boomed from the porch, followed by a crash. More expletives. More threats. And though the voice grew distant, Laurel didn't look back, just kept tugging Jonathan along until they made it to the corncrib.

"What are you doing here? At nightfall of all times." She ducked to enter the small building.

"He . . . he is dangerous." He stood outside the crib, staring back at the house.

"Of course he's dangerous, which is all the more reason for you to stay away."

She breathed out a sigh and collapsed onto the quilt-laden floor of the corncrib, mentally counting the heads of those inside. Good, everyone. Serious but safe and sound. She reached into her pocket and distributed cookies.

"You did real fine, Suzie." She kissed the golden head and was rewarded with her toothless smile.

Jonathan still stood in the doorway of the corncrib, first staring at her, then Isom, and then looking back toward the house. The dark silhouette of the cabin's roofline rose over the hillside, but the uneven terrain and a cluster of trees shrouded their sheltered hideaway from view. It was their older corncrib, smaller and unused, except for times like this.

She ran a hand over her eyes and leaned her head back against the hand-hewn walls. Her insides quivered, her fingers shook. What was wrong with her? She'd been through enough of her daddy's escapades to expect his volatile behavior, so what made the difference? Her gaze traveled back to the doorway. Jonathan.

Isom knew about life with their daddy, but not Jonathan. He stood there, frozen from the shock of seeing Daddy behave in such a contrary way to the man he'd first met. Confused. Bewildered.

Down deep, she knew her daddy wouldn't

intentionally hurt any of the children, but she wasn't sure how the same sliver of sanity might carry over to an outsider. Especially when his drunk senses told him Jonathan was cut from the same cloth as the man who "stole" Kizzie from their family.

"Did you at least bring your rifle, if you're going to traipse about the woods at night?"

"What?" His hands clutched nothing else but a small box, and unless they had a new kind of rifle in England that fit inside a jacket, then that answered her gun question.

"Well, that settles it. If you ain't got your rifle, you're going to have to cozy up with us in the corncrib tonight, 'cause there's no way I'm leaving the young'uns to walk you back down to the mission house."

His gaze fastened on her, focusing. "You're going to sleep here?"

"That's exactly right, and so are you, so you might as well have a seat." She gestured toward the quilt at her side.

He shuffled forward, dazed, stumbling a little before he settled beside her. "Maggie said he was better."

"And there's a good chance he'll be better in the next second or two, but there's no tellin' when he'll go off again. That's why you can't just show up here until after winter is over." She shook her head and groaned. "And for heaven's sake, if you're going to come up the mountainside of a evenin', bring your rifle. I don't want to remind you of your first night in the mountains and the cougar that was just waiting to take a taste of the new teacher."

He shuddered, his shoulder bumping against hers in the close quarters. "This world is much different from mine. I forget, sometimes, the real dangers."

Laurel's pulse finally started to slow. She placed her elbows on her knees and leaned her chin in her hand, staring over at the addlepated man. "There better be something like a gold brick or a healing remedy for drunkenness, if you came all the way up the mountain with it tonight."

He looked down at the box in his hands. "The glasses." He sat up straight. "These are Isom's new glasses."

His eyes lit with boyish excitement. Crazy man. He'd gotten so excited about delivering Isom's glasses, he'd nearly gotten himself killed. That was about as sweet as it came.

She nudged his shoulder with her own. "Next time, carry your rifle in one hand and the glasses in the other. You don't have enough meat on your bones to satisfy a hungry cougar anyhow, and I'd hate for our school to be out of a good teacher."

It was an awkward sort of fitting, maneuvering around the cramped area to adjust how those spectacles sat on Isom's nose, but the reward was worth the effort . . . and the terror. Not only Isom's response — his amazement at looking at his sister Maggie's art and differentiating the slopes and colors with more clarity — but observing firsthand the closeness of Laurel's family.

Isom told some tall tale about a rabbit so big it chased after Butter and nearly "licked" him in a fight. Suzie sang her alphabet song three times. And finally, after the cookies were gone and stories told, James crawled onto Laurel's lap and John onto Jonathan's and fell asleep.

"How can you manage this sort of life for your family every night?" He whispered, his palm resting on sleeping John's golden head.

Laurel leaned her head back against the wall and turned to look at him, the lantern light flickering in her eyes. "It's not every night. Only the bad ones."

"There shouldn't be any this bad." He looked around the corncrib and the little bodies huddled together in quilts. Suzie curled up in a quilted ball at Laurel's side, while Isom sat across from them, staring with amazement at the picture book in his hands, his glasses sitting a little crooked on his small nose. "How could he do this to his children? And your mother? Is she safe?"

"He'd never hurt Mama."

"How do you know?"

"He's drunk, but ain't *that* drunk. She's the best thing in his life. If he ever hurt her, she'd leave without lookin' back, and he'd die of a broken heart."

None of it made sense. Laurel spoke of her father with such warm regard, such kindness, and yet here the children were, sleeping in the corncrib on a late October evening because their home wasn't safe. His father stoked and brewed unkindness, but he'd never resort to something like this, yet Laurel and all the children were close to their father. How could that be? He could barely stand to stay in the same room with his father.

The thought paused him. Perhaps there were some similarities in the situations.

"Aren't you angry with him, that your father would do this?"

Laurel rubbed her hand in a gentle rhythm over James's sleeping head, hesitating. "I've not known any different, so it became the expectation, not the surprise. I pray God would take the love of drink away from him, save him. Every day, I pray, but until then, what's the good of wasting all that energy on anger? It don't hurt him any, does it?"

The idea jolted Jonathan to attention.

"I reckon that's why the Bible's always talkin' about love, because it's the only thing to bring change — and we have to be reminded of the power of it all the time. The sacrifice."

"What do you mean?"

"Well, being angry comes easy. It's what our hearts want to do straightaway. Mama says letting hate fester inside causes our hearts to callous, so love is harder to find. We don't have to work hard to hate or be angry or even let fear cause us to do painful things like burn up a beautiful library of books." Her gaze traveled over his face. She had golden freckles in her eyes the same color as the ones across her nose. The loose golden curls of hair framing her face brought out the flecks. His breath slowed, and he embraced the unexpected moment. Funny how a corncrib could become one of the tenderest memories of his life.

"Fear is easy. And anger," he whispered, resting his own head back against the wall, staring down at her. Content to do so.

"But really loving somebody? Really trying to do the right thing, to forgive and to help even when it's hard? That takes a whole lot of strength and courage. I reckon my mama is one of the most courageous people I know."

"I reckon you're right. I'd like that sort of courage."

"Seems your daddy's hard on you," she said, continuing to watch him.

He swallowed and looked up at the low ceiling, faint slips of moonlight filtering through the cracks into their little hiding spot. "Ever since I was seven and a riding accident left me with a broken ankle and foot, I've never been able to please my father. Of course, I wasn't exactly his favorite before the accident. The quiet brother of the three. Not . . . influential enough, I suppose. But when the bones in my leg grew back in a misshapen way, it impacted everything. My walk, my ability to compete in sports, even the way I held myself in society. Everyone knew. And Father saw it as an embarrassment. Despite my mother's insistence and pleas, Father began conveniently leaving me home from parties or other outings, referring to me in private conversations as the lame one."

"That's rotten, if I ever heard of it." He turned his head to watch the injustice fire up her eyes. Her brows crinkled, but she kept her voice low. "So what? You got a bum leg. Why does that matter so much? My grandpa had one eye. My uncle, Coe, he lost an arm in the war, but that didn't slow neither one of them down. You're *you* on the inside. That's what a parent loves."

And she felt that, from both of her parents. Securely. Even if one of her parents lost his mind for three months out of the year. To quote Isom, "Ain't that a wonder."

No, there was the difference. In his right mind, Sam McAdams cultivated a solid, loving relationship with his children, and that memory held them through nights in a corncrib. Unbelievable. Powerful.

"I've always known my mother loved me."

"And your uncle. He's as proud as a rooster of you."

He grinned at her description and the sentiment. "Indeed, he is, and he's been more like a father."

"And that's why you came here? To be near him?"

He pulled a long breath through his nose and looked back to the ceiling. "In part." Somehow admitting weakness to Laurel came easily, perhaps because he knew she'd accept him, brokenness and all. Just as she did her father. Like most of the people on the mountain seemed to do. No social stigma. No class battles. "My inability to join the war as a soldier, because of my leg, caused another blot against my father's name in his mind. As other families sent their sons to fight without any certainty they'd return, he had at least one at home. He never spoke of it, but it was there, in the glances, in the unbearable silence. So when my uncle suggested I employ my talents here, I took the offer to my father, readied for the chance to feel useful."

"What did he do?"

"He laughed. Told me I was too weak to bear such a wild responsibility, so I accepted, in part because I wanted to prove him wrong and in part because I wanted to . . . do some good somewhere."

"And be with someone who loved you, even in the middle of this wild place."

He turned his face back to hers and became caught in her lantern-lit eyes. *Love.* What a small word, yet . . . appropriate, especially as he stared into Laurel's face. "Yes."

"You're strong."

He scoffed and shook his head.

"Listen to me, Jonathan Taylor." The edge in her voice brought his gaze back to hers. "You may not be as strong as some men, here." She patted his arm. "But you're a whole lot stronger than most men, here." She placed a palm over his chest. "And that's what God counts most, and so should you."

Her conviction, her faith, caught and held him. To have known a friend such as her in his childhood, perhaps he'd have been a different man. A braver one. He raised a palm to her cheek and brushed his thumb against her skin before ending the caress. "Thank you, Laurel. Thank you."

## Chapter Eighteen

The last week of October brought a sudden dip in temperatures as well as a flash of activity. Everyone on the mountain seemed energized by the upcoming holiday and infamous corn shuckin'. The time flashed by in a flurry of teaching, grading, and "mountain classes," as the children started calling Jonathan's after-school sessions. Despite every inclination of his heart, Jonathan reduced his cooking lessons with Laurel down to once a week in order to offer a "doctorin' " class, as the students termed it. He'd spent days after the corncrib seeing her face in his dreams, wondering what it would be like to have such a woman by his side, but he had to squelch the musings. Pursuing a relationship with her was not only selfish but poor planning. He only survived on his teaching salary because of the allowance his father bestowed on him — an allowance in place until Jonathan took a wife. A financially beneficial one, as Cora reminded in her letters.

But if Jonathan could finish college and become a physician, he'd free himself from his father's control, paying his own way. Then, he'd also be free to pursue the woman he wanted by his side. His thoughts shifted back to the corncrib and waking up to the McAdamses' rooster with John curled up against his chest, and Laurel's head resting on his shoulder. He pushed away the warmth. He didn't even have an inkling whether she reciprocated any of these feelings, but if she did . . . Nothing would stop him from coming back for her.

Jonathan, Enoch, and new-cohort Bent Morgan brought back three crates of books from their trip to Wilkesboro, and one crate of writing utensils and paper. He even found a very reasonably priced art set, a book on wood carving, and a cookbook for southern delicacies. Laurel laughed with delight when he presented it to her. Maggie hugged him and thanked him profusely, all the while wiping away tears. His "trade" for the art supplies was a new painting for the new room in his house — the mountains at sunset in the autumn. He presented her with a massive canvas on which to paint it, and the girl's eyes nearly bugged out of her head.

"Good gracious, that painting's gonna be about the size of the wall," Laurel had teased.

The barren bookshelves in the school swelled with new bindings. Of course, there was the residual pang of missing those old, well-loved books, pages worn from generations' enjoyment of story, but Jonathan kept too busy to mourn the loss for long. He was finding his rhythm, sensing his belonging among these people, and even celebrated the beginning of his weeklong holiday by cooking dinner for his uncle after church on Sunday. Uncle Edward stayed over Sunday night to accompany Jonathan over the ridge to the Spencer cabin for the corn shuckin' activities, an experience for which his students attempted to prepare him.

"You make sure to wear your finest church clothes, Teacher, 'cause there's gonna be some rousin' music."

"Law, Teacher, you ain't never been to a corn shuckin' until you been to one of our'n."

"Dancin', singin', all kinds of de-licious vittles."

"And some games to keep things interestin'," came another's response, a mischievous wink included.

"Wouldn't be surprised if you didn't meet your sweetheart there." The final comment had caught him off guard. His sweetheart?

But the students had become so comfortable with him after these two months, he'd come to expect their kinship and teasing.

"It's good to see you finding your place here, Jon, for however long that might be," Uncle Edward said as they made their way through the forest. "It's not a world for everyone, but for some, it fits." He grinned. "Not just fits, but grows us in the best ways. Calms the restlessness, I think."

He was right. Whether from the mountain air, good wholesome work, or the joy of connecting on a very real level with others, his life in this isolated place brought a deep calm. A contented purpose. "It's strange, Uncle. I came here expecting to feel sorry for these people. Their lack of necessities and education and experiences, and there are times when I still find myself wishing I could offer them more." Jonathan breathed in the cool air. "But I never expected to almost envy parts of their lives. The freedom in living and loving with such authenticity and voracity."

"The joy in simple things," his uncle added.

Jonathan nodded. "The ingenuity, determination, and . . ." He thought of Laurel and her father. "The fierceness of their loyalty."

"Both good and bad."

Jonathan grinned. "True. Loyal enough to protect their children from the evil designs of a flatlander teacher."

His uncle raised a playful brow. "Or magnanimous enough to love someone who isn't lovable at the moment."

"Yes," he whispered, his father's stern face coming to mind. "The more difficult choice."

"And the only one to encourage lasting changes." Uncle Edward faced ahead, taking the turns and climbs through the mountain as easily as a man half his age. "If change doesn't come, at least you know you offered an opportunity."

They heard the music long before they ever reached the Spencers', but when they finally topped the ridge, Jonathan froze to take in the sight. He'd seen a few of the farms but never one like this. The Spencer cabin stood in a large, open field, its conglomeration of various outbuildings and barns all neatly encapsulated by a tidy split-rail fence. Mountains framed the view on every side. No, this wasn't a half-shod, poverty-stricken homeplace.

"It's the largest farm on the mountain, so the corn shucking always happens here. Tradition." His uncle added with a twinkle in his eyes, "And we do not shake up tradition here."

Jonathan chuckled and then took in the view again. Amazing. The farm held many more buildings than he'd seen at any of the other cabins, even the McAdamses, who had a small barn, corncrib, smokehouse, springhouse, and pigpen. What were all the other structures at the Spencers'?

"The Spencers have been in Maple Springs the longest of any family. They came wealthy but with a desire for privacy, so when they were passing through North Carolina for the warmer climates south, Artair Spencer, the clan leader, saw these hills and they reminded him so much of his Scottish homeland, he stopped their journey here and built the first homestead. This spot has been occupied by a firstborn son of the Spencer family ever since, and tended with care and pride, as you can see."

"It's beautiful," Jonathan said, staring, wondering, and then he turned his attention to his uncle. "Wait, Enoch is the firstborn son."

Uncle Edward nodded. "He is."

"Can college be an option for him?"

Uncle Edward's face sobered. "I don't know, but if there's anyone willing to see beyond these mountains for their child, it's Cade Spencer."

As soon as they stepped into the clearing from the forest, a loud "haloo" called out to greet them from the crowd of gatherers. They were ushered into a mass of activity. Makeshift tables ran the length of the massive barn with every possible food the mountain had to offer. Liquor flowed without reserve, and an enormous pile of corn stood in the center of a circle of chairs and blankets, waiting for the work to begin.

Everyone turned out for the event, even the reclusive Ozaiah Greer and the less austere Cort Carter.

"Glad to see you, Preacher." Cade pushed through the gatherers, his hand out in welcome. His pale gaze turned to Jonathan, warm and inviting. "Teacher, real glad you could be with us today." He gestured toward the complex. "The womenfolk brought the food, yonder. Dranks." He eyed Jonathan. "Springwater and tea is by the food tables, but if you're interested in tryin' something new, my woman, Lizzie, makes the best elderberry wine this side of the Blue Ridge. Otherwise, grab y'all a plate or a dance and join round the pile. We'll get started here shortly."

The rousin' music enlivened the mood all around. Even Jonathan felt the temptation to join a few of the youngsters who'd made a dance floor out of a flattened area of land in front of the barn. He followed his uncle through the crowd, stopping to have conversations here and there on the way, and meeting some of the parents of the younger students he'd never met. The Rippeys and the Morgans gave a warm welcome, even Pearl Jacobs approached him to thank him for selling Luanne's dresses.

"I ain't never seen my girl so happy as she is sewin'." Jonathan stared at the woman's retreating back, her voice as fragile as the rest of her. She wore the weariness of this life like so many of the other women. He'd come to understand there were three camps of mountain women. The hardened, suspicious ones, much like their male counterparts. The healthy, vibrant, joyful ones, the definite minority. And the wearied, defeated ones, who aged much faster than their years. Pearl Jacobs exemplified the latter.

"Lookie here, Teacher." Laurel passed by, her arms laden with a large dish. "I made some Yorkshire pudding in your honor."

Maggie followed behind, her grin as wide

as her sister's and her arms as full. "And a treacle tart. Laurel rode Clementine all the way down to Bert's store outside the train depot to make sure she had lemons for just the thing."

Yorkshire pudding? Treacle tart? The words, so out of place here, finally met comprehension. His feet cemented to the ground as his gaze followed Laurel's form toward the food tables. She made him English food? His grin slowly expanded with the emotion in his chest. He was in love with Laurel McAdams. What on earth would he do with all his good intentions?

"She was plumb fixed on tryin' her hand at an English dish or two." Mrs. McAdams came along next, her voice holding its usual gentleness. "We pulled out two of my granny's recipes and doctored 'em up a bit with what we had handy."

His attention drifted from Mrs. McAdams back to Laurel. "I can't express how kind it was of you to think of me in this special way."

"Now, Teacher." She brought his attention back to her face, her grin brightening as if she wanted to laugh, and a sudden awareness of what Laurel might look like in twenty-so years filled his thoughts. "You've been sprayed by a polecat, chased by a mountain lion, and slept in our corncrib. I reckon you've earned your place here, but that's no cause to forget your homeplace."

A young woman, face new to him, waited behind Caroline McAdams, her features undeniably McAdams.

"I don't reckon you've met Betsy, have you?" She turned to allow the woman to step into the conversation. "This here's my eldest, Betsy Smith. She moved with her husband over the Patton Ridge last year, but she wouldn't miss a corn shuckin'."

Betsy smiled and took Jonathan's outstretched hand, her loose-fitting dress showing her advanced pregnancy. "I should be seein' more of you for the time bein', Teacher. Gable, my husband, is set on me stayin' with his mama till the baby's born so I won't be alone while he's gone workin' or huntin'. Leastways, I'll see you at church."

"It's nice to meet another member of the McAdams family." Jonathan gestured toward Caroline. "They've been so welcoming to me."

"Well," Caroline added, "when we all are in our right minds, we've been."

Her reference to her husband gave a levity to the situation to curb Jonathan's irritation at the man's behavior. "Yes, he was very kind to me."

Her gaze softened in silent appreciation.

"Woo-hoo!" Cade Spencer stood up on a tree stump, and the music stopped along with the talking. "I thank y'all for comin' to this here corn shuckin'. Everybody's brung so much eats there'll be plenty for each family to take home. Gather round and let's get this shuckin' started."

"Rules!" someone in the crowd yelled. "Gotta call the rules."

Cade slammed a palm down on his thigh and laughed. "Well, we all know that music, eatin', and dancin' can commence along with shuckin'. This is a time for celebratin' our crop and people. I'm feelin' generous because of y'all's generosity, so I buried two jugs of white lightnin' in the corn pile."

The crowd gave their boisterous support.

"And don't forget," Cade continued, his volume rising into the excitement. "If 'n you find a red ear, you gotta kiss a girl of your choosin', but you best kiss a girl who don't belong to none other, or you'll get into a heap of trouble with her mister."

Everyone laughed with good-natured merriment.

"Let's fill our plates and take a seat, Jon." Uncle Edward leaned close to speak over the noise. "The safest place for those of us who don't wish to dance is sitting far away from the music."

He'd almost made it to the end of the food table, making certain to add a double portion of both Yorkshire pudding and treacle tart to his plate, when a soft hand slipped around his arm.

"How nice to see you here, Mr. Taylor."

Danette Simms smiled up at him. He stepped back, and her hand dropped from its hold. "Good afternoon, Miss Simms. What a turnout, isn't it? Quite the excitement."

She sent a perfunctory glance around. "It's better than having nothing happen at all, the usual for Maple Springs." Her smile fell. "Which is why I'd like a few moments to speak with you."

He braced himself, keeping his expression neutral. "Of course."

"I've decided to leave Maple Springs once this school session is finished."

Laurel's concerns about Danette Simms had been prophetic. "That's only four weeks away. What about the children!"

She looked at him as if he'd grown antlers from his forehead. "The children? Half of them don't care what I'm teaching, let alone learning anything. I'm wasting away back here in this isolated, dark, and ignorant place." She drew in a breath, calming. "At any rate, I thought it the professional thing to let you know first, as my colleague, and I plan to speak to your uncle next."

Jonathan felt sick. "I'm sorry to have you go. I believe the children have learned much more than you realize, just through exposure, if nothing else." Though her constant frustrations with her students and emotional distance didn't help bridge the chasm of understanding between her and the children.

"I also thought it my duty to warn you."

"Warn me?"

She leaned close. "You've been spending a lot of time with Laurel McAdams, and it hasn't gone unnoticed."

Heat crawled up his neck. "We're friends, and she and her family have been a great help to me."

"Folks are talking that it's much more than friendship between the two of you." Her brow rose in challenge.

He refused to take the bait. "Folks always talk. We can choose to listen or not."

She waved her fingers as if dismissing his words. "I told these folks that you were too smart to align yourself with a mountain woman and her drunkard daddy."

A flame shot through his chest, but he

managed to keep his voice controlled. "I don't know, Miss Simms. I suppose if the Son of God made friends with sinners and outcasts, I could do far worse by extending the hand of friendship to kind and generous mountain people who have done nothing but open their homes and hearts to me."

The sweet facade fled her expression. "They're not *our* kind. None of them. No matter how sweet and generous. They are poor, stinking, uneducated people. Peddling dreams to them is a waste of your time and mind. You're throwing your talents away on some mission that will make no difference in the grand scheme of things. So what if you teach a handful of them to read? Does it really matter? They'll skulk back to their hollows and drown in their traditions and liquor anyway. You should leave while you can, as I'm doing."

"Miss Simms, I cannot disagree with you more. I think it is very wise that you are leaving Maple Springs." His body tensed under the strain to keep his anger amiably housed. "It is evident from your harsh words that you have neither the heart nor the understanding to make a real difference here. The sooner you leave, the better it will be for both you and these children." He tipped his head. "Good day."

He nearly shook from enclosed fury. Of course, his perspective had been colored by his uncle's letters, softened, balanced, but Miss Simms's response reflected the misconception of the larger population. Even in Wilkesboro, people seemed surprised at Enoch's manners and affability, not to mention his ready wit and money sense. They couldn't sort out any logical reason for Jonathan to leave his home in England to teach mountain children, let alone find pleasure in doing it.

They didn't need more teachers or business owners or doctors in Maple Springs just to have them here. They needed people with a bigger vision and understanding of the mountain culture to really make a difference.

He sat down next to his uncle and started eating, as people around him commenced shucking the pile of corn in front of him. Bent Morgan was the first to find a red ear of corn, and without one bit of shyness, amid the whoops and hollers around him, he marched around the circle, took Mary Rippey by the hand, and gave her a sound, though immature, kiss on the mouth.

The crowd applauded and laughed, while Mary stood frozen to the spot, her cheeks the color of ripe strawberries.

Jonathan caught Laurel's gaze as he raised a forkful of the treacle tart to his mouth. She had her bottom lip caught between her teeth, watching him as if her life teetered on his reaction to the taste. He raised a brow, placed the tart in his mouth, and . . . it tasted wonderful, the sweet syrup blending in with the tart lemon for a perfect combination. He mouthed the words *thank you* to her from across the crowd and her smile split so wide, it pinched into her cheeks. Thankfully, she'd caught him eating the tart. Yorkshire pudding had never been a favorite dish of his, and the Appalachian version didn't prove any tastier.

After finishing their meals, he and his uncle moved closer to the circle to join the shucking. People laughed and held light-hearted conversations, while the music played in the background, the children ran all about, and everyone removed, piece by piece, the outer shells of the corn, creating one pile of shucks and another of golden ears. Jonathan had barely shucked ten ears of corn before he opened up a red one. Heat rushed to his face and he tried to hide the ear behind his back, but Enoch noticed. "Teacher's gotta red one."

The crowd nearly exploded with "Woo-wee, Teacher. Go find a sweetheart to kiss" and "He's got the book learnin', but does he have the kissin' smarts" to "He's in for a real education now."

With each goading, his face grew hotter. Sunburnt hot, in fact. His uncle didn't help at all, shoving him to a stand. Jonathan shook his head, but the calling grew louder.

"Now don't be yella, Teacher. There's gotta be a gal who's worth kissin'."

"You're long past marryin' age. Shore 'nough, you've had kissin' practice afore."

*Not enough to really talk about.* With a helpless shrug, he started an uncertain walk within the circle of the crowd. His attention pulled, despite himself, toward Laurel. She sat next to her daddy, his red-rimmed and bleary eyes showing his continued state. Jonathan could choose her. Truth be told, he wanted to. And since it was all part of the game, what would she do? Miss Simms's accusation resounded in his head. He'd prove folks right if he did. Would that make her decision for college more difficult? Would she end their friendship?

"He's stallin'." Cade Spencer laughed.

"Maybe he sees so many pretty women, he don't know which to choose," another voice shouted.

"Or he don't know nothin' about sparkin' a woman."

Jonathan glared at Dan Morgan, whose grin perched unrepentantly.

With his jaw set, he marched toward the McAdams family, gaze fixed on Laurel. The sounds around him rose into a roar. Laurel's eyes grew as wide as saucers, but just before he reached her, he dropped to his knee in front of Suzie, and with the gentlest of movements he took her hand and gave it a chivalrous peck. Suzie's sweet trill of a giggle broke through the silence.

A round of protests mixed with laughter as he stood and bowed to the crowd.

"That ain't no doin', Teacher. Don't count."

He raised his palms in the air. "The rules said nothing about where a kiss should take place."

"I see I need to be clearer in my declarations next year, boys," Cade called out with another laugh. "The Teacher's outsmarted us. Ain't that a sight."

The crowd continued on and Jonathan took his seat, another red-ear discovery overshadowing his within a few seconds. When he found Laurel's gaze again, she stared at him with such confusion, he wanted to breach the crowd and sort it all out.

"Help!" A child's voice pierced into the

festivities. "He's sick."

Two boys, about Isom's age, ran into the center of the crowd, pulling a wheelbarrow behind them. "He's swellin' like a melon."

People rose to their feet, blocking Jonathan's view.

"He got bee stung. We was sneakin' some of Mr. Spencer's honey, and a whole crowd of bees lit into us something awful."

Jonathan pushed forward through the crowd.

"He's got the blue look," a woman screamed. "No, no!"

Jonathan finally made it to the rim of the circle, and in the wheelbarrow, face swollen and discolored, lay Lark Carter, pulling at the collar of his shirt and wheezing.

"He's gonna die." Imogene Carter rushed forward, taking hold of him. "I seen it afore. He's gonna die. No, no. Keep the shadows at bay, good Lord. Help! Please help!"

# Chapter Nineteen

Laurel sat stunned, her breath shallow. She'd thought Jonathan Taylor was going to cross the circle and kiss her. He'd stared at her long and hard like he'd considered it likely. Her mouth had gone dry from the speculation, and then her mind came to a firm conclusion: if she was bound to get kissed by somebody, she wanted him to be that somebody. She squeezed her eyes closed. She wasn't certain how she felt about that particular conclusion. Or the giddiness dancing around inside her chest at the contemplation of kissing Jonathan Taylor.

What would it feel like to be sparked by a man like him? Would he ever choose to stay in the mountains? She could teach and then they could sit by the fire and talk, read, or play music till nightfall. The whole idea lit like lightning bugs . . . and blinked out just as fast.

Lane Jacobs's cries for help broke into her fanciful musings. The crowd moved forward. A woman's desperate voice, a man's booming command, a child's frantic explanation.

"Honey. Bees."

Laurel made her way through the crowd, a horrendous wheezing noise growing louder and more desperate the farther she went. A smaller gathering circled a body on the ground. Lark Carter, though she barely recognized him. His lean face bulged three sizes, so big you could barely make out where his eyes were. Red and purple blotches covered his skin. And the wheezing. Laurel pressed her palm into her stomach. She'd heard that death sound before.

"Go get the doctor."

"There's not time for a doctor." Laurel turned to the sound of Jonathan's voice. He stood by Cade Spencer, closer to the body. "He's having an allergic reaction to the bee sting."

"No!" Imogene wailed and buried her face into the motionless boy's chest.

"I ain't listenin' to no flatlander." Cort Carter stepped toe-to-toe with Jonathan. "Leastways, one who runs a devil school with them devil books." He flipped his gaze to Allen, his eldest. "Run for the doc."

"I can help him, I think." Jonathan stood

tall, confident.

The plea in his expression was met with stone. "We don't want none of your work here, Teacher. You'll kill him for sure."

"Cort, Jonathan has medical training." Preacher Anderson stepped between the two men. "This type of reaction has to be treated quickly or Lark will die. Do you remember Topy Lawson, last spring?"

Cort shot his attention to the preacher, a flicker of fear softening the hard lines of his anger. Laurel looked down at the boy, no older than Isom. Yes, his face looked the same as Topy's, his breathing an eerie echo of the past.

A quiet fell over the group. Too quiet.

The wheezing had stopped.

"He ain't breathin', Cort!" Imogene cried. "He ain't breathin'." She turned on her knees and clutched her husband's leg. "Let Teacher try. Please, Cort. Let him try."

The man's steely face warred through expressions until grief won out. He stepped back, giving his permission for Jonathan to pass. Laurel stood with an excellent view of Jonathan's face. He was afraid too. Was it too late?

"I need a sharp knife. The sharpest you have." His voice quavered and then steeled. "If there's still a pot of hot water boiling over the fire, bring some of that. And some cloth."

He looked up at Laurel, and his chin firmed. He turned to the Carter parents and the crowd. "I've only done this procedure once in my training and seen it twice. Lark isn't breathing right now because his throat is swollen on the inside from the bee sting and his air can't get in."

Imogene whimpered.

"I'm going to make a small incision." He cleared his throat. "A small hole in the lower part of his neck to let the air in." He turned back to the parents. "If I don't do this, there is no way he'll live, and there's no assurance he will, even if I do. You understand?"

Cort stood stock-still, a standoff between the two, and then with the slightest movement, he inclined his head.

Jonathan nodded. "As long as we all understand."

Cade Spencer entered the circle, knife in hand, his wife next to him carrying cloths and a pot of steaming water.

"Does anyone have a tube? Something thin and hollow," Jonathan called out. "Maybe the size of a pencil?"

The crowd looked at each other and back at him, faces blank. Laurel's thoughts skittered over possibilities. *Lord, help me. Help me.* "What about makin' one? With hard paper?"

Jonathan shrugged. "Hard paper?"

"The art book. Maggie's art book. The paper's thicker. It'll hold better."

His eyes widened. "Yes, let's try it at least, unless someone else has another idea."

Maggie shoved her art book into Laurel's hands, and she ripped two pages out, running to Jonathan's side with them.

"Stay." He placed his hand on her arm, keeping her at his side. "I'll need help."

She searched his face for strength, then leaned over the body with him. The knife in his hand shook as he lowered it to Lark's neck.

"Hold back the collar."

She complied, the boy's skin hot to the touch. Jonathan's free hand rested on Lark's neck, pressing around as if in search of something. "There's a small space in between bone and cartilage of the neck that can open the lower airway if the upper airway is obstructed." His voice shook in the whisper, but she got the gist of his plan.

"All right. Do you need me to hold his head still?"

He didn't take his eyes off the boy. "Yes, lift his chin so his neck is fully exposed."

She tilted Lark's head back, and Jonathan

moved closer, knife lowering, hand steadying.

The red rim of blood shone from the cut, but Jonathan quickly pinched the incision into a pucker. "Hurry, roll the paper into a tube shape."

As he pinched the opening with one hand, he inserted the tubed paper with another. All at once, a large exhalation of air vibrated the paper and Lark's chest moved in response.

Jonathan looked over at Laurel. "He's breathing."

Laurel turned to the Carters. "He's breathing."

Imogene darted forward, but Laurel caught her. "No, you can't touch him yet. Teacher has to hold that tube in place for him to breathe."

"But I fear the paper won't last long enough for the swelling to go down," Jonathan said, without turning. "I have a very odd idea of something that might work."

Laurel lowered to his side. "You have good ideas. What's this one?"

He quirked a brow. "Could we get our hands on a few violin pegs? I believe they're hollow."

Jonathan couldn't wait to write his professors a letter with his account of the day. And the violin peg had worked as a breathing tube! He sent another grateful glance heavenward and collapsed into his reading chair by the fire. Once Lark's swelling subsided and Jonathan sutured his neck in what he hoped was the right way, folks began approaching Jonathan to share stories of children and adults who'd died from the same kind of allergic reaction. Then their tales unfolded into recollections of illnesses and deaths so rampant, it proved Jonathan's first assumption when he'd joined Dr. Hensley on his house calls. Maple Springs needed more help. Trained help.

Perhaps one of his professors would volunteer to come to Maple Springs as a research possibility? Or a new graduate who felt a call to America and adventure would see the good of such an endeavor?

He groaned and lowered his head in his hands. If only he'd been able to finish his degree. He could have . . . His thoughts stalled. No, he'd never have considered Maple Springs if war and rejection hadn't sent him on this journey. He leaned back in his chair and closed his eyes, his smile turning into a chuckle. At least until Jonathan gained the training he needed to return.

Only God could have designed such a

detour. A perfect plan much bigger and better than anything he'd have conjured up.

A knock at his door pulled him from his thoughts.

Cort Carter stood on the porch, a bundle in his arms and a crate by his feet, but his expression proved the most curious. The hardened lines in his face had gentled, slightly. He pulled his felt hat off his head and cleared his throat, shoving the bundle forward. "My woman made this. She wanted you to have it."

Jonathan took the offering, the lantern light revealing an exquisite quilt of autumn colors. "Thank her for me, Mr. Carter. It's beautiful."

He gave a curt nod, his gaze darting to Jonathan's face and away. "Brought some cannin'." He gestured to the crate on the porch floor. "Help stock your larder for winter."

"Thank you, again."

The man rocked back on his heels, silent, but not taking his leave.

"Would you like to come in?" Jonathan stepped back and opened the door wider. "I have some bread and jam Mrs. Spencer sent home with me, and —"

"Naw," he drawled, but didn't move. Finally, he raised his head. "I'm much obliged to you for what you did to my boy." The man worked his jaw and rocked back and forth, twisting his hat between his hands. "We done you wrong. Ozaiah and me. I ain't keen on you learnin' our young'uns to go beyond the mountains, but you ain't runnin' a devil school, and . . . my Rebecca's taken a shine to readin' like I ain't never seen." He cleared his throat again and nodded. "I'm much obliged."

Jonathan held in a victory cry of joy and instead offered his hand. "I care about these children, Mr. Carter. I want to do right by them *and* you."

He stared at Jonathan's outstretched hand. Then whatever reservation bound him broke, and he wrapped his work-worn fingers around Jonathan's. "This don't mean I agree with all the things you're teachin'."

"Of course not."

"And if 'n I have a cause with you, I won't shy away from speakin' my mind."

Jonathan's grin grew wider. "I'd have it no other way, sir."

Mr. Carter gave another firm shake and then released Jonathan's hand. "Right, then." He gestured back to the crate. "Our place is one of the only ones around that's got peach trees. Gene sent some preserves."

"I'm certain I'll enjoy them."

The man looked back at his shoes, crammed his hat back on his head, and walked to his horse. Jonathan placed the quilt down and moved the crate inside then closed the door. Two conquests happened today — saving a life and salvaging his reputation, and both secured his dream to become a doctor in these mountains.

Laurel massaged the back of her neck, sore from another night in the corncrib. She wiped down the counter at Mrs. Cappy's and checked the barrels of flour and sugar to make sure they were sealed tight for the night. Oh, how she loved the smell of brown sugar!

She sighed. Brown sugar, butter, and cinnamon. The trinity of delight to her taste buds.

She took the broom from the closet and began sweeping, peeking out the window to study the sky. All afternoon, the air had tingled with the scent of snow.

Her smile returned, and she leaned against the broom, staring out the window like a dazed fool. Snow, cinnamon . . . and then her mind turned back to the idea of Jonathan Taylor's kiss. *Brown sugar, for certain.*

She blinked and shook her head, face

blooming hot.

"Number one," she said aloud. "He's got a whole life in England with a trail of possible wives who could make his daddy a whole lot happier than a poor mountain girl. Besides, he's leavin' Maple Springs come summer, and that is that."

As if she needed any further reasons to refuse the blushing thoughts access in her head, she continued. "Number two, kissin' leads to marryin', and college don't come to married gals."

She pushed the broom around the floor and then swept the dust out the side door, recalling one of the letters Jonathan shared from his sister. "And third, no rich, handsome city fella is gonna want a mountain girl for a wife when he can have some daughter of a salt mine to . . ." She snickered. "Spice up his life."

She rolled her eyes and locked the side door. Cora Taylor sounded like a spitfire. Laurel liked her already. After placing the broom in the closet and giving the front of the store a final look, she crossed to lock the front door and retire upstairs for a nice long hour of reading her newest Emily Cabot mystery, but a flash of pale blue through the window stopped her cold. Someone was running across the field toward the store. Laurel leaned closer to the window, squinting to make out the face.

Maggie!

Laurel slung open the door and met her sister at the bottom of the steps. "Is it Mama? Daddy?"

Maggie shook her head, leaning over to catch her breath.

"Isom?" Her breath caught in her throat. "Jeb?"

"Betsy," she gasped.

"Betsy?" What on earth would be wrong with . . . Laurel grabbed Maggie by the shoulders. "The baby ain't due for another month."

"Don't matter. The baby's comin' now, and Mama can't leave Daddy after the fit he had last night."

Laurel closed her eyes, remembering the madness followed by the seizure. No, Mama couldn't leave him.

"Dr. Hensley's gone to Wilkesboro, and Granny Burcham's left for Harley this morning to deliver Rilla March's babe. Betsy's all alone with her mama-in-law, and you know that ain't gonna help Betsy none."

Laurel ran her hands down her face, trying to sort out what to do. "Preacher?" She shook her head. "No, it's Wednesday. He's over in Yella Hill."

"And he's a preacher, not a doctor," Maggie added.

A doctor. Laurel's gaze shot to the thin tree line across the field. "No, Preacher isn't a doctor, but I know someone who wants to be."

## CHAPTER TWENTY

The natives called it "wind snow," and the name fit. The snow hurled against them in haphazard swirls, dancing through the sky in a magical distraction as Jonathan trekked up the steep mountainside toward Norie Smith's house. He pulled his coat more tightly around his neck, attempting to keep out as much of the frigid air as possible. Only a half hour ago, he'd been sitting by his warm fire reading Dumas's *The Three Musketeers* and sipping a fresh cup of tea.

How could Danette Simms say life in these mountains was mundane?

He'd never traveled to this part of the mountains, with its rocky cliffs and narrow ledges twisting up a slender slope between mountainside and deadly drop. No doubt the path proved tricky in good weather, but with the wind beating ice against his face, it turned almost treacherous. Even Laurel, leading the way, appeared less confident in her ascent. Maggie kept quiet vigil between them, tucking her dark hair into the knitted scarf covering her head.

"It shouldn't be long now," Laurel called back, her golden hair blowing around her face and sprinkled with snowflakes. "I haven't been to the Smiths' in years, but if my memory's clear, the cabin should be at the top of the ridge, right, Maggie?"

Maggie nodded. "But there wasn't one hint of snow afore I came down the mountain. Looks a heap different in the snow."

Well, what they could see at any rate. The "top of the ridge" proved to be another twenty-minute climb. By the time the small party finally reached the front porch of the windowless cabin, Jonathan's weak leg ached from hip to toe.

"It'll be faster on the way back." Laurel shot a grin over her shoulder.

"Of course. We can sled down."

"With the wind a howlin' like a banshee, we might even fly."

A moan from inside the house interrupted her light laugh. She turned and knocked on the door, Maggie at her side. "Mrs. Smith. It's Laurel McAdams. We brought the teacher."

The door cracked open, and a thin, bent-over woman with a hollow-cheeked face peered out. She examined each of them, her black eyes pausing on Jonathan. "We don't need no teacher. Ain't learnin' about birthin'. Already know."

"Mr. Taylor's had medical trainin'. Did you hear about him saving the life of the Carter boy at the corn shuckin'?"

"That was him?" Her eyes narrowed behind her black-rimmed glasses, examining him for the truth.

"Yes ma'am. And he's had some teaching about birthin' babies." Laurel looked back at him with a shrug.

Yes, he'd seen dozens of deliveries. Two of them were human. He pulled his medical bag into view. "Can we at least see Betsy to sort out if there's anything I can do to ease her discomfort?"

The older woman hesitated before swinging the door wide and ushering them inside. The house consisted of one room with two beds, a small table with three chairs, and a massive fireplace. A wonderfully warm massive fireplace. Betsy Smith occupied the larger bed in the far corner of the room, her face blotched red from exertion, and the same pale hair as Laurel now stuck to her sweaty face.

"I don't sees why we need no doctor here. Betsy kept callin' for one, but in my time, womenfolks gave birth on their own as much as they did with a granny midwife or" — Mrs. Smith's gaze narrowed on him again — "some flatlander teacher-doctor."

Quite the title.

"It's your first grandbaby, ain't it, Mrs. Smith?" Laurel drew the woman's attention away.

"That's so."

"And it's Betsy's first child. I don't see no harm in making sure both have as much help to get along as possible."

"Don't need more than the good Lord's help, is all I'm sayin', but the girl wouldn't be quiet 'bout it. When that one came by for a visit" — she nodded toward Maggie — "Betsy told her to fetch her mama. I birthed one of my young'uns alone in this here cabin." She raised her chin and tapped the edge of the rocking chair she finally settled into. "Didn't need nobody else."

Laurel's annoyance pinned a frown to her face, and she marched over to her older sister's bedside, voice soft and comforting, but Betsy writhed through what must have been another contraction.

Jonathan had been replaying in his mind the two human birthing experiences he'd witnessed in school. His satchel carried bandages, a few excellent cutting knives, and a small vial of morphine, but all the other necessaries would have to be provided by Mrs. Smith. He scanned the room. Nothing was prepared. Not even a pot of water over the fire. He stared over at the older woman, now knitting as if a woman wasn't in labor in the bed nearby. She'd not prepared one thing for her daughter-in-law?

Well, even if he wasn't a real doctor, he could do much better than nothing at all.

"Maggie, Laurel, I need you two to help me prepare for the baby's birth."

They both turned to him, ready for orders.

"We need hot water and lots of cloths." He nailed Mrs. Smith with a prying look. "Rags? Towels? Clean ones."

"There's a bin, yonder." She waved toward a chest by the wall but made no attempt to assist them.

Jonathan drew in a deep breath and met Laurel's gaze as she walked past him to the fireplace. "Thank you," she whispered.

He stood taller, looking over at Betsy and setting his jaw for action. This was what he wanted to do. This called him. And ready or not, he'd do his very best to help as he could.

Laurel had witnessed the twins' births, helping Granny Burcham by fetching this or that, but that had been Mama, and her eighth and ninth young'uns. Seeing her sister Betsy struggling with the pains, and crying out for help, nearly sent her into a panic.

But Jonathan kept a cool head, his voice never showing any signs of concern. At one point, he took out a small vial and placed the tiniest drop of liquid on Betsy's tongue. She calmed a little, still awake but not as restless.

Maggie paced, flinching with each cry. Norie Smith sat in the corner in a rocking chair, knitting, as if the day wasn't different from any other. Laurel wanted to shake the woman until her wiry gray bun fell off the back of her head. Even Laurel, with her little experience, knew to boil water and get cloths ready for a birth, but Mrs. Smith had done nothing. *Nothing.*

"We're close now, Betsy." Jonathan's words flowed with comfort. He'd told her he didn't know much about delivering babies, but he'd sure fool her. "You're doing excellent." He turned back to Laurel. "Bring a large towel, Laurel. I see the head. It shouldn't be long now."

Laurel obeyed and stepped close, marveling at the miracle happening before her. Betsy cried out.

"You can do this, Betsy. Push."

Within seconds, Jonathan held a wriggling, red, crying baby in the towel in his arms. He laughed. "It's a boy, Betsy. You have a boy." His smiling eyes, bright with the wonder of a child, met hers. "A crying, breathing baby boy."

Laurel released her held breath and nearly kissed Jonathan on the cheek. Their gazes held, and something in her heart melted like ice cream in summer.

"It's a fine boy?" Betsy's weak voice shook them from their stare.

Jonathan handed Laurel the wiggling bundle, and with careful steps, she carried the baby to her sister. The pain, the agonizing, suddenly turned to wonder as her sister cradled the little bundle in her arms, close to her chest.

"He's mine. Look at that, Laurel. Just look at him."

"He's the handsomest baby boy in Maple Springs." Laurel grinned. "And you're one of the strongest gals." She leaned down and kissed her sister on the forehead, her eyes brimming with grateful tears.

Maggie had stepped close to the bedside, watching the interaction as Jonathan finished with her sister. Tears streamed down the younger sister's face. She reached to stroke the tiny fingers of their first nephew.

Laurel's thoughts hitched. Except for Kizzie's baby. Wherever she was.

"Laurel, would you toss out this dirty water and get me some clean?" Jonathan asked.

She blinked back to the present and followed through with his request. When she opened the cabin door, a white wonderland met her view in all directions. At least two inches covered the ground, and the snow still fell in a heavy cascade. She came back inside and moved toward the fireplace.

"Maggie, I need you to get on home. You've got the farthest piece to travel, and the snow doesn't look to let up anytime soon. Mama will be hankerin' for some news, and you need to get home before dark."

Though Laurel doubted she'd make it.

Maggie looked back at Betsy, reluctant to leave.

"Go on now, girl. You can tell Mama she's got herself a grandbaby," Betsy whispered.

Laurel walked over to her satchel and pulled out her gloves, placing them in Maggie's hands as the girl pulled on her coat. "Move as fast as you can, you hear? It ain't too cold, but the darker it gets, the colder. You can stop off at the store to warm up, if you need to. I'll help Teacher finish here, and then we'll make it back down the mountainside, all right?"

Maggie nodded, wrapping her scarf around her head and giving one last look back at Betsy and the baby before she slid out the front door.

They worked in silence, with sounds of a new baby and mama together, along with Norie Smith's snoring, keeping them company. At first, Jonathan helping her with the cleanin' almost sent her into protest, but he'd proved different in so many other ways than what she'd grown up knowing, maybe this was part of who he was too. A servant.

Her gaze drifted back to his, over and over, as they continued working. Would a man like him wait for a girl like her? Didn't seem likely, but he'd proved far more than "likely" since he'd arrived in Maple Springs.

An hour or so later, after Laurel and Jonathan had cleaned up as much of the mess as they could, the cabin door burst open and in walked a snow-covered Granny Burcham.

"Well now, I see I missed all the excitement."

"Granny Burcham!" Laurel rushed to her. "How on earth did you know?"

Her gray eyes twinkled and her whole face crinkled into a smile. "I've been doin' this for nigh forty years. Don't you think I got my ways?" She winked and lowered her voice. "Your sister passed me at the bottom of the mountain. Told me what was what."

Her happy cackle filled the small room, waking Mrs. Smith from her nap in the rocking chair but Betsy and the baby slept clean through. Laurel breathed out some relief at hearing that Maggie made it down the rugged mountainside safely. The familiar path up to their cabin wasn't near as steep or dangerous as the one to the Smith cabin, especially in the snow.

"Well, well, I heard tell we got us a new doctor in these parts." Granny Burcham rounded Jonathan, giving him the once-over with those keen eyes of hers.

Laurel covered her grin as Jonathan stepped back from the woman's close perusal.

"My oh my, you're much nicer on the eyes than our old doctor." She chuckled, and he shot a wide-eyed look to Laurel, who lost control of her laugh.

Even with his disheveled hair, stained shirt, and ruffled clothes, he stayed easy on the eyes. So easy, Laurel just wanted to keep lookin'.

"Well, lookie here." She whistled and approached the bed where Betsy slept with the baby in her arms. "That's a fine-lookin' sight if I ever saw one. A boy?" Granny Burcham turned back to Laurel for confirmation.

"Yes, ma'am."

She nodded and clicked her tongue. "A fine-lookin' boy. Good color in the mama's face too." She turned her gaze back to Jonathan. "Nice to know we have another set of hands to help in these parts, Teacher-Doctor." She chuckled and shook her head. "Teacher-Doctor. What in law! Well, I reckon I'll stay on for the night to help with the first sleep-through, since y'all have done my work for me." She tugged off her coat and cap and settled in a chair by the fire. "Y'all better git on down the mountain before things get worse, 'cause the snow ain't stoppin' for a good bit yet. Clouds are too heavy."

"Right!" Laurel walked to where her coat and satchel hung on wooden pegs by the door. Jonathan met her there, following her urgency. She looked back at the sleeping mother and baby. "You'll tell her I'll be back up tomorrow to visit, won't you, Granny Burcham?"

"I'll tell her you'll be back as soon as you can." The woman nodded. "This snow ain't gonna get many folks anywhere fast." She waved a hand to them. "Go on now. Shoo."

They stepped onto the tiny porch, everything covered in a blanket of fresh white. The whole world looked different and new, like some daydream out of the stories Laurel loved so well. She'd never outgrown the magic of snow. She hoped she never would.

"This . . . this is remarkable," Jonathan said, stepping out from under the shelter of the porch, face raised to the falling snow.

Like a child, his arms spread wide and he circled, laughing. The sight nearly topped seeing that brand-new, healthy baby in her sister's arms.

"Don't you have snow in England?"

He nodded. "Some, but in London it never looks like this." He gave the surroundings another panoramic appreciation. "This is pristine and beautiful."

She chuckled and stomped off the porch, the snow crunching with a layer of ice on the top. A slippery walk home. She marched toward the direction they'd come. "Well, admire the beauty on the way. We got a tricky path to tread."

He ran to catch up with her, the fading light bringing an added chill to the air. Laurel increased her pace, slipping a little as her foot hit a rock beneath the snow. "You did good work back there, Teacher, but once this story gets out along with what you did at the shuckin', I don't know how many more free afternoons you're gonna have."

"I feel alive when I do that sort of work," he said from behind her, the path too narrow for side-by-side walking, especially as the bend in the mountain opened to a sharp ledge to their left.

"Well, it's clear God's got a calling on you, for sure. You talked so easy and gentle. It kept me calm too."

"That's good, because on the inside I was terrified."

She looked back at him. "Truly? You didn't show one sign of bein' nerve-racked."

"Well, if you ever want a hint, my mother says I scratch behind my right ear repetitively when I'm nervous."

She laughed so hard she almost slipped again. "Yeah, Butter does that too, but we always thought it was due to fleas."

"Ha ha," he mocked from behind her. "I could say the same about you and your father. You keep such a steady head."

She shrugged. "Years of practice, I reckon, but, like you, sometimes I'm shakin' on the inside like a dog from the creek."

The path widened a little, so that Jonathan moved to her side. "How on earth can you tell this is the way down? The entire forest looks different in the snow."

She didn't hide her eye roll at all; in fact, she exaggerated it. "Teacher, we're on top of a mountain. Every way is the way down."

She marched forward a little, his pace slacking in the snow, and then . . . a sudden thump hit her in the back. She swiveled around to see Jonathan staring out into the distance with a much too guilty expression on his face.

He did not! She reached down to fill her hands with snow and then resumed her walk. "Don't start somethin' you can't finish, flatlander."

Another thump hit her, this time in the leg.

She balled up the snow in her hand, turned around, and threw it — hitting him hard against the shoulder.

His grin spread, and he reached down for another handful. She increased her pace, stopping only long enough to grip her own snow. On they went for only a few minutes, dodging, laughing, slipping on the trail. They'd made it to the sharpest curves in the mountain pass when Jonathan hit her with a snowball in the back of her knee. The contact dislodged her leg from beneath her. She buckled to the slanted ground and hit hard, the impact putting her into a fast slide. Her palms flew to her sides, grasping for something, anything, to slow her speed, but the ice slipped through her fingers like water. *Oh Lord, help me.* She attempted to shove her boots deep, but nothing helped as the edge drew closer. The last thing she saw before she skidded over the rocky ledge was Jonathan running toward her, calling her name.

# Chapter Twenty-One

Jonathan would never forgive himself. He'd caused Laurel's fall. Air whooshed from his lungs as she slipped over the edge of the mountain into nothing but sky and snow, her eyes wide and locked with his.

He raced to the ledge and peered over. There she lay on a snow-covered outcropping about ten feet below him, trying to push herself up but failing. Warmth flew back into his limbs. *She was alive!*

"Laurel!" He slipped over the ledge and slid down to her side, easing her up to a full sitting position. "Forgive me. I never meant to —"

"Didn't you get enough doctorin' practice on my sister?" She grinned at him, but it was through gritted teeth.

"Where are you hurt?"

"My right leg, I think. It's what's stingin' the most. My body hit the rocks beneath the snow and my leg caught the worst of it."

Already the snow stained with her blood beneath her right leg. Jonathan held in a wince and moved down to examine her, pushing back her skirt to the knee.

"It's a good thing you're a teacher-doctor right now, ain't it?"

He tried to smile at her attempt to lighten the mood, but the gash running from the top of her calf down to her ankle looked serious. Very serious. She'd already lost too much blood.

He jerked his coat off and began unbuttoning his shirt. Her eyes grew wide.

"Jonathan?"

"You have a deep gash on the back of your leg, Laurel. You're losing a lot of blood." He slid the shirt off and began wrapping it around her wound. Hopefully, the cold from the snow might help slow the bleeding a little, but he had to get her warm, and to a place where he could suture the wound. At this rate, she may not remain conscious for much longer, and he needed better bandages than a Sinclair with adjustable cuffs.

"What do you need me to do?" She searched his face, hers even paler than usual.

"I need you to stay awake and work with me to get to my house. It's the closest place with the proper supplies. I need bandages and a suture kit, neither of which I have right now."

She nodded, her face void of the previous humor.

They worked together to make it back onto the path, the expended energy clearly taking its toll on Laurel from the heaviness in her step.

"That sled sure would come in handy right now."

He forced a chuckle, trying to keep with her mood. "You mean to tell me you can't whip one up from a felled tree even now?"

Her smile flickered, too quickly. "Well, once I get my magic wand, or at the very least, my seven dwarves."

They continued downward, closer to his home with each step, but she was faltering.

"I reckon I know what happens if I lose too much blood." She leaned into him, less on her own now. "I've read *Dracula*."

"How can you joke at a time like this?"

She sighed and gave a little groan of pain. "I think I'd rather meet hardships with a smile than a frown." Her head bobbed over to his shoulder for a second before she righted it. "You've seen my people. There's enough frowns around here to fill a funeral march."

The words *funeral march* from her lips didn't do anything to lighten his mood, but he played along for her sake. "You take many things with a smile. Your life has been so difficult compared to mine, but you're always positive and filled with such spirit. I've had worlds of opportunities compared to you, and your life is sometimes a very wild and dark place, yet I've seen more love and light and hope in this world in you than I've ever known in mine."

Her gaze found his, searching, a glint of pixie mingled in with the sweet. "You're getting all sentimental on me. I *must* be dyin'."

His throat constricted. "I'm not going to let you die."

Her head leaned against his shoulder again, remaining there longer, body sagging. "I'll take your word for it, Teacher."

His rooftop came into view just as her body gave way to the loss. He slipped his arms beneath her and struggled down the hillside as fast as his limp and the snow would allow. *Dear Lord, please keep her safe. Please don't let her die.*

Laurel's entire body felt heavy. She could barely move her arms. How many quilts did Mama put on her? She drew in a deep breath, her chest giving a slight protest of

350

pain at the interruption. What was that smell? Sweet. Vanilla? She forced her eyes open and blinked the room into view. New wood walls all around. One of Maggie's paintings hanging nearby. The giant one of a rainbow sunset. Laurel blinked again, and a sudden throb surged from her left leg up her side. The fall! Betsy's baby! Jonathan!

She tried to sit up, but the only thing that changed was the rhythm of her pulse in her ears. What was she doing in Jonathan's house? Footsteps in the next room drew closer. Laurel fisted the quilt and made another attempt to sit straighter, making a small adjustment. *Well, at least that was progress.*

Jonathan rounded the doorway, head down over a book. A very thick book. Must be an interesting one from the way his brows pinched into a tense V. He looked a mess. Untucked shirt, wrinkled trousers, and a thick head of hair pointing in all directions. She decided right then and there that she liked messes.

"Good book?"

He looked up, his eyes wide, and then the most beautiful smile bloomed alive on his face. She liked smiles too.

"You're awake."

"Well, I think I am. Is this your house?"

He nodded. "It was the closest place, and I had supplies here to treat your wound." He shifted closer, taking a seat by the bed. "The store was locked, but I finally knocked loudly enough to wake Mrs. Cappy so I could gather a few of your clothes, for when you feel well enough to change."

Warmth rushed into her cheeks at the thought of him gathering her clothes, what little there were. "Thank you kindly."

He stared at her with a soft look that tugged something loose around her heart. "I'm only thankful I could help. Laurel, I'm so sorry."

"It was an accident, pure and simple. Do you think, living in these mountains, I've never had a bad fall before?"

"Not by me." Anguished lines deepened around his eyes. "Not by me."

"As far as I can tell, besides feeling too tired to stand, you made up for the mistake quite well."

His grin returned, wiping away the creases in his forehead. "You should have seen Mrs. Cappy with her hair all rolled in curlers as she looked at me through the window."

"She's scary in those curlers."

"I didn't want to stay away from you for too long, so I asked her to bring any of your other things over as soon as possible. She wasn't too happy about getting out in the snow, but I thought it would be important to at least let her know where you were, so she could tell your family if they came looking for you."

Laurel nodded and struggled to a better sitting position with Jonathan's help. Her leg throbbed from the movement, but she bit back the pain. "They won't come lookin' for a few days. They know I'm at the store."

"You've been asleep for two days."

Laurel's gaze shot to his. "Two days?"

"You lost a lot of blood."

"I've been laying in this bed for two days?"

"And I don't think Mrs. Cappy will be back until the snow melts a little more. There's two feet of it, at least." He stepped to one of the two windows in the room and drew back the curtains. The white shone bright into the room. "If you are feeling better later on today, I'll walk to your house to let your parents know where you are."

"You don't think I'll be fit to walk today?"

"I'm only glad you're fit for sitting already." He leaned close, grin tilted. "But I imagine you're hungry, and I happen to know how to cook a few things you might like to eat."

She offered a weak laugh, her stomach responding to his offer. "I *am* hungry. Just wait to make biscuits when I can help, all right?"

He stood and bowed. "Your wish is my command, my lady."

She laughed, her face growing warm from his attention. A good kind of warm. Her stomach let out a growl louder than a mountain lion.

"And that's my cue to get to work." He clapped his hands together and backed toward the door. "I've left a copy of *Emma* by your bedstead. I thought a lighter read, considering the circumstances, would be a better choice to encourage healing."

The dark blue bound book waited on a beautiful bedside table that matched the wood of the bed. She felt a little like a princess in her fancy surroundings with such service. "I don't think a lady in the entire mountain has had a recovery room like this."

"You should have the best." He nodded, his grin like a little boy's with a secret. "I'll be back with something to eat shortly." He wiggled his brows on the way out. "And a spot of tea."

Laurel picked up the book to read, but between the banging of pots and pans in the next room and an occasional hiss of water on fire followed by an unmanly exclamation, she had a hard time keeping her focus on frivolous Emma and dashing Mr. Knightley. After all their cooking lessons, she could almost envision what steps he was trying to take to cook her something to eat. No matter what he fixed or how it looked, she was going to enjoy it as if it was fit for a queen.

She must have fallen asleep at some point during the novel and the experimental cooking, because she startled awake by a loud pounding at the door. A muffled sound followed and then the creak of an open door. Laurel blinked the room into focus.

"Teacher, you need to pack a bag and get out of Maple Springs. Now."

The voice pulled her up straight. Was that Mama? So tense and agitated?

"What's wrong?" came Jonathan's reply. "What's the matter? Do I need to get my doctor's bag?"

"No, you need to leave." Another shuffle followed in the next room and then her mother stepped into the doorway, pausing with her hand on the frame to stare at Laurel. "Law, girl, we got to get you out of that bed. There might be some hope yet."

Laurel pushed back the coverlet. "What's wrong?"

"We ain't got time to talk right now." She turned back to Jonathan. "Teacher, get your bag together. If he gets here before you leave, then there ain't no hope a'tall."

Jonathan looked to Laurel for an interpretation of this wild behavior, but Laurel was at as much of a loss.

Mama walked across the room and pulled the curtains closed. "Come on, let me help you to stand. Leastways we can get you into a sittin' chair."

Before Laurel could respond, her mama slipped an arm beneath Laurel and scooted her to the end of the bed. As soon as Laurel rose to her feet, the world started to spin. She groaned from the ache gravity forged on her leg but tried to push through it to abate the desperation in her mama's eyes.

"You can't even stand." Mama returned Laurel to the bed, and then she turned away, searching the room like some frantic animal hiding from a predator.

"Caroline, I don't understand —"

"Where's your bag?" Mama scanned the room, finally focusing on the small door near the bed.

Laurel stared, wondering if she was somehow still dreaming, because she'd never have imagined her mother pushing her way into a man's house and rummaging through his closet. She reentered the room with a leather bag in hand and shoved it into Jonathan's chest. "Pack what you need and quick. My husband is on his way here with one point in mind."

"Daddy's coming here?" Laurel's breath caught, and she met Jonathan's gaze.

"He's gonna make you two marry."

"He's going to what?" Jonathan exclaimed, dropping the bag to the floor.

Everything slowed down. Noises. Movements. Thoughts. Laurel had spent the night, two if not three, in Jonathan's house, in his bed, and the only person who knew about their situation was Mrs. Cappy. One misplaced word to the right person spiraled a mountain-wide gossip trail that distorted truth into fiction, with everyone drawing their own conclusions.

And there was only one conclusion they'd draw.

Daddy already lost one daughter to the ways of the world. He'd make sure not to lose another.

Laurel drew from what little strength she had and pushed herself to the edge of the bed, groaning as her leg tipped over the edge, pulsing a deep ache.

Jonathan ran to her side, checking her bandage. "Laurel, you need to stay in bed.

Those sutures have to hold."

She grabbed the sleeve of his shirt and pulled his attention to her. "Get out of here."

He shook his head, running a hand over her bandages. "Your father can't make me marry you."

"He'll do everything in his power to either marry us or —"

"Kill me?" Jonathan stood and turned to Mama, palms raised. "Surely we can reason with him. This is ridiculous."

Mama placed clothes in Jonathan's bag without any rhyme or reason. "There ain't no reasoning with a drunk. Here's what you can do. Get your bag and hightail it down to the train station. You can come back to teach after winter. When my man's got his clear head on." She nailed him with a look. "See sense, boy. I'm trying to save you."

The urgency in Mama's voice must have spurred him forward, because he began to collect things and add them to the bag. "I can't believe this. I'm coming back. I'm going to set things right." His gaze met Laurel's and he paused. "Wait, what about Laurel? What will happen to her?"

She knew, oh, did she know. If her daddy let her stay at home, she'd be shunned by most of the people in town. Probably lose her job at the store. Whether she and Jonathan did what the rumor said or not didn't matter. All that mattered was what people believed.

"I'll be fine," she said, wondering if she lied or not. "You need to go."

He hesitated before grabbing a few more items and shoving them into his bag. With a last look from the doorway, he turned the corner and walked out of her life, probably forever, if he knew what was best for him.

## Chapter Twenty-Two

Jonathan had to be dreaming. He marched to the front door, satchel over his shoulder and bag in hand, replaying the last ten minutes in his head. No, his imagination couldn't conjure up something this bizarre. With one last look at the place he'd begun to call home, he opened the front door, only to meet the barrel of a shotgun.

"Well, I figured you for a fornicator, but are ya gonna be a coward too?"

Jonathan dropped his bag and raised his palms in the air. Mr. McAdams stood with the gun, and beside him, Hezekiah Cane held Uncle Edward in a viselike grip.

"Sam, there's no reason to bring my uncle into this situation." Jonathan kept his voice calm despite the rush of fury shooting through him.

"Can't have a wedding without a preacher," the man said from behind his gun, and gestured with his head for Hezekiah to go inside.

Mr. Cane shoved Uncle Edward through the front door, and Sam used his gun to motion for Jonathan to follow. Jonathan stumbled back into the house behind them, searching the man's stone-cold expression. "You can't want this for your daughter, Sam. Forcing her to marry, not if you really loved her. You know what her dreams are, and she'd never forf—"

"You're gonna make things right, boy." His lips tilted into an even grimmer line. "And don't think of runnin, 'cause drunk or sober, I'm still one of the best shots around."

Heat fled Jonathan's face.

"What if we wait a few days, Sam. Let me get back on my way to Hot Springs." His uncle pulled free of Hezekiah's hold, turning to Sam with entreaty. "The Spanish flu has hit our part of the world and lots of people need medical help. I could even take Jonathan with me to give assistance, then once we've finished helping, you can —"

"I won't have another young'un make a mockery of my family."

"Nothing *has* happened, Sam. Nothing that would lead you to force a wedding. Laurel fell on our way back from the Smith cabin and lost a lot of blood. I brought her here to —"

"I know what I heard, boy. I know what that means." The man's voice boomed through the room. He pushed past Jonathan and rounded the corner to the bedroom. "And she's in your bed yet."

"I told you, she was wounded —"

"Sam," came Caroline's voice. "Can't you see she's not well. Laurel ain't the type of young'un to —"

"Ain't no use, woman," he stopped her plea. "I saw him sneakin' from the house a few weeks back. Sneakin' out in the mornin' like he knew his own sin."

The night in the corncrib! Jonathan pinched his eyes closed.

"Daddy, it's not —"

" 'Twas more when I seen how he looked at you at the shuckin'. Now the whole mountain knows the wrong of both of you." He growled, raising his rifle back to Jonathan. "And the whole mountain's gonna know you set things right too. This time, we will set things right."

This time? Jonathan's eyes pressed closed. Their daughter Kizzie!

"Please, Daddy."

"Move on into that there bedroom, Teacher. We got a wedding to do."

"See reason, Sam. Wait a few days." Uncle

tried again, but all hope began to suffocate beneath Sam's steely determination.

"Now, Preacher. Marry 'em."

"Sam, please." Caroline tried again.

Jonathan met Laurel's tear-filled gaze, staring as helpless as him.

"This is not the right thing —"

A click sounded from the gun as he trained the rifle at Jonathan's head. Jonathan pinched his eyes closed, his stomach clenched.

"Marry 'em or bury 'em, Preacher. What's your choice?"

His uncle's resigned sigh answered.

"And make it quick."

Uncle cast a sorrowful look between Jonathan and Laurel then pulled a small book from his inner jacket pocket and opened it.

"Laurel McAdams, will you take Jonathan Reginald Taylor to be your lawfully wedded husband for as long as you both shall live?"

He'd never seen her cry. She'd always seemed too strong for crying, even with a leg wound that must have caused tremendous pain, but as a tear trickled over one of her cheeks, Jonathan had the sudden urge to turn to Sam McAdams and take the bullet. Whatever it took for her to be free. She was still pale from her loss of blood, almost fragile looking now.

Her attention switched to her father. "Daddy, please."

"Answer the preacher, girl."

"I will," she whispered, but her expression apologized to him, asked forgiveness.

Uncle cleared his throat. "Do you, Jonathan Reginald Taylor, take Laurel —"

"Lilabeth," Caroline spoke softly, adding the word into the almost nightmarish proceedings.

Uncle Edward peaked a brow.

"Her second name," Caroline clarified. "Laurel Lilabeth."

Laurel sat up a little straighter, as if the name somehow brought additional courage with it. Jonathan would have married her, freely. If given the time, he'd have come back to these mountains and made her his bride, if she'd have had him, but now?

She didn't want this.

"— Laurel Lilabeth McAdams to be your lawfully wedded wife."

Jonathan hesitated, holding Laurel's gaze, praying for another option. Would she ever be able to forgive him for ruining her dreams with a simple snowball? How could she?

"Forgive me, Laurel," he whispered.

"Stop stallin', Teacher." The tip of the gun pressed into his back.

Jonathan sent a glare to Sam and then turned to his uncle. "I do."

Uncle Edward drew in a deep breath, his gaze fastened to Jonathan's, offering some strength. "By the power vested in me, I pronounce you man and wife. What God has joined together let no man put asunder."

The pronouncement resounded, somber, more like a death knell than a wedding march.

Sam McAdams lowered his gun and nodded. "Y'all here be witnesses to this fact. Go on, Preacher. Your horse and man are still waitin' outside, yonder. Git on."

Uncle Edward looked between Jonathan and Laurel, as if he had more to say.

"Don't worry none," Mr. McAdams added. His pale eyes, red-rimmed, settled on Jonathan. "Me and my boys plan to watch the house for the next few days to make sure nobody takes a notion to leave afore the whole mountain knows my girl's married."

Uncle Edward held Jonathan's attention. "I'll be back as soon as I can. Stay strong, son."

*Son.* A sense of comfort pooled over a few of the ragged shards of loss as his uncle left.

"Move on now." Sam ushered Caroline forward.

Everyone filed out of the house. Jonathan stood at the front door, staring out into the snowy wilderness blindly. He couldn't see Mr. McAdams's "boys" but knew they waited within the forest, keeping watch.

Married *and* a prisoner?

He stepped back inside, closing the door, and a deafening silence ensued. Breaths came, in and out. Steady. *Stay strong.* He listened for sobs, even sniffles from the bedroom, but met only quiet. How had everything gone wrong within minutes?

And Laurel? He pinched his eyes closed in silent prayer. How could he be strong for her?

He rounded the doorway, and the view gripped him. Laurel sat on the edge of the bed, head down, hands in her lap, staring toward the curtained window. Her long, loose hair fell around her shoulders in untamed abandon, her face pale and sober. Words escaped him.

"Lilabeth was my granny's name." Her voice was low, controlled. She kept her attention focused on the window. "Outlived three husbands and learned how to blacksmith." Her sad smile pierced through him. "Strong woman."

He sighed and stepped into the room, taking a seat in a wooden high-back at the end of the bed. "I'm sorry, Laurel."

She looked up at him, her eyes void of their usual sparkle. "Me too." She looked back down at her hands. "Me too."

He ran a palm through his hair, fighting some unseen enemy he couldn't even name. "What are we going to do?"

"What do you mean? We're married. What do you think we can do to change that?"

He shot to his feet, needing to move, desperate to do something. "I don't know how we're going to do this. If my father finds out that I've married outside his approval, I will lose my allowance. We can't live on my teacher's pay." He groaned and dropped back into the chair, as helpless as when he'd stood. "If it had been two years from now, when I'd finished medical school, then I wouldn't need his support, but even now, he's financially supporting what the teaching pay doesn't cover. I don't know how to make this work."

She slammed a palm down on the bed and turned to him, eyes flashing. "Do you think I don't feel the helplessness of this situation too? I'm grieved to my core." Her fist pressed into her chest, her voice breaking. "For a good man to be *forced* to marry me? No girl wants that sort of tragedy. To have my name drug through the rumor mire as a . . . loose woman?" She waved her palm in the air as she searched for a description. "They're not gonna let me work in Mrs. Cappy's anymore with that sort of reputation, I bet." Her gaze widened, her jaw dropping wide with a gasp. "And college?"

The realization in her eyes knifed through him with a fresh sting.

She shook her head, new tears blurring the gold in her eyes. "There's no college for me now."

Oh, the pain! Her expression, so alive, so transparent, broke him. This was wrong! Devastating. He'd ruined her future, her dreams, all from one misfired snowball that ended in this life-altering avalanche. How would he ever make this up to her? How could she ever forgive him? He surged to a stand. "I need air." Without another word, eyes searing with unfamiliar tears, Jonathan grabbed his coat on a hook by the door and left.

Let Sam McAdams and his men watch him lose control of his emotions, but the last thing Laurel needed was another opportunity to see him fail.

Laurel forced breaths in and out as tears heated her vision. Her thoughts halted and spun, unable to find a landing space. The walls closed in. She pushed herself up, grappling for furniture as a crutch to free her from the small room, blinking as weakness tempted to press her to the floor. Halfway through the sitting room to the kitchen, she collapsed, burying her face into the rug in front of the fire. What was God doing? Didn't He love her dreams at all? Everything was lost! First her money for college and now college itself.

What good were hopes and dreams if they were stripped away so easily? Why even have them a'tall? Spurned by frustration, she pulled herself up by the wingback, held to the doorframe of the kitchen, and finally collapsed in a wooden ladder-back by the tiny kitchen table. A loaf of store-bought bread waited, half-eaten. Her stomach groaned. She peeled off a piece and raised it to her lips, only to let it fall back to the table. It wasn't as if she was selfishly dreaming. She wanted to help her entire mountain. Now . . . now, as a wife, her future stared back at her, the course as certain as the morning light. Cooking, cleaning, babies. Hard work. Not that any of those things were bad. No, they were blessings in their own way and time, but she'd longed for more. Hadn't God carved this longing to teach deep within her?

"Why, Lord? Why?"

The tears spilled over then, dripping down her cheeks. A cloth waited on the counter nearby. She took it in hand, the scent of lye hitting her nostrils. With a fury born from sorrow, she scrubbed the small table then moved to the pine floor. Work. Mindless work. She couldn't give in to the sorrow or the emptiness steeling through her in a way she'd never encountered before. Hopelessness.

Jonathan marched through the snow, faster and faster, blindly forcing one foot in front of another. He felt eyes watching from somewhere in the woods, Sam's men, but it didn't matter. He needed to walk, breathe, attempt to understand this broken page of his life.

The air, crisp from the new-fallen snow, cooled the inner heat and cleared his head. He slowed his pace and drew in a deep breath of the clean air. A startling blue sky contrasted against the wintery world around him, distracting him for the faintest second from the horrible reality of the last half hour. Though the snow had stopped, flakes dropped from the trees as he passed by, flittering down with soft, fragile elegance. His eyes stung. His lungs pressed with a need to scream at someone for the injustice of what happened. Two lives impacted forever.

And it had been his fault. His ridiculous actions. All of it. He'd crippled her dreams. How could she ever see him as a friend again, let alone her husband?

The trees fell away as a stage curtain, and he found himself on a rocky outcropping — the same ledge he'd stood on with Laurel the first night he'd arrived in Maple Springs. The view stretched to the horizon in a powdery white patchwork of cloud and snow, with random peeks of an indigo sky, a stark contrast to the clear blue.

The vastness, which always captured him at such a view, suddenly pulled a snarl instead. If God heard — if God saw, then . . .

"Why?" he called into the empty horizon. His voice echoed back, edged with blame. If he'd been the only one impacted by such a catastrophe, it wouldn't have made so much of a difference, but the fact this situation wounded Laurel ripped through him with a dozen accusations toward the One who controlled it all.

"Don't You care?" He screamed again, and the word *care . . . care* came back.

He scoffed. Where was the care right now, especially for Laurel? If God loved her, why did He allow this? What did He plan to do with these shattered dreams?

"You let this happen. How can You love her?"

*Love her . . . love her . . .*

The words returned almost as a question. Yes, he loved her. He'd turn back time, if possible, to make amends for the pain he'd caused. Do anything. How could he make her happy with all the loss? The pain?

*Love her . . . love her . . .* still echoed in the valley below.

"There's too much hurt. Love can't be enough."

And the simple challenge echoed back. *Enough . . . enough.*

Jonathan pushed open the door, his chest weary from the internal battle. He'd walked much longer than he'd planned, half praying, half begging for some answers.

The quiet of the house ushered his own hushed entry. A low fire lit the room, scaring back any afternoon shadows. He moved with quiet steps to the bedroom, but Laurel wasn't there. He froze, his mind reeling through possibilities. Where could she have gone?

He rushed into the sitting room again, scanning the chairs for any evidence. She couldn't have gotten far. Besides the guards keeping watch, her wound wouldn't have allowed it.

The scent of lye drew him toward the back of the house. The kitchen floor shone with the handiwork of a good cleaning, the countertops were tidied, and over at the small table in the corner, Laurel sat with her head resting on her arm . . . asleep.

How had she managed to garner enough strength? The loaf of bread lay almost finished next to her. He sighed. At least she'd eaten something.

He stepped closer, his shoulders slumping with the weight of the day. Tears clung to the tips of her eyelashes, evidence of the same ragged disappointment he'd struggled with for the past few hours alone in the forest. *Love her . . . love her.* The whisper echoed back to his mind.

A challenge.

A calling.

Could that really be enough to repair the wounds he'd caused?

One golden curl fell from her braid, slipping against her cheek and over one eye. With the gentlest of movements, Jonathan took the piece between his fingers and tucked it back into the masses of her hair. Silky. Soft. He hadn't imagined how soft it would feel.

His chest constricted with another pang mixed with . . . tenderness? She'd worked hard and probably wept even harder. This strong, brave girl, weeping? A groan resurrected from the core of his own hurt.

With a careful touch, he slipped his arms beneath her, but she didn't stir, only tipped her head until it settled against his shoulder. The same honeysuckle scent that always accompanied her presence swelled around him with a stronger hold. Her palm rested haphazardly against his chest, and something fierce surged to life within him.

A protectiveness. Bright and alive as a fanned flame. He couldn't explain it and certainly didn't understand it, but somehow the knowledge tempered the residual fury from this upturned world.

Even after her loss of blood and the emotional assault of her father's forceful decision, she'd cleaned his kitchen, probably with as many tears as water, and in her weakened state, even his presence didn't wake her.

He pressed his lips against her hair, breathing in the sweet scent, closing his eyes to pray for peace for both of them. He couldn't change the details of the past, but he could reshape the future.

He carried her to the bed, tucking the autumn quilt around her.

Whatever it took, he'd find a way to bring her dreams back to life.

# Chapter Twenty-Three

By the second day after their makeshift wedding, Laurel was able to walk unassisted, though not for long and with a decided limp. She found some satisfaction in waking up, dressing herself, and getting into the kitchen without disturbing Jonathan, who slept on the couch bed in the main room. The poor man. He was too long for that couch. And his body curled in some contorted way in an attempt to get comfortable. She'd fit better on that couch than he would. And she'd let him know that tonight.

Her chest ached, like her heart was sore, lonely. Two days, and they'd barely spoken to each other. Neither had said anything harsh or mean. Just lots of quiet. Lots of painful quiet filled with so many unsaid things, so many lost conversations. She stood in the doorway of the kitchen watching him sleep. Having poured out her grief through prayer and anger and more prayer and more anger, she felt her loss settle into a familiarity around her heart, a weary acceptance of dying dreams. But she grieved for something else too. Had she lost the sweet friendship between the two of them when they'd exchanged vows? The very thought seemed so wrong. Could he still be her friend when his entire future had been altered, and by her father's own hand?

Her mama had sent comfort in the only way she could. The morning after the wedding, she'd left a crate on the front porch filled with jams, canned goods, flour, sugar, and her own wonderful concoction of honeysuckle water. The perfumed water recipe came all the way from Laurel's great-granny, who'd worked in a flower shop in the Old World. The motto passed to each generation of girls — there's no reason why a lady couldn't smell nice. God's perfume makers filled the earth.

Inside the crate, her mama left something extra special — an iron skillet passed down from her granny Lilabeth. Laurel knew this pan. Her mother's favorite. And she knew the phrase scratched on the bottom in an attempt to encourage or remind.

*"God is bigger."*

She pinched her eyes closed and pushed the grief back. Hardships happened to everyone. Some change the day, others change the future. Her vision blurred, but she stilled the onslaught of tears. *Help me trust. Help me trust beyond my broken heart.*

With quick work, she quietly cleaned up the dishes from the night before, almost smiling at Jonathan's attempt to make cobbler. Burnt on one side and not done on the other. Well, at least now, as his wife, she could keep him fed with fully cooked meals.

After sitting a spell, she started frying some bacon, the delicious and familiar aroma filling the house, bringing a little of home with it. She looked through the cabinets and found the ingredients for biscuits, smiling again at the thought of his dozens of failed attempts to make the perfect biscuit.

He was such a good man. How could God allow the situation to ruin his life? There was no happy ending for this choice, was there? They both lost. And how could she ever make up the loss to him?

"I see you're moving around better." He stood in the doorway, scratching his head and looking around the kitchen with a grimace. "I'm sorry I didn't clean up last night. I was so tired and then forgot."

"You don't have to apologize. These are

things I can do now that I'm back on my feet."

He didn't respond, and she swallowed back a sudden urge to cry again. Law, she'd cried more tears in the past two days than she'd cried since Kizzie disappeared.

She went back to her work on breakfast, and the rigid silence swelled to an almost unbearable volume. She hated it, and even banged around a few things in the kitchen to make some noise. But the silence continued, with only the sound of Jonathan walking here or there from one room to the next.

Each second the silence grew, increasing a longing she didn't quite understand. Would this be life? Silence? Where had their conversations gone? She bit back the sadness and slammed a plate down on the counter. She'd choose anger over crying any day.

He reentered the kitchen, book in hand. Quiet. But she felt his gaze on her. *Talk, Jonathan. Please don't leave me in this silence alone.*

He dropped his attention back to the book, and she bit the insides of her cheeks to keep from screaming at him. She couldn't recall her mama ever screaming at her daddy. With a wobble and gritted teeth, she carried the plate of biscuits to the table and placed them down a little harder than necessary.

His gaze shot to hers.

"I can't stand this quiet between us."

He lowered the book slowly, refusing to break their eye contact. "Neither can I, but I . . . I didn't know what to say. I caused this, Laurel." Grief laced those golden eyes. "Me."

She dropped into the seat across from him. "I'm not blaming you. Neither one of us wished for this. We both lost our freedom and dreams, so it hurts. It hurts somethin' awful." She pressed her palm into her chest. "But it'll hurt a whole lot worse if we lose our friendship too."

His face funneled through so many expressions, she lost count, but it finally paused on understanding — a sad sort of understanding. Probably a whole lot like what she felt on the inside.

"You're right. That would be much worse."

For the first time since this tragedy occurred, she smiled. A real smile. One that felt slow and difficult because it meant more than a smile had meant before. "I don't see why getting married should end our friendship, do you?"

He shook his head, his own smile softening the pain in his eyes. "I'd always hoped marriage would be a lifelong friendship."

She studied him and pushed up from the table to retrieve the rest of breakfast. "That's a nice notion, for sure." After placing the jam beside the biscuits, she returned to her seat. "We got a pretty good start at a friendship, I think. Don't you?"

"I do." He nodded. "This lifelong friendship certainly works well for me in one particular way."

"What's that?"

He gestured toward the table. "Biscuits with you here are decidedly more edible than when you are not."

And her grin loosed. There was the Jonathan Taylor she knew.

The next few days, Jonathan found various items left on their porch each morning. Gifts, Laurel told him. For their wedding. So evidently, news had spread to the uttermost reaches of Maple Springs, because the Spencers, Morgans, Carters, even Norie Smith, left various items in celebration. He and Laurel had found two routines within the first week of their marriage. Reading from the Bible together at breakfast, and then reading their separate novels at night by the fire.

Their close proximity in the small house heightened every sense. He listened for her to settle in the bed at night. Grinned at her habit of whistling while she cooked. Even the simple way she twirled the end of her braid when she read by the evening fire became a fascinating study.

She found the fact that he helped her wash up laughable. No one in her world expected a man to do "woman's work," but he liked the opportunity to be near her, and as the week went on they found their banter again.

Jonathan thought he'd see his uncle by Sunday, but he never showed, sending a message that the flu epidemic throughout the mountain communities was much worse than anyone anticipated.

"The snow's melted enough that you reckon you'll have school tomorrow?" Laurel asked, clearing the table from their supper. She'd cooked something simple. Corn pone, side meat, and green beans. No complaints from him.

"I hope so." He carried their plates to the wash bin.

"Oh, I'm sure the young'uns will all be curious about your bein' a married man now."

With a few hand pumps, water flowed from the sink faucet, and Laurel shook her head. "I don't know how on this earth I'm gonna ever get used to having pumped water on the inside of the house. It's a wonder."

"You'll be the envy of every mountain wife." He chuckled, thankful that one thing in life made the predicament easier. He took a dish towel and began drying the few dishes as she finished them. "And since we're properly married . . . I think you ought to see if you can keep your job at the store."

She stopped scrubbing on a plate and looked over at him, her brow crinkled. "Why? I'll have work to do around here and —"

"I can help with the work around here, but I don't want you to give up on college, Laurel."

She stood so close, her hands still in the bubbly water, her eyes fastened on his, and the same bond he'd always felt with her twisted more securely.

"Married women don't go to college." The tiniest bit of hope tinged her whisper. Their shoulders brushed together. She was so close.

He pushed a damp strand of hair from her cheek, those eyes softening with wonder and curiosity. "You can become one of the first."

She kept staring, face upturned, lips parted. What would she do if he kissed her?

He watched her face for guidance, but she didn't move, didn't back away. With careful deliberation, he lowered his lips to hers for the gentlest of kisses. Her lips proved as soft as he'd imagined, an untouched delicacy.

The kiss ended much too quickly, but he needed to gauge her response. When he pulled back, she remained unmoving, eyes closed, hands in the pot of water. With a tip of her smile, her gaze fluttered to his. "That was . . . the sweetest thing."

He'd heard there could be far sweeter, but she wasn't prepared for that yet, he didn't think. "Indeed, it was."

She still stared at him, almost dazed. "I reckon I'd do about anything for you with such sweetness as that." Her grin crooked in its impish way. "Even work for Mrs. Cappy."

"I think you should work for Mrs. Cappy." He tipped her chin up and took another kiss; this time, her lips coaxed him to linger a little longer.

"All right then. I reckon I will."

He fought the urge to return for another kiss and resumed his work. "But you wouldn't stay overnight with her, surely?"

She chuckled and went back to her work. "I'll see what she says, but I'd trade your mornin' kisses for her poached eggs any day of the week."

Sure enough, Mrs. Cappy took Laurel right back. Laurel even made her case that Danette Simms was in the house for the next three weeks before the session ended, so Mrs. Cappy didn't need her or Maggie to sleep over. Mrs. Cappy reluctantly agreed after saying, "That woman ain't no help a'tall with vagrants. She can't even swing a skillet."

Between a morning kiss and a renewed dream, Laurel found her steps lighter and her attention continually pulled to the schoolhouse on the hillside. The ache of her broken future somehow began to piece back together in a different picture than it had before, and something told her the end result might prove even prettier than the initial. Could Jonathan find happiness in this simple mountain life?

The postman arrived at the store in the afternoon while Laurel and Mrs. Cappy wrapped freshly baked fried apple pies, his bag of mail backed up from the snow delay. Nine letters and a small package.

Mrs. Cappy gave her usual perusal of the mail, making conjectures as to what news each piece held for which mountain recipient, and then she narrowed her attention on the package. With a grunt, she looked over at Laurel and raised the package. "This one's yourn."

"Are you joshin' me, Mrs. Cappy?"

The woman nailed Laurel with a stare and slid the package across the counter to her. Sure enough, there in pretty ink scrawled Laurel's name. She looked back up at Mrs. Cappy, then down at the package. Who on earth would send her something? The package wasn't large, the size of a regular envelope, but it was packed a half-inch thick. That must be one long letter.

The return address listed *The People's Daily*. Where had she read the name before? She sent another glance to Mrs. Cappy and sighed. No use trying to be private about it. Laurel peeled open the package.

Fifty dollars fell out.

Laurel gasped. Mrs. Cappy's crinkled frown unfolded into shock. "What in all creation are you doin' getting fifty dollars cash money by mail?"

Laurel shook her head, staring back down at the money as if it might jump up and bite her. "I . . . I ain't got the faintest idea in all the world." A slip of paper blended in with the stack of bills, along with five magazines with the same title as the business name. She flipped open the letter. Typed.

Dear Miss McAdams,
   We are pleased to award you the first-place prize in our annual fiction contest for new writers for your charming story "Honeysuckle Summer." We have included five copies of your published story in our circulation along with the fifty dollar first-place prize. The colorful prose and your quality of writing set you apart from the other entrants and highlighted your unique gift of storytelling. Our circulation seeks to promote new talent and would enjoy seeing more of your work to inspire and entertain our readership. Please do not fail to contact us at the address below. Congratulations.
                                    Sincerely,
                              Mr. J. B. Haynes

Laurel reread the letter in her head, unable to fully comprehend.
"You mean to say that city fella paid you for them stories you write down?"
Laurel blinked up to Mrs. Cappy, looked

down at the letter, the cash, and the magazines, and then back to Mrs. Cappy. "I reckon so."

Mrs. Cappy's brows shot to her red kerchief. "Well, ain't that a marvel."

The truth began to sink in. Laurel couldn't tame her smile. It spread so wide it pierced into her cheeks and transformed into a giggle. "A true marvel, Mrs. Cappy. I never heard the likes of it before in all my life."

Jonathan had been right. Her attention shifted to the window, the faint silhouette of the schoolhouse on the hillside showing through the winter veil of trees.

"Well, what are you waitin' for, girl?" Mrs. Cappy waved toward the door. "Go on and show him."

Laurel didn't need one more ounce of encouragement. She stuffed the cash and papers back into the envelope and raced out of the store up the hillside.

The children played out in the schoolyard and welcomed her as she passed. It took everything in her not to scream out her news as she passed each smiling face. She bounded up the school steps two at a time, ending up in the doorway of the upper-grades classroom. Jonathan sat at his desk, head down, pencil out, most likely grading.

She worried her bottom lip, waiting. He seemed to sense her presence, because he looked up, and the smile he gave her warmed her all over. A welcome smile. One that felt like summer sun and fresh strawberries and soft quilts by a warm winter fire. She reckoned he had the best smile in the whole world. Nice lips too. Surely it was proper to think warming thoughts about a husband's lips and smile, wasn't it?

"Well, hello there, Mrs. Taylor."

The reference to her new name caught her off guard. She almost forgot to hide the prized envelope behind her back. Laurel Taylor had a nice sound to it, especially the way he said it. All rumbling and precious.

She pinched the envelope tight and stepped into the room. "Hello there, Mr. Taylor."

He placed his paper and pencil down. "To what do I owe this special visit?"

She took a deep breath, unable to hold in her excitement anymore, and rushed forward, slamming the envelope against his desk. "You were right. I did what you said, and look what happened."

He tilted his head and stared at her, eyes filled with question, then he pulled the envelope close. The cash money fell out first. His eyes widened. Then the paper and magazines followed. He took the letter, reading over it, his grin growing into a laugh.

He shot up from his chair, rounded the desk, and lifted her off the ground, twirling her around. She couldn't help but laugh. It felt good, wonderful. After all the loss and pain, to laugh . . . with Jonathan.

"This is excellent news." He set her down. "You know I'm not surprised at all."

His palms rested on her waist, his body so close as he stared down at her. Something vibrant and alive swelled into a strange sort of tender joy, like the soft flame in a tinted lantern. Warm, bright, but . . . gentle. "I couldn't have done it without you encouraging me."

"We make a fine team, don't we?"

The warmth expanded into her eyes, stinging. She belonged here, with this man from another world yet still so much a part of her own. Could they learn to belong to each other? "That's a truth."

He tilted his face closer, his palm coming up to rest against her cheek. Her breath dissipated. Would he kiss her again? She dropped her attention to his mighty fine lips. She'd entertained lots of thoughts in her head, but kissing thoughts distracted like no other.

He watched her eyes, as if seeking permission, his palm trailing from her cheek to the side of her neck as he closed in. Her breath caught, and her body pressed against his, anticipating another round of lip-locking sweetness.

The sound of children outside stopped his approach.

He cleared his throat and stepped back. "I think we should celebrate your news this evening. I'll even attempt a cobbler with those canned raspberries your mother sent."

She shook the heated fog from her thoughts and placed a hand on her hip, ignoring the residual tingles on her neck from his fingertips. "And I'll be there to make sure we don't have burnt cobbler."

He shrugged a shoulder, his gaze dropping to her mouth again, almost as if his thoughts turned in the same direction as hers. Yep, kissing thoughts could give a coon dog competition for perseverance.

"Like I said, we make a good team."

## Chapter Twenty-Four

Laurel searched through the cabin for a second time, but Jonathan was nowhere to be seen. Knowing Laurel remained useless from distraction the rest of the afternoon, Mrs. Cappy sent her home a little early, but instead of finding her husband — she grinned at the title — home reading or working on lessons, he'd disappeared.

She didn't know his full routine yet, so perhaps he visited families on his free afternoon from after-school sessions, but as she took another look in the kitchen, her gaze fell on a jar of honeysuckle water. Her hand skimmed down her braid. Wouldn't it be nice to make her hair smell pleasant for him? She smiled. In fact, an entire bath sounded excellent. Perhaps some honeysuckle sweetness might encourage some honey-sweet kisses.

Taking a bath proved a lot easier when she didn't have to walk to the springhouse and back. Gathering water from the pump in the kitchen, warming it, and then taking her bath took half the time, and in the cozy surroundings of Jonathan's beautiful cabin, it felt different. Not sneaky, exactly, but certainly different. She was drying out her hair with a towel when someone attempted to open the door she had bolted before her bath.

Feet still bare, she tiptoed over to the door and opened it to find Jonathan, rubbing at his arms to keep warm, his hair a mess of wet ringlets like hers.

"There you are." She stepped back for him to enter. "Why is your hair wet?" She peered out after him at the clear sky, now fading into dusk.

He shuffled past her and bent over at the fire, rubbing a hand through his damp hair in front of its warmth. "The snow, and certain unforeseen circumstances last week, got me off my schedule." He peered at her, upside down. "But the path had cleared up from the snow and the walk wasn't unbearably cold, so I went to the hot springs for a bath."

Her eyes shot wide. "The hot springs?"

He straightened, his curls all wild. "It's much less bothersome than heating water and cleaning up afterward twice a week."

"You take a bath twice a week?" She shook her head, taking in the idea with a revelation. "No wonder you smell so good all the time."

His grin twitched wider, his gaze studying her, heating her cheeks. "And you? I smell honeysuckle. Did you use some of your mother's water?"

"I washed my hair with it," she said, looking away from his darkening expression. Something about the look caused her skin to tingle all over. "Ain't you the least bit afraid of someone spying on you down at the springs?"

"Should I be?" He laughed, taking a step closer to her.

She narrowed her eyes at him. "There are sneaky folks in these mountains. I'm not one of them, but I know a few."

"I imagine you can be especially sneaky when you want to." He moved close enough to reach out and touch her if he wanted to. His smile tilted ever so slightly, and somehow his gaze did its magic again, bringing a buzz like thousands of hummingbirds in her stomach. Was this what it felt like to be sweet on someone? To have him be sweet on you too? She was pretty sure it had to make marriage nicer when the folks were sweet on each other.

He reached out and touched her wet hair then raised a handful to his nose, keeping his gaze fastened on hers the entire time. The look in his eyes seemed to beckon her body nearer, and her feet answered the unspoken call.

"Honeysuckle," he whispered.

A sizzle sounded from the kitchen, and she blinked out of her daze. "Chicken's boiling."

Heaven and all its angels. If this was being sweet on a man, she was maple syrup and brown sugar with peaches on top.

They worked together for supper, a strange sort of dance. A brush of hands here. A lingering glance there. Her body stood on edge, aware of every movement, almost anticipating another smile, another touch. After simple conversation and washing up, they found their way to the sitting room, as they'd done the past three nights, to talk and read in companionable silence. He seemed hesitant to sit in his usual chair by the fire, but when she took her spot in the facing wingback, he sat, watching her.

Did he want to talk?

Well, she wanted something too, but apart from another kiss, she didn't know what it was. Her body, her breath, hummed with an anticipation she couldn't define, leaving her stomach knotted and her skin prickling for reprieve. With a frustrated huff, she reopened a copy of Doyle's *The White Company* and stared at the page, unseeing. The fire crackled. The clock on the mantel ticked. Jonathan turned a page of his book. He breathed out a sigh into the quiet.

She studied him. His handsome profile, his drying curls, his lips. Especially his lips. And her skin lit again.

Was it right for a wife to ask for a kiss from her husband? Could she just go right up and kiss him silly if she wanted to without a single word?

He caught her staring, so she cleared her throat and nodded toward his book. "What are you reading?"

He raised a brow and tilted the little red book in her direction. "Shakespeare."

"Shakespeare?" She frowned. "You like Shakespeare?"

"You don't?"

"I've never been interested in all the moonin' and pinin', the rivalry and dyin'. This man thinks he's in love with this woman, but really he's in love with this one. The man is too mad to live so he kills everybody." She shook her head. "I don't reckon it's my style."

He laughed, low and content. "Not everything he writes is that way. Some of it, even the plays, is art through words."

Her doubt must have shown on her face, because he lifted his book higher and began to read.

" 'Let us not to the marriage of true minds admit impediments. Love is not love which alters when it alteration finds, or bends with the remover to remove. Oh no! It is an ever-fixed mark, that looks on tempests and is not shaken . . . Love alters not with his brief hours and weeks, but bears it out, even to the edge of doom. If this be error and upon me prove, I never writ nor no man ever loved.' "

She sat in silence, staring at him, her soul whirring from the sound of his voice, the depth of his words, the tenderness in his eyes.

"Law," she breathed out. "I could listen to you read to world's end."

He slowly closed the book and stood, his gaze never leaving hers.

A sudden nervousness stole over her. "I reckon I wasn't fair to Shakespeare."

He wasn't smiling, but not frowning either. He looked . . . serious, but not mad, and whatever he communicated captivated her. He stopped in front of her chair and held out his hand.

Her throat tightened. For some reason the idea of taking his hand at this moment carried a promise of something she didn't fully know but wanted. She slid her fingers into his and he drew her up to her feet. Breaths shivered from her as he drew her closer, his tenderness nearly buckling her to the ground. He was such a fine man. She'd never known a solitary person like him. "I . . . I like spending time in your company more than I have words to say," she whispered into the small space between them.

He touched her chin, his warm fingers slipping over her cheek and into her hair. "I like spending time in your company too," he muttered, low and raspy. "More than I have words to say."

Her attention flickered to his eyes, searching for . . . well, she wasn't quite sure, but her heart seemed to find it, because all her uncertainty dissipated. Her palms came to rest on his chest, warm and soft beneath her fingers. The sound of her pulse rushed to her ears. He was so close, and movin' closer at the pace of sunrise. His breath fanned her face, so she closed her eyes to enjoy his touch and within that moment, his lips covered hers. Gentle, as smooth as the petal of a flower. The simple contact spilled a sweet heat, a tingling spark over her skin. She could hardly breathe, barely move. Her books never prepared her for something this . . . this wonderful.

His palm cradled her cheek, nudging her to linger, which wasn't a hardship, because she couldn't think of anywhere else she wanted to be. She'd waited all day for him to finish what he started at breakfast. His arms engulfed her, moving through her hair and down her back to pin her against him, each new kiss lingering longer, asking for more. His hands slid down her body. Her fingers gripped at his shirt. He claimed her . . . and she claimed him right back. Man and wife.

Kissing thoughts couldn't compare to the real thing.

As quickly as the kiss started, Jonathan stumbled back, leaving Laurel's brain as foggy as an August morning. She blinked her eyes wide and stared at the man who was much too far away for her peace of mind . . . and body.

A whole host of emotions crashed through her as he drew back from their embrace: kind of hungry, a little mad, completely in awe, and a teensy bit lonely.

He stared at her as if he knew she was crazy hungry for more kisses. "I . . . became overzealous. I . . . I'm sorry."

"You are?" she squeaked. Something felt wrong about an apology over a kiss from man to wife, but then again, the heat behind that kiss might be the trouble. Overzealous sounded like a great way to continue their kissing conversations.

"Well, no, I'm not really."

She shifted a step toward him. "You're not?"

With each blink of his eyes the uncertainty began to clear. "No." He gave his head a shake, his very fine lips crooking up on one side. "No, I'm not."

"Well, I'm sure as sunrise not sorry," she said, aching to close the distance between them to nothing. "I think my whole soul's been waiting for a kiss like that from you."

He stared at her, his breath still pumping his chest up and down. "Yes. I believe you're right."

He looked at her. She looked at him. Neither stirred.

What did they do now? She knew what she *wanted* to do, but somehow diving across the room at the gentle, tenderhearted man seemed unladylike and a little desperate. Silence yawned into the discomfort and then Jonathan walked forward.

Not really walked. Kind of charged at her like a wild boar. Without any hesitation at all, he cupped her face in his hands and took her lips with his. Great day in the mornin', she loved this man. Every piece of him. His mind, his laugh, his heart, and, without one solitary doubt, his lips.

She wrapped her arms around his waist and flattened her palms against his back. Warmth from his skin pressed through his shirt, as muscles moved beneath her trembling hands. One kiss led to a more urgent one, then another. His fingers slid over her shoulders and back up, trailing her neck until she gasped against his mouth.

He pulled her closer and heated up the kiss till death seemed inevitable. Was it his lips that had caused her whole body to burn from the inside out? Or was it some unyielding need inside of her? Either way, breath was coming in short supply.

Just about the time she thought she might survive, his lips left her mouth and traveled a smooth path from her cheek to her ear. Her legs grew weak, but he seemed prepared for it, because one arm slipped around her waist to keep her from collapsing on the floor in a heap of tears and heat.

Oh sweet heaven, was God watching?

The idea nearly pushed her back from Jonathan's strong arms, but his thumb trailed a gentle line from her chin down the front of her neck, distracting her with a feeling like butterflies dancing over her shoulders. His kisses alternated between deep and soft flutters against her waiting mouth. She explored his taut back with her hands, and finally her curious fingers reached the skin just above his collar at the nape of his neck. He inhaled quickly at her touch, a sound that somehow encouraged her fingers into his thick curls.

This was holy matrimony?

*Lord, have mercy. Ain't no way something this hot could be holy.*

She buried her face against his neck, holding tight, their bodies pressed together like the pages of a book.

A knock pounded into the quiet of their whispered breaths.

Was that her heartbeat?

Jonathan's?

It sounded again — heavier — from the front door.

They froze in place, their wide-eyed gazes meeting, and then they jumped back from each other as if somebody's hand had been caught stealing stack cake. Jonathan stared at her, face flushed, and no doubt tryin' to catch his breath same as her.

The knock came again. Louder.

"Jonathan? Laurel? You home?"

Jonathan pushed a hand through his hair and stepped back, nearly falling over the stool in the middle of the sitting room. His attention still fastened on hers, as if he was tryin' to read her mind. She closed her eyes. Her mind really wasn't fit for readin', because the idea of the two of them stickin' together like pages of a book sounded like the best happily-ever-after in the world.

No, it was bad enough the good Lord read her thoughts. Adding Jonathan to the mess just made it nigh unbearable.

The knock came again.

He moved to the door, patting down his unruly curls on his way. Her fingers tingled from the memory of untidying it. She breathed out a long stream of air and steadied herself with a palm to the wingback nearby. Darkness shrouded any light from outside. Who was visiting them so late? She growled. And with such inconvenient timing.

Preacher stood in the doorway, looking like a wild man, from the growth on his chin to the strange assortment of patchwork clothes he wore.

"Uncle." Jonathan grabbed him in a hug. "You're safe."

The man walked in, his body moving slowly, wearily. He pushed a palm over his face and raised tired eyes to Laurel, taking off his felt hat and nodding to her. "Only by God's mercy. This illness is like none I've ever seen. It's taken entire families overnight." He collapsed in the nearest chair and dropped his satchel to the floor.

Laurel broke out of her stupor and collected a cup of coffee as Preacher continued to talk. "I came home for some new clothes. I bought these makeshift things after stopping in town last night for a shower. I didn't want to bring any of my old clothes into Maple Springs for fear I'd carry the disease with me."

Laurel handed him the cup, which he took with a smile. "Thank you, Laurel." He studied her. "You look well."

She smiled at him and glanced up at Jonathan, pretty sure her face burned bright red from the spark in her cheeks. Her eyes popped wide. No wonder sparkin' was called sparkin'.

She turned her attention back to Preacher. "I'm much better than when you left."

The man's attention shifted between the two of them. "I can see that." He sipped his coffee and then set it down on the small table beside his chair. "I took the liberty to stop by the post office in town before riding into Maple Springs because I knew you'd ordered more books, Jonathan." He reached into his jacket and drew out an envelope. "You'd received a telegram yesterday. So had I."

"A telegram?" Jonathan stepped forward and took the proffered paper. He looked over it and then to Laurel, a sudden chill dousing the previous warmth in her middle. " 'Charles killed in action. Father needs you home immediately. Not well.' "

"I took the liberty of purchasing a ticket for the first train out in the morning." He looked to Laurel. "I only had enough cash on me for one, Laurel, or I'd have bought another for you."

She shook her head, trying to comprehend the sudden shift in her world. "I can't leave too, Preacher. Somebody's gotta stay and keep house." Her gaze found Jonathan's again. "Keep an eye on the chickens."

"You have chickens now?" the man asked with a grin.

Laurel answered, absently. "A wedding gift from the Spencers."

Preacher took another sip of his coffee and stood. "Perhaps I could leave Gideon with you, Laurel, while I take the train back to Hot Springs for another week. Would you mind tending him?"

She shook her head, still refusing to digest

the fact that the husband she just learned how to kiss was going to go back to England. "That's fine, Preacher. I don't mind."

"You can even ride him, if you'd like. He's an easy horse."

She smiled absently and looked back over at Jonathan, whose head bent low. How could she be so selfish. He'd just found out his brother passed. Of course he needed to go home.

"I'm going to ride home, gather a change of clothes and more supplies, and attempt to get a few hours of sleep. The train leaves at six in the morning. I'll meet you back here by four."

Jonathan nodded without looking up. "Thank you, Uncle."

Preacher placed his palm on Jonathan's shoulder as he passed and then paused at the door, looking back at Laurel before walking outside.

The silence returned. Deep and loud. Laurel slipped back into her reading chair, her fist pressed against her chest, taking in the unwanted information, accepting what she couldn't change.

"I'm sorry about your brother, Jonathan."

He squeezed his clasped fingers together, keeping his face downturned. "Charles. Sadly enough, we'd never been close."

"Then I'm sorry all the more," Laurel whispered, drawing his attention to her. His eyes reflected the same weariness she'd seen in his uncle's. Her heart ached for him, even more. His father! Her face went cold. He didn't want to face him, especially now, with an unwanted wife. Her pulse hammered against the thoughts spiraling in her mind. Would he want to be free of her? To please his father. All the pent-up kissing-heat whooshed from her face. No one in England ever need know of this week-long marriage. He could disappear from Maple Springs and return to the fancy life he once knew.

Without any ties to the mountains . . . or her.

## Chapter Twenty-Five

She'd helped him pack his bag, a quiet assistant, moving here and there to gather items he requested or she thought he'd need. Jonathan hated the distance the telegram created between them, the uncertainty. Only an hour before, they'd not only accepted their married circumstances but embraced them. Quite literally. In fact, he'd embraced his circumstances with such gusto, the last thing he wanted to do was travel away from them . . . from *her*. He closed the bag and took her hand, drawing her down on the bed beside him.

"Laurel, I won't be gone long."

She kept her focus on his chin. "You ought to try and get some sleep before you travel." Her voice sounded small, too weak. "I'll sleep on the couch bed so you can get some proper rest."

She unwound her hand from his and made to stand, but he caught her fingers again. "I'd rather you stay here with me in my arms before I go, whether we sleep or talk. An ocean will be between us soon enough. And . . . I'd like you to do me a favor while I'm gone."

Her face lifted, golden hair spilling over her shoulders. He smiled. She was beautiful.

"I have the lessons for the last two weeks of school charted out. They're on my desk here at the house. Would you be willing to finish out this session for me while I'm gone?"

Her eyes widened. "Teach your upper-grade class?"

He nodded, his smile growing. "I can think of no one else as ready for this opportunity as you."

A flicker of a smile softened the sadness in her expression. Ah, yes, at least he could offer her something. "I will try my very best."

"I have no doubt."

Her smile faded too quickly.

"I'm sorry to leave you like this."

"I've been studying on something about this trip for you . . . and your future." She hesitated, refusing to sit. "London's a long ways off," she continued. "They won't know what happened here, us being married, and . . . they don't ever need to know."

His fingers tightened on hers, and he tugged her down beside him. "What do you mean? You can't —"

"You can be free, don't you see?" She raised her face to him, eyes watery and bright. "You don't have to be ashamed when you visit your family. You made a difference here, just like you wanted, and you can hold your head high without any strings fastening you to Maple Springs. This marriage." Her breath shivered out. "It . . . it doesn't have to follow you."

"Is that what you want? To be free of this marriage?" He searched those eyes that had become the best thing he saw every morning. Was she taking the entire responsibility of her father's drunken choice on herself? Or worse, did she regret their relationship?

"You were forced into something you didn't plan." She cleared the emotions rasping her words. "We both were, but it's *my* daddy that held you to it." She tried to stand again, but he only tightened his grip, willing her to confirm her feelings. "I don't ever want you to regret being with me. Ever."

"And you think I'd do that?"

She drew in a deep breath, succeeding in freeing her hold from his. "You have doctorin' gifts. God's given them to you to save people's lives. You love it." Her smile grew sad. "It shows in every action you make. Beautiful and perfect and good." She wiped a finger over her eyes and shook her head. "I won't be the one that holds you back from that dream. I need you to have an untied heart so" — her gaze lifted to his, intense, certain — "if you choose to come back, it's all of you. No regrets." She paused. "And if you choose to stay away, then that's all of you too. Life's too hard for a split-up heart."

"Laurel," he breathed her name, weakening her at the knees, but she shook away the temptation to withdraw her words.

"You get some sleep." She stepped away. "But know this, Jonathan Taylor. You don't have to do nothing else to make your daddy proud. Your Father in heaven looks down on you, smilin'. He's already proud because you love Him, and you are walking in the calling He's put on your life. Whether doctorin' or teaching. And He's so happy with what you've done to show love to my people."

"Please, Laurel, stay with me."

She hesitated, as if she might take his outstretched hand, but then she shook her head, body stiffening back another step. "I won't hold you back. You *have* to be free."

She left the room without looking back, and he placed his head in his hands, praying God kept her heart strong, hopeful, until his return. Because he *would* return.

He heard the clock on the fireplace mantel strike every hour. Was Laurel asleep, or did she stare at the ceiling, counting the minutes, as he did? The shuffle of boots on the porch alerted him to his uncle's arrival, but Jonathan had already gotten dressed, ready for him.

Laurel opened the door for his uncle, her robe pulled around her, her hair long and loose down her back. Uncle Edward didn't enter but tipped his hat to her. "I've corralled Gideon in your fence in the back, Laurel, if that's fine."

She nodded, pinching the front of her robe together from the night's chill. "I'll get Mr. Morgan to halve one of the extra barrels at the store to make a waterin' can for him, and the wood shed's small but can provide shelter, if he needs it."

"Thank you." His uncle turned to Jonathan, who had his bag in hand.

Jonathan hadn't packed much. He didn't have to. He had a room in London filled with clothes and necessaries.

"I'm glad you packed light, son. It's a long

walk to the station, especially this early in the morning." Uncle looked between the two of them. "I'll wait on the porch so you can say your goodbyes."

Jonathan closed the door. Laurel stood beside him, fidgeting with the hold on her robe.

"Safe travels, Jonathan," she whispered, her eyes down. "I packed you some side meat and a biscuit in your satchel if you get hungry."

He didn't respond, only looked at her mussed hair, all golden in the lantern light. An ache squeezed his chest, words evading him. His silence must have piqued her interest, because she looked. That was all it took. He captured her cheeks with his palms and drew her into a kiss, stamping her with the promise of his return. She thawed into him, gripping the front of his coat. Salt mingled with the taste of her lips. Her tears.

He pressed into her, refusing to break the connection but knowing he had to. With a last lingering touch, he drew back, lowering his forehead to hers. "You will never be a regret."

Her gaze found his, and with a timid motion, she touched her fingers to his lips, almost as if memorizing them by contact. Her palm dropped to his chest. "Don't forget who you are, here. Strong."

He gathered her fingers into his hand and kissed them, then with one last look at her framed in the doorway, he walked away.

Teaching school provided welcome distraction from the sudden emptiness in Laurel's life. How could Jonathan have already taken up so much room in her life in every place? The children challenged her, but having a solid thumb on their ways as well as their family dynamics, she knew how to take control.

And the studies? The teaching? Each subject energized her. She knew much of the information in the texts, but teaching it, and then drawing from the culture to use examples, created a myriad of opportunities for discussions.

Growing up in a family of eleven, she'd never been alone — and now, every night, after helping Mrs. Cappy close up her store, she'd locked the door to a cabin filled with quiet and the scent of oakmoss and leather.

She used the time — working on school lessons and writing more stories — but when she finally settled down to sleep, her mind wandered to England. Jonathan had told her it would take a full week to travel, first by train and then by ship to London.

With a deep breath, she drew back the curtains of the bedroom and glanced out over the only sea she'd ever known — a sea of mountains.

She replayed their last day together over and over in her mind. He'd kissed her like he wanted to stay. Like he wanted *her*.

Her eyes stung. Oh, how she longed for him. A man couldn't kiss . . . She closed her eyes, remembering his caress, his teasing, his friendship . . . No, a man couldn't love a woman like that without leaving a mark on her heart. Would he come back to her, or would his dreams, his father, pull him away and end up leaving a place inside her heart that no amount of time or teaching could fill?

The evening shadows fell across the valley below, and a melody filtered through her thoughts.

> The heart is strong at rememberin'
> The heart holds fast to what's true
> And days may pass and miles grow long
> But nothin' can keep my love from you.
> No, nothin' can keep my love from you.

She pressed her eyes closed. *Let it be so, Lord.*

In the quiet of the house, all alone, she

prayed for Jonathan, for his family, for their grief, for Preacher and the people stricken by the Spanish flu, for her mama, daddy, and siblings, and for Kizzie, wherever she was.

And she asked God to bring Jonathan home. She drew in a quivering breath. Wherever "home" might be.

London's streets seemed more crowded than when he'd left, noisier, and the air cloaked with gritty smog. But some things didn't change. Before Masters, the butler, could even announce Jonathan's arrival, rushed footsteps hurried from the other room and Cora came into view, wreathed in smiles, making her mourning black look fashionable.

"You're here?" Cora covered her mouth with her hands, her bright umber eyes flashing wide. With a squeal, she ran forward into his waiting arms, burying deep as she'd always done. "I didn't know if you'd come. When you didn't arrive for the funeral, I thought you might have chosen to stay in America."

"I missed the funeral?" Jonathan tipped back to see her face. "I came as soon as I received Father's telegram."

Cora's expression tightened. "Father

pushed to have Charles's funeral as soon as possible. He's not talked about it, but I can tell he's sad, especially because it was Charles."

The melancholy in her confession resurrected the general air of their home. Everything good, every future dream, hung on the eldest Taylor son. His father's dreams. Richard, second. At least his father still had Richard.

"Will you stay long?"

Jonathan hesitated, and Cora's smile softened. "I didn't think so. Every line of your letters glowed with your admiration for your work and the people there, and, if I'm right" — her grin peaked with mischief — "you're particularly fond of a certain mountain girl who has an infectious smile and intelligent sparkle in her eyes."

He rubbed the back of his neck and winced. "Did I truly write that?"

"I can show you the exact letter, if you doubt me. It's a particular favorite of mine." She slid her arm through his and guided him through the house, the familiar scents and sights calling to his past. Electric lights. Indoor plumbing. Servants. All so different from where he'd lived the past three months.

"I have a lot to share with you and

Mother, some surprising developments."

She laughed. "I love surprises, and I have a few things to share with you too, besides the additional list of brides Father has for your choosing." She grimaced, crinkling her perfectly tipped nose. "He's become much more adamant about your future since Charles's death, almost desperate. There's been increased talk about his failing business. He even sacked Edith and Ross."

Jonathan stopped, a sudden dread whooshing through him. His father hadn't called him home to mourn Charles; he needed a scapegoat. "They've been with this household for a decade at least."

"I know." Cora shook her head. "He's tightened the purse straps on me too, though I thought at first it was due to the fact he despised my work at the hospital, but now I don't think so."

"Is he home?"

"No, he's away on business until Friday, but I know he'll be relieved to see you, especially with Richard still at the front." Cora squeezed his arm. "Mother and I shall have you all to ourselves for three days before Father brings his dreariness into the house. Oh what fun we'll have! And we'll have to tell Cousin Colin of your arrival. He's needed some cheering up after returning from the front with the loss of his right hand."

Jonathan turned to his sister. "What? But . . . but his work?" Colin's odd degree in botany required an artist's hand to sketch the wildlife he so passionately studied.

Cora's expression sobered. "He's learning to use his left hand."

His cousin had always been a singular person, focused and driven by a long list of unusual interests, but his gentle nature fit with Jonathan's well and they'd become friends throughout the years. Yes, he'd definitely wish to see his cousin, but more than anyone, he wanted to see his mother . . . and, at some point, tell her about his bride.

The days with his mother and sister proved restful and sweet. He regaled them with stories from Appalachia, Cora shared tales from her work at the hospital and then laughed about the parade of unfit suitors Father kept introducing to her, and Mother, with her usual gentleness, glowed as a woman content with the sight of her child.

He'd missed them. He'd always been able to speak with his mother and sister honestly, express his dreams without fear of ridicule. He shared his heart about his care for the mountain people, their need for a doctor and simple basics, and, particularly, his love for Laurel, though something kept him from revealing the forced marriage details.

Colin visited a few times, but his ready smile rarely reached his eyes. War had impacted him to the heart, a similar tale for so many soldiers. The Blue Ridge Mountains might do Colin some good too, once he'd healed more from his time at the front.

A few overheard conversations among old acquaintances, along with information shared by Cora and Mother, filled Jonathan in on the declining success of his father's investments, partially due to the war and partially to his father's mismanagement. His mother shared the news with relative contentment, simply saying, "Do not worry. We are taken care of."

With her usual passion and spontaneity, Cora took him on a shopping spree for items for his cabin — rugs, curtains, cooking utensils . . . laughing as she spoke of imagining him attempting to cook — and in a quiet instant with her, he revealed the truth about his marriage to Laurel. After a moment's shock, his sister fell into laughter, and then she pulled him into a few women's shops to purchase special gifts to take back to Laurel.

Oh, what would Cora do in those mountains!

# Chapter Twenty-Six

Jonathan entered his father's study after breakfast on Friday morning, adjusting his suit and swallowing to wet his dry throat. After more strategically placed questions paired with a few conjectures of his own, he entered this confrontation with an idea of his father's plan. Enlist Jonathan into helping him salvage the business. Take Charles's place at the helm, as if that was even possible.

And he'd keep Laurel far from the conversation. The longer he received his allowance, the more money he could save to send her to college. By the time Jonathan completed the rest of the school year, he'd have enough money saved to fulfill Laurel's dream.

His father stood from behind his massive oak desk, dark hair slicked back in his usual fashion and gaze commanding the room with one look. He gestured Jonathan toward a chair, without so much as a welcome.

"You look well, Father." Jonathan spoke first, offering his hand to his father across the desk, seeking some way to connect with him. Conversations from Laurel and his uncle Edward proved to soften a little of the edge in Jonathan's heart against his father's coldness. Love held power, not resentment. "I know the past few weeks could not have been easy for you."

His father remained stoic. "Yes, which is why we must prepare for every eventuality, especially in these times. Family must remain our priority."

Jonathan tensed. Family had never been his father's focus, except when used as a pawn or influence. "Family is important." His mind went to Laurel, and an idea shot to realization. Laurel was *his* family now.

His father stared at Jonathan's hand and, with hesitation, took it.

"Let us have a drink together."

His father ushered a footman forward, but Jonathan waved the man away. "No thank you."

"Drink with me." His father's gaze leveled him, no request in his tone. "In memory of your brother and in celebration of your homecoming."

Caution rose, and Jonathan took a proffered drink from the tray.

His father pressed the glass to his lips, sipped, and set it back on his desk. "Your brother will be missed in this family, as you well know. He worked hard and made his family proud by his sacrifice, a faithful son."

His tone dripped with unswerving expectations. Jonathan lowered his glass without taking a drink and attempted to prepare for a confrontation for which he came ill-equipped. Jonathan had returned to England to comfort his family, not conform to them. "He was always a gifted leader. I am sorry Charles and I weren't closer near the end."

"Yes." The word elongated, measuring, a warning glint coming to life in his father's dark gaze. "But there is time to remediate your failings to your surviving family."

Jonathan gripped the arm of his chair with his free hand. Ah, the knife began to twist.

"Now that you're home, I expect you to take over your brother's responsibilities in the business."

Jonathan refused to shift an eyebrow, keeping his voice controlled. "We can discuss those responsibilities when I complete my duties to Uncle Edward and the people in Maple Springs."

His father raised a cigar and lit it, unfazed by Jonathan's statement. "Nonsense, teachers for such a backwater school are found in any corner of any street in the world. They'll make do. Your responsibility is here. With your family."

Jonathan straightened for the battle. "You have always emphasized the importance of completing our tasks to the end. A duty of any Taylor, I believe is the way of it." Jonathan took a sip of his drink, as if his stomach wasn't knotted into near-nausea. "Uncle Edward hired me as the teacher for the school year. I agreed to complete it, and I mean to do that."

"It seems you will have to disappoint your uncle. Your responsibility is here now."

"I *will* keep my word." Jonathan refused to budge. "And I am no businessman, Father."

"No, you are not." He released a puff from his cigar, eyeing Jonathan without emotion. "But I don't need your business sense, or lack thereof." He lowered his cigar to the tray and placed his elbows on the desk, making a tepee of his fingers. "Despite appearances, this war has taken a toll on my business, and your brother's death . . ." His father cleared his throat, the only sign of emotion. "I've decided that Miss Daphne Rivers would make a good match for you. Her father's reputation in business, not to mention the social circles the family will draw us into, should make a significant difference in our current circumstances and increase our business prospects."

Jonathan drew in a deep breath. A year ago, Jonathan would have kowtowed to the power and intimidation surging from his father's steely expression. He'd have rushed for an opportunity to receive a kind word or thought from this man he barely knew, but a year ago he hadn't lived in Maple Springs or loved Laurel McAdams.

He firmed his heart toward his decision, knowing the possible consequences. Jonathan would work harder and longer to secure Laurel's dream of college. He'd find a way. "I won't marry her, Father."

His father's smile held no kindness. "It has been a long-held dream of yours to become a doctor. Indeed, you are halfway through your studies. Who funded that coveted education?"

Jonathan knew this confrontational terrain. "You did."

"And who provides an allowance that exceeds your paltry teacher's pay?"

Jonathan almost smiled; the impending threat lost its sting in the light of his certainty. "You do."

"Indeed, *I* do," came the low reply. "And who will ensure that you live in comfort and reasonable happiness as long as you do as expected of you?"

"Comfort and happiness are not two characteristics which I would place in your hands, Father. You've shown nor given either to me." Jonathan eased back into his chair, suddenly aware of his own freedom from his father's manipulation. God held Jonathan's future, and He'd placed Laurel directly in the path to show Jonathan where true strength lay. "What I've learned has been through Mother, Uncle Edward, and my grandparents. Not from you. And my life in Maple Springs has only taught me more. Given me more."

His father stood, bracing himself against the desk, expression hardened to steel. "You are weak. You've always been weak. Even now, you're not man enough to step into the shoes you were meant to fill and save this family."

Jonathan stood, eye level with his father. "You know as well as I that a marriage to Miss Rivers isn't going to save your business, and certainly not this family. It's nothing more than a bandage around a cancer sore. The business has been failing for years. This war only showed the weaknesses within the foundation."

His father slammed his palms against the

desk. "How dare you?"

"Weak men bully others into submission by threats and intimidation. I am neither weak *nor* the scapegoat for your mismanagement."

"You ungrateful, ill —"

"And I won't marry Miss Rivers." Jonathan smiled, showing his slight height advantage over his father. "Because I was married three weeks ago to Laurel Lilabeth McAdams."

His father released a humorless laugh. "If you're trying to lie your way out of this, then you're more of a coward than I —"

"You are welcome to wire Uncle Edward for confirmation, since he officiated the ceremony." Jonathan reached into his pocket, retrieving the certificate his uncle created for him — a paper he'd requested as a gift for Laurel, but it would serve its purpose now as well. "Or, I can procure the marriage certificate for you now."

"What?" His father snatched the paper, sneered at it, and then, without warning, tossed it into the flames of the fireplace.

"No." Jonathan stumbled a few steps toward the fireplace, his hands fisted at his sides. Pointless. The paper was already consumed.

"An easy enough remedy to our little

problem."

Jonathan's gaze flew back to his father's. "That changes nothing. I know my own heart, and I will not comply to your wishes."

The sneer on his father's face somehow aged the man before Jonathan's eyes. The graying hair. The crinkled brow. A man withering as much on the outside as within. "Then you will have nothing. I'll strip you of any allowance or financial support. No inheritance. Your name will be blotted from the family's lives."

Jonathan blinked from the sting. "Do you see what you're doing? What you're choosing? You alienate the people who would love you by your cruelty. I may not cower beneath your demands, but that does not mean I wish to quit this family. You are my *father.*"

"You are not my son." His voice held no hint of welcome or regret.

Jonathan closed his eyes, accepting his fate. "How many more relationships will you sever before you wake up to your own cold loneliness? Open your eyes to what you have. You cannot redeem the loss of Charles, but God has given you time, yet, to bring happiness to those around you, instead of despair. Think of Cora and Mother —"

"Our conversation is finished. You are

dead to me." His father crossed his arms and turned his back.

Would this be the last time he saw his father? Jonathan prayed for compassion even as his heart struggled to round the desk and shake some sense into the man. Love exacted change, not anger. "You haven't the power to expunge my name from this family any more than you do the existence of a God who would hold you accountable for your hard heart, but, whether you acknowledge Him or not, He is there. And whether you acknowledge me or not, I will be praying that God will break your heart of stone so that you can seize what time you still have." Jonathan bowed his head and, without another glance back, walked toward the door.

"I want you out of this house within the hour." His father's voice followed him. "You are no longer welcome here."

Jonathan paused only a moment, drew in a deep breath, lifted his head, and left the room.

He alerted the butler to his immediate departure as Jonathan walked up the stairs to his bedroom. His eyes stung, and his breaths pulsed for control of his emotions. Even if his father never created a loving home for Jonathan, the idea of severing their relationship altogether incited a resounding ache in his chest.

As he pulled an unused trunk from his closet, he prayed for his broken father and the wounds only Christ could reach. Jonathan packed what little he had brought and a few keepsakes, and instructed Masters to package the dozens of things Cora and his mother had purchased for shipment to Maple Springs.

He could only imagine Laurel's face at the wild assortment of gifts and decorations.

"Laurel." He breathed in her name.

Yes, it was time to leave London. Time to go . . . home.

At light tap on the bedroom door preceded his mother and Cora's entrance. There was a gentleness in his mother's expression, her usual countenance except something deeper. A lingering sadness. She'd overheard his father's conversation.

"Do you love her? Your bride?" Her voice smoothed over the question, accepting his future, his choice.

"I do." Jonathan took her into his arms and placed a kiss on her cheek. "And you would love her." He glanced to Cora. "You both would."

"She's the Laurel from Jonathan's letters, Mother," Cora added, dark brow perched high. "Smart, a writer, funny, strong." Cora released a light laugh. "I have an American sister-in-law."

Mother took one of his hands into hers and touched his cheek with the other. "Despite what your father mandated, dear boy, you will always have family here."

He closed his eyes and covered her hand against his cheek. "I never doubted that, Mother. I'm only sorry things did not turn out better for your sake."

"We will be fine." Her gaze bore into his, searching, until her smile bloomed. "And I see that you already are. When you spoke of Laurel, your eyes brightened with affection."

"Besides present company, she is truly the best woman I've ever known."

His mother patted his cheek and lowered her hand. "Only the best will do for you, my dear boy."

"And you must keep writing to us," Cora said. "We'll make certain Masters delivers the letters to my room. Father never enters there." She stepped close, leaning her head against his shoulder. "And someday I'll have my own place, then you and Laurel can come and stay with me regardless of what Father says."

He grinned down at his plucky little sister.

"Introduce Laurel to London? What an adventure that would be."

"And do not worry for money." His mother's smile peaked to one side. "Your father is not the only one with finances." She placed an envelope in his hand. "I support a great many charitable organizations from my own purse. Your professional future seems an excellent addition to my list."

"What? How?" He took the envelope, looking inside at the handsome amount.

"Your father has no control of my inheritance, which I dole out as I choose." She grinned. "And I choose you . . . and Laurel and the mission at Maple Springs."

He laughed and pulled her into his arms. "Thank you, Mother. I will bring Laurel here one day."

"Or we'll travel to you," Cora added. "Besides, I'm a trained nurse, or at least I'm a trained volunteer. I could help you in your wild world of polecats and cougars."

"I'd rather not introduce you to either of those, but there are a host of other things and people I'd love to show you." He cupped his little sister's cheek, the little girl in her face bowing to the woman she was becoming. "I'm still learning that world myself, Cora. But maybe someday, someday soon, I'll send for you."

■ ■ ■ ■

Laurel finished working on the lessons for the last day of school before the winter break. She'd taken some of the students' newest work and placed it out on tables or pinned it to the walls so that when they arrived for their last day tomorrow, they would see their best pieces on display. A literature essay here. A poem there. A detailed sketch of the anatomy of a frog. A few paintings, some excellent dresses, a half dozen wood crafts. She smiled at the eclectic display. Yes, her people had a great many skills, and ones to celebrate.

Jonathan had encouraged this celebration.

Her fingers slid over the pages of handwritten lessons on Jonathan's school desk. He had lovely penmanship. Almost artistic.

He never strayed too far from her thoughts. Always as close as the scent in their home or the memory of his kiss.

She breathed out a long sigh and stood from the desk. He'd been gone for three weeks. *Three.* Each night she prayed for his return, and every morning greeted her with an empty house and an aching heart. How could her simple world and old-fashioned ways compare with his life in London? She pinched her eyes closed. And she *wanted* him to fulfill his dream of being a doctor. He'd make an excellent one. She just wanted to be the woman by his side along the way.

She shook the niggling doubt from her mind and walked to the blackboard, writing out the devotional verse for the last morning of school.

*"Now the God of hope fill you with all joy and peace in believing, that ye may abound in hope, through the power of the Holy Ghost."*

Hope. Oh God, help her cling to hope.

"You asked me once to describe my home."

She froze at the voice, *his* voice. Her hand shook, trembling the chalk.

"It's a beautiful sight, one of the best places on earth, nestled at the edge of a wood."

She braced her palm against the board, afraid he might disappear if she turned. Her eyes burned. Her breath seized.

"Its fieldstone exterior sets it apart from other houses in the area, a true work of art among the oaks and pines, and the view..."

Laurel placed the chalk down and drew in a deep breath as she turned. He stood just within the doorway, afternoon sunlight framing him like some sort of dream or angel. Was he real? Truly him?

He took a few steps forward out of the sun's glow and nearer to her. His gaze searched hers, his familiar smile spreading. "But, my favorite part of home is — even better than the layers of mountains that reach out to touch the sunset — my favorite part is this girl."

She caught a sob in her palm.

He approached a few more steps. "She's smart and beautiful with enough joy in her smile to brighten up any life, especially mine, and wherever she is, that's where I belong."

She shook her head. "No regrets."

"Not one." He grinned. "I've learned the value of a fair trade."

"A fair trade?" Her voice raked across her emotion-clogged throat. What on earth was her handsome-and-addled husband talking about?

He neared to touching distance. "You see, I've given you my heart, and I think it only right that you give me your heart in return. A fair trade."

She sniffled, shaking her head. "I can't do that."

A burst of air escaped him, like she'd punched him in the stomach. "Why not?"

"Because, you already have it. I reckon

you've had it since the first week we met, and I didn't know until I had to tell you goodbye."

Sunrays filtered through the windows, creating a patchwork on the floor between them. His smile burst wide and he closed the distance between them. He captured her in his arms, his lips finding hers.

She laughed against his smile, even as tears warmed her cheeks. He may have been the one to return to Maple Springs, but in his arms, she found her home, her dreams.

He pulled back, cradling her face, his eyes so filled with love they almost glowed. "Mrs. Laurel Taylor, will you *choose* to be my wife, from this day forward?"

Her smiled tugged wide. She stood on tiptoe and kissed him again, because she could. "I will, Mr. Jonathan Taylor. From this day forward."

# ABOUT THE AUTHOR

**Pepper Basham** is an award-winning author who writes romance peppered with grace and humor. She currently resides in the lovely mountains of Asheville, North Carolina, where she is the mom of five great kids, a speech-pathologist to about fifty more, and a lover of chocolate, jazz, and Jesus. Her Penned in Time historical romance series has garnered recognition in the Grace Awards, Inpsy, and the ACFW's Carol Awards, with *The Thorn Healer* recently listed as a finalist in the RT awards. Her contemporary romance novels such as *A Twist of Faith, Just the Way You Are,* and *Charming the Troublemaker* have received high ratings from *Romantic Times.* You can get to know Pepper on her website, www.pepperdbasham.com, on Facebook, Instagram, or over at her group blog, The Writer's Alley.

The employees of Thorndike Press hope you have enjoyed this Large Print book. All our Thorndike, Wheeler, and Kennebec Large Print titles are designed for easy reading, and all our books are made to last. Other Thorndike Press Large Print books are available at your library, through selected bookstores, or directly from us.

For information about titles, please call:
 (800) 223-1244

or visit our website at:
 gale.com/thorndike

To share your comments, please write:
 Publisher
 Thorndike Press
 10 Water St., Suite 310
 Waterville, ME 04901